If I Surrender
Prescott High Book One
Kristin MacQueen

If I Surrender – Prescott High Book One.

First edition. January 1, 2023.

Copyright ©2023 Kristin MacQueen.

Written by Kristin MacQueen.

Contents

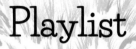

Playlist

Spotify

You Broke Me First – Conor Maynard

Wolf in Sheep's Clothing – Set It Off, William Beckett

Don't Let Me – Jake Scott

Sticks + Stones – Jeris Johnson

Dark Side – Iris Grey

Piece by Piece – Kurt Hugo Schneider, Sam Trui, Kirsten Collins

Never Ending Nightmare – Citizen Soldier, Kellin Quinn

Let Me Hate You – Alexander Stewart

Walked Through Hell – Anson Seabra

I Guess I'm In Love – Clinton Kans

Give Me A Reason – Jullian Rossi

If I Surrender – Citizen Soldier

Monsters – All Time Low, Blackbear

Chapter 1
Grayson

We move as one down the hallways of Prescott High. Everyone watches us and moves out of our way, but no one says a damn word. That's the way I like it. I don't need people to pretend they know me or act like they want to be friends with me. I've got my two friends at my side. I don't need anyone else.

I stop in front of my locker and toss a piece of cinnamon gum in my mouth. It's my one vice. The one thing I can't live without.

"Hey, boys," Cherie practically purrs as she brushes a finger down Connor's chest. He stares at her with disinterest before turning his attention to the locker in front of him. He twists the knob on the lock until he gets to the right number, then twists it the other way.

None of us like the desperate types... well, except Mac. He likes any sort of attention. If you want mine or Connor's attention, you won't get it by fluttering your lashes or constantly flirting. We're above that. We have expensive tastes and like what we can't have or what's just out of our reach. We're the rich assholes of Prescott High who get everything they could possibly want and no one's going to stop us.

"Don't touch me, Cherie." Connor swats her hand away and opens his locker.

He drops everything inside and spins around to face me. He won't take a single book to class. We both know it and so do the teachers. Yet, he'll still get straight A's. I swear he pays the teachers off. Or maybe his dad does.

"You can touch me all you want. In fact, we can find an empty classroom right now and I can show you something special." Mac wiggles his eyebrows.

"There's nothing special about your dick, Mac. Cherie's seen more dick than a porn star. You're not going to impress her." Connor rolls his eyes.

"I'm sure you're quite impressive." She slides her hand down his chest and over the waistband of his jeans, ignoring Connor's insult.

I'm honestly surprised they haven't slept together yet. They're both more than willing to fuck anyone of the opposite sex.

"You're going to get an STD if you let her go any further," I mutter under my breath. Cherie scowls at me, but she doesn't dare argue. No one has the balls to argue with us.

"Hey, Grayson, can I borrow a pen? I don't know where I put mine." Hadley stops next to me and riffles through her backpack again.

"Yeah, let me find one." I open my locker next to Connor's and move a few papers to the side, looking for a pen for her.

"Here, you can have mine." Mac pulls a black pen out of his pocket and holds it out to her.

"Don't touch that, who knows where his hands have been." I push him aside and give Hadley the one I find at the bottom of my locker.

"I know where they've been. They've been down my pants," Mac mutters.

"Thanks!" Hadley stands on her tippy toes and presses a wet kiss to my cheek, ignoring Mac.

"Thanks for licking your lips before you kissed me," I grumble under my breath, wiping at my cheek.

"Anything for you, brother dearest!" She blows me an air kiss.

Mac jumps in front of me, pretending to grab Hadley's kiss and shoves it in his pocket. Hadley rolls her eyes and continues down the hallway.

"She's never going to give you the time of day, especially when you're so desperate for her." Connor eyes him with disgust.

"Who says I want anything to do with Hadley? That's gross, she's Gray's sister." Mac glances at me.

For a split second he looks worried. I stare him down, waiting to see if he's going to squirm under my attention, but he doesn't. He almost looks bored.

"Morning, Will." Connor smirks at Will Cooper as he walks by. Will mutters something back, but I can't hear what he said.

"What's going on there?" I arch a brow. Connor doesn't talk to anyone outside of me and Mac unless you're of use to him.

"I have dirt on him and now he owes me." Connor shrugs and slams his locker shut. "Just another day in the life of money and power." He smirks and moves down the hall, expecting us to follow.

And that's exactly what we do. Mac and I fall in line next to Connor. We're a team. When one of us has a problem with you, you're going to get the wrath of all three.

———

"You're getting a sister?" My eyebrows skyrocket and I glance over my shoulder at Connor. I can't imagine him having a sibling at all. He's not exactly the brotherly type.

"Apparently. I'm super excited, can't you tell?" He deadpans.

"Are you going to be the doting brother now?" I chuckle to myself, climbing off the couch to grab something to drink.

"Honestly, Dad will be lucky if we both survive the first month," Connor grumbles under his breath.

"How old is she?"

"Eighteen. She's a senior, same as us."

"Whoa! Wait. You're getting a stepsister who's our age?" I stop in my tracks, spinning around to face him.

"Yup." He pops the 'p', a scowl forming on his face.

"So... is she hot?" Mac smirks from his spot on the couch.

"I don't know, I've never met her. But she's off limits," Connor growls.

"Seriously? What the hell? She could be the love of my life." Mac falls back onto the couch dramatically. "Gray, tell him to let me date his sister." Mac rolls his head to look at me.

"Stepsister. And she won't be here long enough for you to fall in love with her. You'd have a better chance with Hadley," Connor hisses.

Anger pulsates through me at the thought of anyone touching my sister. She's too innocent for any of these assholes. They need to get the hell away from her.

"I'm going to get rid of her as fast as I can. By the end of the month, her and her mom will be running for the hills." He folds his arms over his chest, determination filling his features.

"What if she's actually cool?" I ask the question both Mac and I are wondering. There's a good chance this girl isn't awful.

Connor doesn't give people chances unless he wants to. He never has and I doubt he ever will. He decided long ago that he's above everyone else and if he wants nothing to do with you, you're screwed.

"They don't come from money. Her mom is only marrying my dad so she can divorce him in a few years and get a payout. She doesn't give a shit about him, none of them ever do. The faster I drive them away, the less money they can get their filthy hands on."

"Have you ever considered actually giving them a chance? They could be awesome people who just happen to be poor." Mac shrugs, barely turning his attention away from his phone.

I don't know why Connor's always so worried about everyone's financial standings, but it's been a thing of his for as long as I can remember. He doesn't believe someone with less money than him should share the same air, let alone the same household.

He's more stuck up than any other person at our school. It's why he rules over everyone else. It's why he believes he's the King of Prescott High. We might go to a public school, but when you're surrounded by nothing but wealthy people, you don't need to pay for private schools.

"So, what's your plan? I'm sure you already have it all figured out." I cross my arms over my broad chest, waiting for this evil plan I'm sure he concocted long before this conversation.

"I do. And it's going to be good. I'm not going after the mom this time. I'm going after her darling princess and you two are going to help me."

Of course we fucking are.

Chapter 2
Piper

"Are you sure about this?" I stare at the passing landscape as we make our way closer and closer to our new home.

"What are you nervous about?" Mom squeezes my thigh.

"I'm a senior, starting at a new school, moving into a new house, and getting a whole new family. What isn't there to be nervous about?"

"I know, honey. I'd appreciate it if you could try to enjoy it though. You only have a few more months of school, then you'll be joining all your friends at college. It's only a short separation."

"I know... I'm just going to miss Tim and the rest of my friends. It's weird to be away from them."

"You know Tim's going to come visit you all the time. He's said that already, plus that boy is crazy about you. I'm fairly certain if I moved you to Japan, he'd still come visit you."

"That would cost a fortune and be ridiculous." I roll my eyes.

"I still think he'd find a way. You're the center of his whole world." Mom pats my hand, keeping her attention on the road.

"What's James' son like?" I ask after a few minutes of silence.

"I'm not really sure. I've only met him in passing, never really had a conversation with him. He seems to keep to himself. He's kinda quiet. I'm sure the two of you will get along just fine. He's going to show you around school."

"Wait... I thought he was like eight." I stare at Mom in horror.

"What? No, Piper!" She giggles, shaking her head. "He's *eighteen*! You're both seniors."

"Mom... this changes everything! I thought I was getting a cute little brother! Not someone my age!"

"Oh, it's fine, Piper. I'm sure the two of you will get along just great. He's quiet and keeps to himself. He's not going to be an issue for you at all." She waves me off, clearly not as worried about this as I am.

A million questions race through my head, making the rest of the drive silent as can be. Who is this guy? What's he like? Is he going to be nice to me? Are we going to become friends? Is he cute?

The last question might be the most important one. I planned to make it through my senior year without a single issue. My sole focus is on college. In college I'll get to be with Tim again. Everything will go back to normal and I don't need a cute step brother screwing all of that up for me.

What if he's a total ass though? He could make my life a living hell.

"We're here!" Mom singsongs, pulling me from my internal questions.

I glance up to find the most elaborate house I've ever seen. It's a cookie cutter mansion, almost identical to every other house on the street. The only difference is this one is my new home. At least for the next few months.

"Can they flaunt their money any more?" I grumble under my breath.

"Piper! Be nice! James doesn't flaunt his money, but that doesn't mean he can't have nice things." Mom scowls over at me as she turns our little beat-up sedan down the long driveway. There's a gate we have to stop at and Mom enters a code before the thick black metal parts for us to continue our journey.

We pull into the circular driveway in front of the house and the door opens almost immediately. A middle-aged man steps outside in a crisp navy-blue suit that probably cost more than this car.

He's handsome, definitely a confident man and he has a large smile spreading from ear to ear. He hurries down the front steps and reaches the driver's side just as Mom shuts the door behind her. He sweeps her into his arms and presses a gentle kiss to her lips.

"I'm so happy you're here. I missed you," he murmurs to her.

When I shut the passenger's door, James' gaze snaps to me. His smile stretches impossibly wider. Mom leads him over to me and makes introductions.

"Piper, it's so nice to meet you." He wraps me in a tight hug and I almost hate to admit how fatherly it feels.

His dark hair has speckles of gray throughout it and his blue eyes sparkle with excitement. I'm not sure how old he is, but he looks on the younger side.

Dad died when I was little. Some sort of heart condition took his life shortly after I was born. I didn't exactly miss having a father. I don't really know what it's like to have one. James will be the first sort of father figure I've ever had.

"It's nice to meet you too," I whisper, hugging him back.

"I know it's kinda weird to meet for the first time on the day you move in, but I promise you're going to love it here... How about I show you both where your rooms are and then I can give you a tour. The moving truck should be here shortly and then Roger can show them where to put your things. Maria can help you unpack also."

"Is Roger your son?" I fall in step beside them as we climb the steps to the front door."

"Oh, no, Piper." James's deep chuckle fills the air. "Roger's our butler and driver. Maria's the housekeeper and Fernando's our chef. If you ever need anything, you can ask the three of them, but don't hesitate to reach out to me too. My door is always open."

"That's a funny joke." A deep snort of laughter comes from the right of us. "I don't know the last time I saw your door open."

I glance over and find a devastatingly attractive guy leaning against the wall. His arms are crossed over his broad chest and his features look like they were chiseled out of stone. He's all angles and sharp lines.

His black hair is carefully styled to look messy, but it probably took him time to achieve the look. His dark brown eyes are full of curiosity and maybe a little bit of resentment.

"Fine, it's not always open, but all you have to do is knock and come in." James rolls his eyes. "Connor, this is Piper, your new step sister. Piper, this is my son, Connor."

"It's nice to meet you." I give him a small smile. I'm not a timid person, but this isn't exactly a comfortable situation. It's awkward and there's a thick layer of tension in the air that I don't think has anything to do with me.

I had no time to prepare myself for this. I thought I was meeting a little kid who would adore me. I could take him out for ice cream or we could sneak downstairs in the middle of the night to watch movies together. I expected a little shadow who would be fun once we got to know each other... not this.

"I'm sure it is... I'm going to Mac's house." Connor pushes off the wall, standing to his full height.

"Ok. I want you home for dinner tonight." James keeps his gaze locked on Connor. His voice is slightly harder when he speaks to his son.

"We'll see. I'm not sure what we're up to. If I'm not here by six, don't wait for me."

"Connor, I told you I expect you at dinner tonight. You'll be here."

Connor closes the distance between the two of them. He's an inch or two taller than James and he has at least twenty pounds of muscle on him.

"And I told you I didn't want a new family. I guess we don't always get what we want in life, huh, Pops?" He pushes his way past James, hitting his shoulder as he goes.

"Connor! You need to be nice and respectful. Piper and Lauren are going to be living here!"

"Oh, my bad." He pauses mid-stride and spins on his heels to face us. "My sincerest apologies." He places a hand over his chest like he's actually sorry. He's not. He's a privileged asshole who needs to be brought down a peg or two.

"It's ok. I understand this will take some adjustments." Mom gives him a sympathetic smile.

"Welcome to the family..." Connor spins back around and jerks open the front door. He glances over his shoulder and meets my gaze. Right before he slams it, he mutters, "I hope you fucking leave just as quickly as you came."

"He seems like a delight," I grumble under my breath as James pinches the bridge of his nose in frustration and Mom places a supportive hand on his shoulder.

This is going to be interesting.

Chapter 3
Grayson

"But what's she like?" Mac drops onto the beanbag next to me in his game room. I toss a remote to him and start the video game.

Connor showed up here about ten minutes ago in a sour mood. I know his new step mom and step sister moved in today, but he hasn't said much about them.

"The mom or the daughter?" Connor arches a brow.

"Both, I guess." He shrugs, not really caring either way.

I begin our game before Mac's ready. He scowls at me, making me chuckle under my breath. I'm able to zoom across the start line before he even has the remote in his hands. He grumbles under his breath about what an ass I am.

"The mom's pretty hot for her age. I'm kinda impressed my dad was able to bag her. She probably does yoga or some shit like that. She's a little too nice for my liking though. She acts like she's walking on eggshells around me."

"Yeah, because I'm sure you're making this *real* easy on them." I roll my eyes.

Connor and Mac have been my best friends for as long as I can remember. It's always been us against the world, but lately Connor's become a pain in the ass. He acts like he's the only one with problems and he's not.

Mac's laid-back. He doesn't give a shit about anything. It's not because his life has been handed to him on a silver platter, it's more because he knows he can't control other people's actions. He sees no point in getting all upset over things you can't change.

From Mac's standpoint, Connor should just be nice and leave the mom and step sister alone. But Mac loves to play games. He loves to watch people squirm and make them uncomfortable. Because of that, Mac will be all over Connor's plan of taking this girl down.

"But what about the stepsister?" Mac pushes again.

He ended things with the last girl begging for his attention. I'm sure he's interested in finding someone new. Someone he can play with. He wants a challenge.

"She's alright. Nothing special though." Connor shrugs, but I can see through his lie. He thinks she's hot and that bothers him even more.

"I still think you should just leave them alone. You have less than a year and we'll be moving to college. Who cares if your dad has someone to share that huge house with?" I change lanes in the game to speed around another character, narrowly avoiding crashing my car into a boulder.

"I do! If she stays a full year, then it will become two. It will keep going until one day when they get divorced, she's going to get half of everything. Or if my dad dies first, she'll get everything and I'll lose my inheritance. She'll probably convince him to split everything between me and Piper and then I'll lose even more. I deserve more than my trust fund!" He throws himself on the couch like a toddler having a temper tantrum.

This is going to be so much fun dealing with Connor. I absolutely hate when he acts like this. His entire focus is going to be figuring out ways to take down Piper. There will be no partying, no fooling around and no having fun this year. I don't know a thing about Piper, but I already hate her for ruining my senior year.

I'm going to take her down and make her regret ever stepping foot in this town or in Prescott High. This is war.

Chapter 4
Piper

Maria helped me unpack all of my things over the past two days. Everyone keeps acting like this place is amazing, but it's not. Sure, the house is gorgeous and it's nice to not have to cook or clean, but it's so empty.

James and Mom are normally cuddled together on the couch. They sit there and talk when James is finished with work every day. It's cute how they want to spend so much time together.

Mom works remotely and doesn't work traditional hours. She often stays up half the night to put together the new websites she creates for her clients. She says she works better when the world around her is asleep. I'm not sure if that's it or if it's just because she's always been a night owl.

Even on the weekends, James is almost always locked away in his office during the day. Sometimes you can hear him yelling at someone on the phone or arguing until he gets his way. He's definitely a force to deal with in the business world… I'm not exactly sure what he does for a living. I think I'd rather not know though.

I hurry through my morning routine, more than ready to get the first day at my new school over and done with. There's nothing fun about being the new girl, especially for my senior year of high school. I'd love nothing more than to go back to my old life and my old school, but Mom deserves this.

She says she loves James and he's the greatest thing that's ever happened to her. I'd never try to take that away from her. She's given up so much for me. It's her turn to be happy.

My cell phone pings with an incoming text. I snatch it off my bed and swing my backpack over my shoulder. I have more than enough time to get breakfast before it's time to go.

Prescott High started school two weeks ago, but this is my first day. They start so much earlier than my old school does.

Now everyone will realize I'm new. Walking into their classrooms two weeks late is going to have a neon sign over my head, blinking 'I'm the new girl'. Can't wait.

Tim: Morning, beautiful. I hope you have a great first day of school.

I smile down at his text. Tim's been my best friend since we were in diapers. We've been there for each other through everything. If he were here with me, things would be so much better.

Piper: Thanks. I miss you.

Tim: I miss you too. How's the new brother?

I let out a loud groan. How do you explain Connor to someone who's never met him?

Piper: Difficult. Stuck up. He hates me. Why didn't she tell me he was my age? I would've fought harder to move in with you.

Tim: Show him Piper Lawson isn't someone to fuck with. Give him hell.

Piper: I'm going to be nice unless he's a dick... then all bets are off. I'll talk to you after school.

Hurrying down the steps and into the dining room, I'm met with a huge breakfast. We aren't allowed to eat in the kitchen. I think if Fernando had it his way, most of us wouldn't be allowed to step foot in there. Every meal is consumed in the dining room.

Fernando sets the last plate on the table and flashes me a huge smile. I think he's one of my favorite people here.

He's younger than I'd expected him to be. In my head, Fernando was this middle-aged man who was overweight and yelled whenever someone entered his kitchen without permission. I couldn't have been more wrong.

Fernando's gorgeous. He's probably in his late twenties and has all the dark characteristics an Italian man should. He's kind and has welcomed me into this home with open arms.

He's told me more than once that he'd be happy to teach me to cook if I'd like to learn. I didn't have the heart to break it to him that I already know how to cook and bake.

"Mornin', Piper."

"Morning, Fernando." I smile sweetly, dropping into the chair he pulls out for me. "Do you always make this much food for breakfast?"

"I make whatever James asks me to make." He rolls his eyes, but it's playful. He's a total flirt with me.

"It looks delicious... Has anyone else eaten yet?"

"No, you're the first to come down. I'm sure Connor will be stomping down the stairs and bitching about something shortly."

"Is he really as terrible as I think he is?" I arch a brow, wanting to know the truth.

Fernando sighs and pulls out the seat beside me. He leans forward, planting his elbows on his knees. I'm surprised when he gathers my hands in his and peeks up at me through his lashes.

"This stays between the two of us, got it?"

I nod my head. I just want to know what I'm up against. I have a feeling he's going to give me trouble. No matter how many times Mom reassures me that everything is going to be great, I have this gut feeling it won't be.

"He's a spoiled rich boy. He gets everything he could ever want. Every time he whines, James throws money at him until he stops. He's never known what it's like to work for something. If he sees you as a threat, he's going to do his best to get rid of you. I'd prepare yourself, Piper. He won't be gentle."

"Thanks, Fernando. I appreciate your honesty."

"If he gets too mean, let me know. I can sprinkle some laxatives in his food." He winks at me before standing and taking his spot at the serving table.

As soon as James strolls into the room, Fernando jumps into action. He makes a big plate for James and places it in front of him.

"Thank you, Fernando." James gives him a smile before turning his attention to me. "Piper, how was your night?"

We continue talking about the house, school, and every other small talk topic we can think of. When Mom walks into the room, I breathe a sigh of relief. Don't get me wrong, James is very kind, but it's still awkward.

Not thirty seconds later, Connor stomps into the room and practically throws himself onto the chair across from me. I glance up at Fernando, catching him rolling his eyes. I have a feeling we're going to become best friends.

"Good morning, Connor," Mom singsongs. She does that whenever she's uncomfortable.

"Mornin'," he mumbles around a bite of food.

"Piper, Connor's going to take you to school today. We can go sometime this week to get you a car."

"I'm not taking her to school." Connor finally glances up from his phone long enough to glare at his father.

"You'll be taking Piper to and from school until she gets her own car or I'll freeze your accounts." James levels him with a stern look.

"Are you fucking kidding me?" Connor slams his hands down on the table.

I watch with wide eyes, wondering what James is going to do. Mom jumps and makes a small gasp. She isn't used to anyone acting like this. For so long it's only been the two of us and I don't really give her trouble.

"Don't speak to me like that, especially in front of people," James growls.

"I see how it is. Those two are now the object of your affection. I'm glad you've finally gotten the little princess you've always wanted." Connor's piercing gaze lands on me and I know it's a warning. He's coming for me and I better prepare myself for war.

"I can just take the bus. It's not that big of a deal. I really don't need a car. I can use Mom's whenever I need to." I wave James off, trying my hardest to calm the anger brewing in the room.

"Sweetheart, we sold your mom's car. I bought her a new one and there are no buses for Prescott High. Most of the students drive or get their chauffeurs to take them."

"Chauffeurs? Seriously?"

"You're not in Kansas anymore, Princess." Connor rolls his eyes. "I'm leaving in five minutes. I'm picking up Gray and Mac on our way... please tell me you're not actually wearing that to school." Connor nods to my outfit.

I chose a pink maxi skirt and a black short sleeved shirt. I glance down at my outfit, trying to figure out what's wrong with it.

"Yes? I thought it was cute."

"Prescott High is going to chew you up and spit you out." He shakes his head with a grimace aimed at me.

Exactly five minutes later – Connor set an alarm and everything – we're walking out to the garage. There are at least seven cars in here. Each are makes or models I've never seen or heard of before. I wonder how much they cost? Do I even want to know?

Connor leads me to an SUV. It seems nicer than most but nothing stands out as being special. I reach for the handle of the passenger's door and he shakes his head.

"You're sitting in the back. The front seat is for Gray."

I nod my head, not wanting to argue with him anymore. As much as I hate being agreeable and going along with what he wants, sometimes it's intelligent to pick your battles and this isn't a battle I feel like fighting.

The drive to his friend's houses is filled with loud angry music. My head is pounding as the car vibrates, but I keep my mouth shut even though I want to scream.

While his focus is on the road, I glance around his Mercedes-Maybach GLS 600. I only know what type of car it is because he told me… five times. He acted like this information should impress me, but I know nothing about cars. I doubt this one is cheap though. The backseat has two chairs that recline. Why do you need reclining seats in your car? But I'm not complaining, this is the most comfortable my butt has ever been.

We pull into the long driveway of another mansion. The front door flies open and a guy hops down the steps. He's cute. He almost looks like a surfer with his strawberry blonde hair hanging in his eyes.

He flings open the backdoor and climbs in next to me. He sweeps his hair out of his face and freezes when he notices me.

"Fucking-a, Connor! You're such a damn liar!" His gaze roams up and down my body, taking in every inch of me.

"What's that supposed to mean?" I quirk a brow, wondering what Connor lied about.

"Off limits. I told you that," Connor growls from the front seat.

Understanding dawns on me. Connor warned his friends to stay away from me. I'm not sure how I feel about that. I highly doubt it was said from a protective brother standpoint. I'm sure there's an alternative reason, I just need to figure out what it is.

"I'm Mac." My backseat partner runs a hand through his shaggy strawberry blonde hair again. His blue eyes sparkle with mischief and I have a feeling he's more trouble than I want to deal with.

When he flashes me a devilish grin that's probably made more panties than I can count disappear from their owners, I know I'm right.

"Piper." I flash him a smile. I don't need to be rude to him just because he's friends with Connor. Though I do have to wonder how good his decision-making skills can possibly be if he willingly hangs out with Connor.

We pull out of the driveway and head down the street to another house. Soon a second guy is climbing into the front seat. I'm assuming he's Gray.

He glances over his shoulder at me. His dark brown hair is just long enough to be tousled. His green eyes are so deep and clear. I swear I could get lost in them. He stares at me for a few seconds until he turns back around to face the road without a single word.

"Oh, it's so nice to meet you too. I'm Piper in case you didn't know." I roll my eyes, already more than annoyed with having to ride in this car with these guys.

Mac chuckles beside me and shakes his head. I think out of the three of these guys, he's going to be my favorite.

"I never said it was nice to meet you. I'm sure it's not." His deep voice rumbles through me, shaking my body to its core.

I fidget in my seat, refusing to acknowledge how his voice stirs something deep inside of me. I'd never go near someone like Gray.

"You're about as delightful as Connor," I murmur under my breath. I swear he huffs out a laugh, but his body is positioned so I can't really see him.

"On the bright side, I'm a delight." Mac wiggles his eyebrows. I swear if we were sitting on a bench seat, he'd scoot over so there was no space between us. He'd probably drape his arm over my shoulders and try to pull me into his side.

"How strict are they with the dress code at Prescott High?" I keep my voice quiet. I don't want Connor in my business any more than he already is.

"They don't care unless you cause problems. Why? Are you worried you're showing too much skin? That skirt is so long I can't even see your feet. I'm sure you're fine." Mac smirks at me. He's so playful and happy. I don't know how he's friends with Satan and his demon lackey.

"Not at all. I'm wondering if I can do this..." I tug the maxi skirt down my legs and stuff it into my bag. As I lift my shirt, I catch Mac's eyes widening to a comical level.

"Con... your sister's stripping back here." Mac swats in Connor's direction, hitting him on the shoulder three times. He never tears his attention away from me.

"She's not my sister! What the fuck are you doing?" Connor snaps his gaze from the road to me, scowling as I tie my shirt just under my breasts. "What the hell happened to the nun skirt?"

"I'm fairly certain nuns don't wear pink." I roll my eyes.

A horn blares at us, pulling Connor's attention back to the road. He swerves to miss another car and growls in frustration. He really shouldn't be allowed to drive.

"You should probably worry more about driving and less about what I'm wearing, *brother*." I watch his jaw clench when I call him brother. He's so easy to rile up.

He hates everything about us coming here and ruining his version of perfection. But guess what? I hate this too. I wanted to stay in my old school for senior year. I never wanted to move three hours away and deal with finding new friends and a new life.

"Why are you changing?" He growls.

"Did you actually think I dress like that? Not even close." I snort out a laugh. "Mom requested I dress nicely for my first day of school. I agreed to make her happy, but I'm not actually going to school in that." I slip my feet into a pair of cute ankle boots and zip them up.

As soon as we pull into a parking spot outside of the high school, I hop out of the fancy SUV and head towards the stairs. I'm more than aware of all the eyes on me. I'm the new girl and no one knows a thing about me. They're going to make it their mission to figure me out. They need to know if I'm a friend or foe and fast.

I only make it a few steps before a hand grips my arm, tugging me back against a solid chest. I peek up and find those same bright green eyes on me again.

"Be careful, Princess. Some people aren't as trustworthy as they seem. Salt and sugar look awfully similar, don't you think?" Gray murmurs in my ear. He drops my arm and steps away from me quickly. So quickly that for a second I wonder if I imagined it.

I blink in surprise, unsure of what to do or say. Gray meets Connor and Mac at the front of the SUV and they head into school together. People step aside, making room for them to walk.

It's like Moses parting the Red Sea. As soon as they pass, students move back to where they were, erasing the space the boys just occupied.

Chapter 5
Grayson

"Dude, you're such a liar. You said she was alright. Nothing special. Did you see her? She's perfection." Mac backhands Connor's stomach, making him let out a low grunt.

"She's temporary," he growls. "And we don't associate with trash."

"She sure doesn't look like trash. She looks like a delicious entrée. One I'd love to sink my teeth into." Mac wiggles his eyebrows, making me grin.

Connor pauses right next to Mac's locker. He whirls around and pins him against the cool metal, gathering Mac's shirt in his fist.

"I swear, Mac, if you touch her, we're done. I said she's off limits. Stay the fuck away." He drops the fabric and marches down the hall without another word.

"What the fuck was that?" Mac straightens his shirt, flashing a passing girl a dazzling smile. He won't let anyone see how much Connor upset him, but I catch the slight worry in his gaze.

"Don't worry about it. He's just stressed out." I wave off his concerns. I don't believe a single word falling from my lips, but Mac doesn't handle stress well. He won't be able to focus on class at all if his mind is on Connor and his outburst.

"I need to get to English. I have to finish my paper before class starts." I pat him on the shoulder.

"Gray, it's the second week of school. How are you already behind?" Mac chuckles, shaking his head.

"Summer reading assignment." I shrug and spin on my heels, walking away to him laughing. I'm the biggest procrastinator you'll ever meet, but it's always done on time. "I'll catch you at lunch. Try not to piss off Connor anymore."

"All I said was that he's a liar!" Mac calls to my retreating back. I chuckle and shake my head. The two of them fight more than an old married couple, but they always have each other's back.

I'm sitting in my third period class when my phone vibrates in my pocket. I tug it out and glance at the screen, trying to hide what I'm doing. Mrs. D hates cell phones and she'll take it for the rest of the day if she catches me on it.

Connor: I got a copy of Piper's schedule from the office.

Gray: How'd you pull that off?

I frown down at my lap. There's no way the office would just give another student's schedule to you.

Connor: I'm her helpful brother. She must've lost her schedule this morning and was having a little bit of a panic attack over it.

Gray: Mac's right. You're such a fucking liar. What's the plan?

I glance up when Mrs. D stops talking and find her staring straight at me.

"Mr. Young, could you please tell me why you keep staring down at your lap? What's so interesting that you aren't paying attention to me?" She arches a brow, knowing exactly what I'm doing.

Mrs. D isn't much older than we are. She told us last year that she's in her mid-twenties. She seems to have a soft spot for me, but I'm not sure if that's going to help in this situation. Slowly an idea takes root and as much as I want to grin, I give her the most innocent expression I can muster. It's the only way I'll be able to pull this off.

"I was just trying to will a problem away."

"What kind of problem? Do you need help?" Her brows draw together.

"Nah, I think you're part of the problem."

"What exactly is this problem, Mr. Young?" She sighs, clearly done with my antics.

"My pants are just a little tight in a certain area this morning. I think it has to do with your shirt. Are you cold, Mrs. D?"

Her gaze snaps to my crotch and her cheeks flame a bright red before she glances down at her own shirt. You can see her nipples through it. She makes a beeline straight to her desk and shrugs on a sweater, zipping it up to her neck.

"Please just pay attention, Grayson."

She avoids looking at me for the rest of the period. I do my part and keep my attention on her, wondering just how much I'm going to regret what I just said. I can't imagine she's going to just let it go.

The rest of the morning is uneventful. Hadley, Mac, and Connor text me throughout my classes and I know I need to stop answering them. I need to focus and keep my grades up.

Last year when we were fighting to get Mr. Ward's last wife to leave, my grades plummeted. Dad said if I do that shit again this year, he won't let me go away for college. He won't let me take my place in the company and he definitely won't let me live out the rest of the year with Connor as my friend.

I can't screw up my entire future just to help Connor. Yet I know I'm going to get pulled into this shit with Piper no matter how hard I try not to. Fucking awesome.

Chapter 6
Piper

"Hey, Piper!" Connor hurries behind me with a tray full of food. "I can't find my ID. Can I use yours to pay for lunch? I'll have Dad add extra money to your account."

I stare at him for a minute. I know there's an unspoken war going on between us, but he seems sincere. I wonder if he actually has lost his ID.

"Sure. Just bring it back to me when you're done." I hand over my card with a smile. As much as I don't enjoy being around Connor, if we can play nice, this year will be a little bit more tolerable.

"Of course. I'll be right back."

He rushes away to pay for his food while I finish picking out what I'm going to eat. As soon as I have a drink and a salad on my tray, I move to stand in the line for the cashier.

Standing on my tippy toes, I try to peer around the people in front of me to find Connor. I need my card or I won't be able to pay for my lunch.

"Next!... I said next!" The cashier's glaring at me when I realize she's talking to me. I move my tray closer to her. "Scan your card." She gestures to the machine in front of me.

"I, uh, I don't have my ID."

"Well, you can't get lunch without it."

"Can't you just add it to my account with my name?"

"Nope. Don't know how to."

"Can't you try?" I try to tamp down my anger. It should be directed at Connor, not the little old lady preventing me from getting lunch.

"Don't worry, Aggie, I got it. Just add it to mine." A guy steps up behind me, scanning his card. The old woman smiles sweetly at him.

"Such a gentleman. Thank you." Aggie winks at my rescuer. He nudges me to grab my tray and get moving.

"Thank you for that." I glance up at him, more than thankful he stepped in and saved me from not only starvation, but also humiliation.

"No problem. I'm Will."

"Piper."

"Well, Piper, seeing as I just bought you lunch, I think I deserve a little lunch date." He winks, placing a hand on my lower back and leading me to an empty table.

"Is that so?"

"Yup. It's only fair, right?"

"Sure." I roll my eyes, but I can't help my amused smile. I wasn't going to have anyone to sit with anyway.

Will's adorable in a boy next door way. He's slightly taller than me and has a nice athletic body. I'm sure he probably plays water polo or some snobby sport like that.

"So, I know you're new and your name is Piper, but that's about it. Tell me about yourself." Will takes a big bite out of his hamburger and stares at me while he chews, waiting for my answer.

"That pretty much sums it up." I shrug.

"Do you have a boyfriend?"

"Nope. Do you?"

"Nah, I like women." He flashes me a pearly white smile.

"Piper, thanks for your card. I finally found mine. Here it was in my wallet the whole time. Crazy, right?" Connor drops my ID in front of my face. I catch it right before it falls into my salad and glare at him.

"Yeah, real crazy," I grumble under my breath.

"I see Will bought you lunch, though. Isn't that so nice of him." His voice is cold and threatening. "Watch your back at football practice, I wouldn't want you to get injured, Will." Connor clamps his hand down on Will's shoulder and squeezes hard. He stares at me for several seconds before heading back to his table in the corner.

Mac and Gray are staring at us when I glance over there. Mac smiles and winks at me, but Gray just glares. His green eyes stand out even from this far away.

I didn't really get a good look at Gray this morning, but he's wearing a tight black sleeveless shirt and gray joggers. His muscles are on full display and I don't think a single person would complain about the sight.

His warning from this morning flashes through my brain. I peek over at Will and wonder if I can really trust him to have good intentions.

Be careful, princess. Some people aren't as trustworthy as they seem. Salt and sugar look awfully similar, don't you think?

Was this an actual warning from him, or was it a way to get inside my head and fuck with me?

"Ignore him. Connor's always been more bark than bite." Will waves him off, picking up a French fry and popping it in his mouth.

"Yeah, well all his barking is directed at me now." I stab my salad and bring it to my mouth.

"Did you make any friends yet?"

"Not really. Who wants to make new friends their senior year of high school? You've probably known all these people for the past twelve years. It's fine though, I don't plan on sticking around here after graduation."

"What am I, chopped liver? I'm making a declaration. I, William Cooper, am officially a friend of Piper... what's your last name?"

"Lawson." I roll my eyes. "We must be fantastic friends if you don't even know my last name."

"Shush... I, William Cooper, am officially a friend of Piper Lawson. Anyone who fucks with her, fucks with me."

"Aren't declarations supposed to be publicly announced?" I quirk a brow.

"I mean I can stand on top of this table right now and shout it loud enough for the whole school to hear. I don't mind one bit." Will shrugs and rises to his full height. One foot gets planted on his seat before I can scramble out of mine and tug him back down.

"Will! Sit down!" I hiss, trying to shove him back into his seat.

"What? I was trying to make my public declaration! I'm not going to hide my friendship with you."

"Please? Just please sit down." I'm practically begging. People around us are starting to notice something is going on at our table. I'd really rather not be the focus of everyone's attention.

Will plants both feet on the ground and pulls me into a hug.

"What are you doing?"

"I think I deserve a hug for obeying like a good little boy. Hug me back, Piper."

I wrap my arms around him and try to hide my annoyance. Will has been nothing but nice to me, he doesn't deserve my anger or frustration. No, all of that should be directed right at Connor Ward and his asshole friends.

Chapter 7
Grayson

"Why's she sitting with Will?" Mac stares across the lunchroom.

"Mr. Goody Two Shoes bought her lunch since I took her ID and just gave it back." Connor glares down at his tray full of food. "That wasn't the plan."

"I really don't know why you're fucking with her. It's not her fault her mom married your dad. I'm sure she didn't want to leave her friends and move here." Grabbing my chicken Caesar wrap, I take a big bite out of it and chew slowly.

I hate dealing with these little vendettas Connor always has against someone. The first time, it was fun, something to keep us busy. Now, I'm tired of it.

I don't think Piper deserves to be put through all of this when she didn't do anything wrong... yet. If that changes and she gives us a reason to attack, then I'll happily help.

But that doesn't mean I'm going to be her friend either. I don't need any more friends.

"It doesn't matter. I want her gone." Connor's attention has been on her the entire lunch period.

People are going to think he has a thing for his new stepsister if he doesn't stop staring. I'd love to hear those rumors and see how Connor responds. He'd make each and every person in this place who breathed a word about him pay. He'd make it his mission to ruin all of their lives. And he's dedicated enough to do it.

"Last period she has swimming. This is what I have planned..."

His plan is stupid and juvenile, but he knows we'll follow his lead and help him. It's what we've always done. The entire school knows if you fuck with one of us, you fuck with all of us.

Honestly, I don't care enough about Piper to stop Connor. If I go against what he wants, it's only going to cause me more issues. Issues I don't have the patience to deal with or the time.

The bell rings and I'm happy to move towards my next class. I'm getting sick of hearing about Piper ruining

Connor's life. I'd rather listen to my teacher drone on and on about science for an hour.

It seems like no matter where I go, everyone is talking about Piper. Rumors are already spreading about the hot new girl and I have a feeling Cherie and Connor are behind most of them.

Cherie's been trying to gain Connor's attention for years. It's her goal to become his girlfriend before the end of senior year. I don't know why she wants him so badly, but she does.

I have no doubt if Connor mentioned wanting to get rid of Piper, Cherie would do just about anything to accomplish it and gain Connor's approval. Like I said, no one likes a desperate girl.

I claim a lab table in the back row of the science room, hoping we won't have assigned seats this year. The tables fill up quickly and I'm happy no one is trying to take the seat next to me.

Every time it seems like someone's going to sit next to me, I glare at them until they change their minds and find somewhere else. I'm more than content with being my own science partner.

Mr. Murphy begins telling us about our next project and what tests we have to look forward to this month. I'm only partly listening. I don't need to know any of this. Science is easy for me.

"Are you Miss Lawson?" I glance up to see Piper walking through the door. She nods her head at Mr. Murphy. "Please find a seat and refrain from being late to my class again."

To her credit, Piper doesn't blush or drop her gaze. She keeps her head held high and searches for an empty seat. The only one left is next to me.

"Oh joy. It's you," she murmurs under her breath as she drops into her seat.

"Don't look so happy to see me. Someone might think you like me."

"It'll be a cold day in hell when I'm happy to see you." She shuffles through her notebooks until she gets to one with *Science* scrawled across the top in a girly handwriting.

"Better bundle up, I'd hate to see you get frostbite." I toss a piece of cinnamon gum into my mouth and chew slowly.

"The seats you're sitting in today are your assigned seats for the rest of the year. I gave you the past two weeks to figure out who you wanted to sit with. I feel like that was more than fair on my part. Your table mate is your partner for all projects. Let's hope you picked wisely."

"I saw you talking to Will," I whisper, not wanting anyone except for Piper to hear me.

"I was, Detective. Is there a problem with that?"

"Nah, I'd just watch your back." I shrug.

"What's that supposed to mean?"

"Don't be afraid of the enemy who you know will attack you, be afraid of the fake friend who holds you and tells you to trust them."

"Do you always speak so cryptically? You keep saying shit that doesn't make sense."

"I'm just warning you, Piper. There are enough wolves in sheep's clothing around here. You can never be too careful."

"Are you one of them?"

"Nah, I don't hide my true colors. What you see is what you get."

"So, you're just a savage wolf?"

"Better watch out for my bite," I growl, turning my attention back to the teacher.

After school, I don't bother going home with Connor. I already have plans with Hadley and I never break commitments to my sister. Climbing into her passenger's seat, I let out a long sigh.

"What's going on with you?" She quirks a brow before starting her car and pulling out of the parking lot.

"It's been a long day. Connor's set on ruining his new stepsister's life and of course he's pulling me into it." I run my hand through my hair.

"I don't understand why you hang out with him. You two couldn't have more different personalities if you tried."

"I'm not the nice guy you pretend I am, Hads. I'm an asshole who doesn't give a shit about people." Crossing my arms over my chest, I stare out the passenger's window.

"You want people to believe that, but deep down, you do care. You're a good person, Grayson, you just have a hard exterior. Like super hard." She grins at me. "You don't need friends like him."

I hate discussing my choice of friends with my family. They don't understand Connor and Mac. For years I've defended them, but at this point I don't know how to defend Connor's actions.

His dad's last wife was a professional model. She lasted a whole week in the Ward mansion before she ran screaming from the property after he added a hair removal cream to her shampoo. Her hair started falling out in clumps the day before a big photo shoot. She told James there was no way she could stay married to a man with such an evil kid living in the same house.

The one before that had a phobia of spiders and he'd constantly hide spiders in her food... they weren't always dead either. She ended up having so many panic attacks, she couldn't handle being in the same house as Connor.

I feel bad for James. Connor's mom was the love of his life and she died when we were in elementary school. He's been lonely for eight long years. He just wants someone to spend the rest of his life with.

"Is Piper Lawson his stepsister?" Hadley glances at me before turning her attention back to the road.

"Yeah, do you know her?"

"Yup. She's in my English class. She seemed nice. I was thinking of asking her if she wanted to come over some time."

"Why?" I scowl at the passing trees.

"Because she deserves to have a friend and I like her."

"She's not a scared little puppy, Hads. You don't need to save her." Rolling my head against the headrest, I face my sister.

"I'm not trying to save her. I'm trying to be nice. One of us should be and clearly it won't be you. It evens out our twin dynamic or some shit like that."

I snort with laughter because that sounds exactly like my sister. She believes in balance and karma. Because I'm mean, she needs to be nice. If I don't accept something offered to us, she has to or the entire world will be thrown off balance.

The second we walk through the door, Mom is on us. She wraps us each in a hug and follows us into the kitchen. She already has snacks laid out and asks us about our day. You'd think we were still toddlers with how she cares for us.

"I met a new friend named Piper. Would it be ok if I invite her over soon for dinner and a movie night?" Hadley eyes me with amusement.

"Of course! I'd love to meet her. Is she new to the school?"

"She's Connor Ward's new stepsister."

"I'll start praying for her now." Mom turns her attention to me. "Gray, is he already torturing her?"

"He's already scheming." I shrug, popping a grape in my mouth.

"I hate that little asshole," Mom grumbles under her breath.

"Tell us how you really feel." I smirk at her. I love the relationship I have with my family. We're very laid-back and candid with each other. "Isn't there some rule that as a parent you aren't supposed to call kids assholes?"

"Pfft, if you knew the number of times I've told your father what an asshole you are you'd be shocked. And I love you so you'd have to push me much harder than someone else to earn that status. Connor's never been the greatest kid, but he's definitely getting worse. I don't even like having that little shit in my house."

"I know, Mom. Dad already told me. I'll cut ties at the end of the year or I won't get the company." I press a kiss to her cheek and tell her and Hadley that I need to go do some homework. We all know I'm lying. I'll do it all tomorrow morning between classes, but they let me go anyway.

I'll hide out in my room while they discuss Piper and Connor. I know it's going to be a long conversation and one I don't want to be a part of.

Once Hadley gets all of her gossiping out of her system, she'll come look for me and then we can go out for dinner and to the movies like we planned.

Chapter 8
Piper

As I make my way down the hallway to my locker, people are snickering at me. They've come up with some many rumors, it's almost funny.

According to my classmates, I'm running from the law and James has the connections to change my name and make it all go away.

I'm actually the one sleeping with James, not my mom. But she's acting like they're married so we can enjoy nice things in life and James won't get in trouble.

My favorite is I used to strip and James adopted me to get me away from my pimp who was threatening to kill me.

I'm sure there are other rumors that haven't made their way to me yet, but I don't care. These people's opinions of me don't matter one bit. I'm here to get my high school diploma so I can go to college and move on with my life. I'm not here to become anyone's best friend or to find some rich boy to marry.

A group of girls huddle together and glance over their shoulders at me every few seconds. They think they're being sneaky, but they might as well stare directly at me the entire time.

"Hey, sweetheart, do you want to meet me behind the big oak tree? I can really rock your world." A guy steps into my personal space, making me take a step back.

"Yeah, I'm good. But thanks so much for asking." I push my way past him and roll my eyes. High school guys are such assholes.

"Hey, babe, where are you going?" A guy slips his arm around my waist and tries to tug me against his chest.

I shove him away with all of my might and glare at him. What the fuck is their problem? I haven't had issues with anyone in this school until now.

"Don't act like you don't want me!" He calls to my retreating back.

"Oh, fuck off. I don't want anything to do with you," I growl, glaring at him over my shoulder.

"That's because Daddy Ward is already giving it to her daily." One of the girls snickers.

I spin around to walk away and run straight into a hard chest. I stumble back a step and blink in surprise. I wasn't looking where I was going.

My bag slips off my shoulder and as it hits the ground, my things slide out and scatter across the floor.

"Fucking great," I groan, squatting down to gather my things.

"Walking down the hallway is slightly easier if you're looking where you're going." Gray stares down his nose at me.

"Well, excuse me for trying to dodge the creepy pervs in this school," I hiss, as I peer up at him.

As soon as all of my things are in my arms, I stand and close the few feet of distance between me and my locker.

Across the front of the metal is a red piece of paper with the word whore scribbled across it. I roll my eyes, not really giving a shit. I don't care what these idiots think of me, I just don't want them to come near me.

I spin the dial and quickly do my combination while trying to balance my books in my arms. I let out a sigh of relief as the lock frees and I open the door.

When things start tumbling out and all around me on the floor, I groan again. There's a sea of condoms at my feet and every time one of the guys bends down to pick some up, they grin at me and wiggled their eyebrows.

"Why? What the hell did I do to deserve this?" I mumble under my breath as I grab my backpack and shove my books inside.

After slamming my locker shut, I spin around to find Grayson staring at me with a pinched brow. I roll my eyes as I step past him. I'm positive he had something to do with this. I ignore him as I step over the pile of condoms and disappear down the hall.

I hope these idiots take all of them and put them to good use. The last thing we need is them having offspring.

―――

Connor was nothing short of a dick on the way home from school. He went on and on about how lucky Mom and I are to be living in *his* house. In *his* life. He acts like he's the most important person in the world and it's really starting to piss me off. I mean doesn't it get a little lonely being so high above everyone else on your pedestal?

I didn't bother calling him out on stuffing my locker full of condoms. It has nothing to do with letting him off the hook, and everything to do with not wanting to spend another second with him.

I practically leap from the car before he even comes to a complete stop. I can't deal with him any longer. I've reached my maximum recommended dosage of Connor Ward for the day. Doctors say you'll lose your mind and get all stabby if you exceed the dosage. I better stay away if I don't want to make him bleed all over *his* house and make him even angrier with me.

I make a beeline for the kitchen, wanting something to drink. I'd love a glass of wine or even whiskey, but I'll settle for a bottle of water.

"You look like you want to stab someone." Fernando leans his back against the island and folds his arms over his chest, smirking at me.

"How angry do you think James would be over blood on the white carpets?"

"I think it'd depend on whose blood it is. He might even hold some people down for you." He winks at me with a devilish grin. "What happened?"

"He's just screwing with me at school. Little things like taking my ID so I couldn't get lunch."

"I'll never understand that kid." Fernando lowers his voice so only I can hear him. I'm sure Connor wouldn't hesitate to fire Fernando if he knew he was speaking badly about him. "He has the world at his fingertips, but he's too worried about someone stealing anything away from him for him to enjoy it... what are you going to do?"

"I'm planning on putting up with it for a while. Right when he thinks I'm going to give up, I'm going to strike back and hard. I'm not going to get pushed around by some rich prick. He might've started this war, but I'm going back down. He's not going to win."

At dinner, only James and Mom are at the table with me. It's kind of nice just being the three of us. I could get used to a life like this. Hell, I could look forward to a life here if Connor weren't in the picture.

"Piper, I wanted to talk to you." James places his fork gently on the table and tugs his wallet out of his pocket.

"Ok... what's going on?"

"Clearly, my son gets everything he could ever want. Now that I'm married to your mother and you're my daughter, I want to make sure you can have everything you want too." He slides a shiny new credit card across the table.

I stare down at it, surprised to find my name on the plastic. I don't touch it. I don't know how to feel about this. Of course I want to be able to get things and enjoy the benefits of my new life, but this feels like too much.

"James... I don't need this."

"Please, Piper? Let me take care of you. Connor isn't wrong. I've always wanted a daughter. My late wife couldn't get pregnant after she had Connor and we were devastated. We were planning on adopting... but then she got sick." James is getting choked up talking about his first wife and my heart breaks for him.

I'm sure losing her was difficult for him. Especially with Satan as his son.

Mom runs a comforting hand up and down his back. He takes a moment to get his emotions under control and when he does, he glances at us with a sad smile and watery eyes.

"I'm sorry. I still miss her dearly, but I love your mother just as much. Anyway... you have a thousand dollar limit every month. If you need more than that, come talk to me. As long as you're not spending it on stupid things, I won't mind you going over."

"A *thousand* dollars a month? Are you crazy? I'd be happy with fifty or a hundred. I don't need this, James. It's too much." I push the plastic card back across the table and shake my head. This man is crazy. Money must do that to people. It's the only explanation.

"You don't need to spend that much." James chuckles at my horrified expression. "I want you to enjoy all the things you couldn't in your old life. Go shopping with your friends and buy all the things you like. Buy yourself the necklace or earrings you've always wanted, but were a little too expensive to get. And homecoming is in a few weeks. You'll need a dress for that. I'm sure you're going to want to get your hair, nails, and make-up done for that too."

"I won't be going to homecoming. You don't need to worry about any of that." I wave him off, taking a bite of my steak.

"Why not?" James' eyebrows pull low into a frown. He glances from Mom to me and back.

"Well, I have no friends here and I don't think there's going to be a line of guys wanting to ask me out." I'm not trying to get sympathy. I've accepted that this last year of high school is going to be vastly different from the previous years.

"You could invite Tim as your date!" Mom stares at me with hopeful eyes. She wants me to be happy and that includes feeling at home in our new life.

"Maybe. I'll see if he can come."

Even though I tell Mom that, I'm not asking Tim to come to homecoming. The people out here would rip him to shreds and he wouldn't be able to handle it. Sure, Tim has a tough exterior, but he's a giant softy on the inside. I don't want to watch him get hurt.

I can only imagine the shit Connor, Gray and Mac would try to pull on him. I know without a doubt, they'd go after him to try to get to me and that isn't something I want. I'd rather sit at home while everyone else goes to a party. I'd rather be lonely than risk my best friend.

I've already told Tim I don't want him coming to visit me here. I wasn't surprised to find out he planned to surprise me with a visit this weekend. It took a while, but I was finally able to convince him the three-hour drive wasn't worth it.

James wordlessly slides the card back in front of me and this time I don't give it back. I slide it in my back pocket and accept the new world I live in. Like he said, I don't have to use it, but it's there if I need it.

"Next week we're going to pick out your car too. This week became a little too busy for me."

"Sounds good." There's no point in arguing. He'll get what he wants or he'll hound me to accept his gifts until I give in. The Ward men always get what they want.

The week passes in a blur. I do my best to learn my way around the school. When and where my classes are, my locker combination and where to avoid. I stay away from Connor and his little minions the best I can, but it's hard. Every morning Mac insists on striking up a conversation with me, and Gray's my partner in science. I can't very well ignore them. I have to remind myself they aren't on my side. No matter what, they'll always have Connor's back.

It's Friday morning and I'm rushing down the steps in the clothes I'd normally wear to school, not what I'd let James see me in.

"Morning, Sweetie." Mom presses a kiss to my hair and settles into a chair at the table.

"Piper, you should really get ready for school. You're going to be late." James peeks at me from over his newspaper.

"I am ready for school. I'm just grabbing breakfast until Connor comes down."

"You're going to wear *that* to school?" His brows look like they're trying to disappear into his hairline. I have to cough to cover my laugh. It doesn't help that Fernando is standing behind James, his entire body shaking from his silent laughter.

"Of course not!" I glance down at my outfit and James visibly relaxes. "I can't leave the house in slippers." James's eyes widen once again and he turns his attention to Mom.

"Are you really going to let her go out in public like that?"

"James... I know you're used to having a son, but let me explain something to you about girls. If I forbid her from wearing that, she's only going to put different clothes on top until she gets out of the house. Then she'll wear whatever she planned on wearing anyway. I guarantee on Monday she had something different on under that maxi skirt. Am I right, Piper?"

"Camo shorts and a crop top," I mumble around a piece of bacon.

"See? It's pointless. Instead, we have guidelines. Like she can't wear miniskirts unless she's wearing boy shorts under it."

James's brows furrow, clearly not understanding what Mom's talking about.

"I'm not allowed to wear a thong with a mini, James." I roll my eyes, feeling a little more like Connor today.

"I don't want to hear about your... panties, Piper!"

"Ew, who calls them panties?" Connor plops into the seat across from me.

"Old people." I roll my eyes.

"If a bikini would cover it, it needs to be covered at all times," Mom adds. "And she has to wear a bra."

James nearly chokes on the last rule. The poor man isn't used to having a daughter at all.

"Don't worry, James. You only have a few months with me, then you can forget all about me being a girl. You can even pretend I'm a boy when I'm off at college."

"Piper... I didn't mean-"

"I know. I'm just not going to change because I'm living here." I shrug and stand from the table. "I'm ready to go whenever you are, Connor."

"About time. I want to pick up a coffee on the way. This shit sucks," he grumbles under his breath, pushing the cup of coffee Fernando made away from him. He stomps out the door to the garage like the world personally offended him. I follow behind him, knowing he'll leave me behind without a second thought.

Chapter 9
Grayson

It's the last period of school and it feels like the day is dragging. I'm more than ready to go home and relax.

The teacher pauses their lecture when the phone rings. He sighs, not liking whatever he's hearing on the other end of the phone.

"Mr. Young, you're wanted in the office."

"Why?" I frown. I hate walking into things unprepared.

"Mr. Young, I'm not your secretary. If I cared about why they wanted to speak to you, I would've asked. Please leave my room so I can finish this lesson."

I gather all of my books and make my way out of the class and down the hall. I'm not rushing, not for him. I know Connor has something to do with it. He always does.

My thoughts drift to Piper and how she handled all of the assholes hitting on her and the locker full of condoms. I expected her to flip out or cry, but she did neither. She held her head high and left without a word.

She's stronger than I thought she would be. She's not backing down from Connor, yet she's taking his shit. I wonder if this is all part of her game. Is she going to eventually strike back, or is she going to take it all with grace?

Eventually Connor will piss her off enough that she'll want revenge or he'll break her completely.

"What's going on?" I quirk a brow at Connor and Mac as I approach them.

Connor shoots me a shit-eating grin and leads us down to the hallway to where the gym and pool are. I know what's going to happen long before he finally spills the details. I have to bite my cheek to keep from groaning. I don't want a thing to do with this.

"Just hurry up and go." Mac waves us into the girl's locker room. "I'll knock twice if someone's coming."

"How are you going to know which locker's hers?" Following Connor into the room, I glance all around. If I get caught in here, Dad will kill me.

He's not thrilled about my friendship with Connor. Over the years, every time I've gotten in trouble was because of Connor. Dad's been wanting to end our relationship for a long time. He told me after we graduate, I need to cut my ties with him entirely. He thinks Connor's nothing but trouble. At this point, I'd have to agree.

"I'm just looking for the stupid red pants. There are only a dozen people in each swim class. It can't be that hard."

All of the locker doors are metal mesh to let more air into them. The swim team keeps wet bathing suits in there and they need to dry somehow.

"I really think you should just leave her alone. Go after the mom if you want, but torturing Piper isn't going to solve anything."

Connor pauses mid step and spins around to face me. His brows draw low and his gaze hardens. Awesome. When I was thinking about my day and what it was missing, dealing with a pissed off Connor was definitely at the top of my list.

"Do you have a thing for Piper?"

"What? No. I just think this is a little much." I shrug. It's laughable to think I could have a thing for her.

Who could possibly have a thing for the beautiful girl with chocolate brown hair and light blue eyes? Who could be attracted to someone who doesn't cower when faced with someone like Connor? Someone who has a breathtaking smile and the longest legs I've ever seen. Not me. Not even a little.

"Let me handle this. She's my lovely step sister after all... you search that side and I'll check this one." Connor nods to the lockers in front of him.

I keep my frustration to myself and begin searching for Piper's red pants. I let out a sigh of relief when I don't find any on this side of the lockers. It makes me feel slightly better to know I'm not the one to find her things.

"What are you doing with her clothes?"

"I'm going to throw them in the hamper at home. Maria can wash them and put them back. That way I can't get in trouble for any of this. There's no way for anyone to pin it on me."

Connor's nearly giddy with excitement when we exit the locker room with all of Piper's things. Leaving her with no option except her bathing suit.

"I don't understand how this is that big of a deal. She's still going to have her bathing suit. Piper doesn't strike me as the type of girl to care about people seeing her in it."

Mac kicks a pencil someone must have dropped down the hall.

"Cherie's going to steal her bathing suit and towel when she's showering. She'll be left with nothing." Connor wiggles his brows with a devilish grin. Sometimes I swear the guy really is the devil in the flesh.

"She's going to know you did it," I say in a bored tone. I need him to believe I don't care about any of this.

In reality, I feel bad for Piper. Hadley said she's really nice and Hads is never wrong when it comes to people. She always sees through the bullshit and straight into a person's heart.

"Who cares? She can't prove anything."

"You're supposed to give her a ride home." Mac frowns at him.

"Yeah, I'm not doing that either." Connor picks up his pace.

"You can leave without me. I have to go with Hadley this afternoon to get a gift for my mom's birthday."

My brain scrambles with how to fix this. I thought Piper was going to be stuck with wearing her bathing suit. Sure, that would've been embarrassing, but it's nothing compared to being stranded naked.

We don't live in a bad area by any means, but she still can't walk home naked. It's not going to end well if a bunch of high schoolers see her without any clothes on.

I whip my phone out of my pocket and text my sister. I don't know how else to help Piper without the guys knowing.

Grayson: Do you have a set of spare clothes in your locker?

"Seriously? You're ditching us for Hadley?" Mac whines like a baby.

"She's my sister, so yeah. We shared the womb for nine months, she's kinda grown on me." I roll my eyes at them.

They always give me a hard time about spending time with Hadley, but I love my sister and want to spend time with her. I know one day we won't live in the same house anymore, we might not even live close to each other, and I want to make sure we have a strong relationship when that happens because I'm not losing Hadley.

"Whatever, we can have more fun without him." Connor nudges Mac forward. They disappear around the corner a few seconds later and I scramble to read the text from Hadley.

Hadley: Yup. I have a few. Why do you need girl's clothes? Are you trying to tell me something?

Grayson: Give me your combo. I'm trying to help someone.

Hadley: 3-25-19. Go rescue the girl on your white horse, prince charming.

Grayson: You must have me confused with someone else. There's nothing charming about me, Hads.

Hadley: Only because you don't let people see that side of you.

My sister has it in her head that I'm the greatest guy in the world. I've always taken care of her and treated her well. Maybe that's why I don't share Connor's view on Piper. I'd kill for Hadley. I'd do anything in my power to make her life easier. I've never done anything to hurt her and I don't plan on changing that.

I waste no time getting to Hadley's locker and tugging out an outfit that should fit Piper. She's lucky she's about the same size as my sister.

I hurry to the hallway that the pool is in and slow my pace. I don't want anyone to realize why I'm here. I stuff the clothes in my backpack and I lean against the wall like I'm waiting for someone. I use my phone as a distraction, but also to warn people I'm not interested in a conversation.

"Hey, Gray. What are you doing down here?" Cherie purrs as she steps next to me.

"Hey, Cher. I'm just waiting for Hadley."

"She isn't in our class." Cherie frowns.

"Damn, I must've mixed up her schedule. I guess I'll text her and figure out where I'm supposed to meet her then." I lift my phone, shaking it in her face. "See ya later."

Cherie and her friends take the hint and walk away calling goodbyes over their shoulders. Damn, that was actually easier to get rid of them than I thought it would be.

"Are you freaking kidding me!" Muttered curses follow Piper's yelling. A slow smile spreads over my lips. And let the fun begin.

Chapter 10

Piper

"Hello?" I peek around the corner of the showers when I hear the door open and close. I can't see anyone, but that does nothing to ease the panic I'm feeling.

My towel is missing from where I left it and my bathing suit is missing from where I hung it on the hook in the shower. I don't know how he pulled it off, but I know Connor's responsible for this!

I listen for a few more seconds before I chance moving to my locker. I let out a loud groan when I find my things missing from there too. Fucking Connor!

I move from one locker to the next, trying the doors to see if they'll open. Of course everyone was careful to lock up before they left, or the lockers are empty.

I get to the last little alcove of lockers, right by the door, and hold my breath as I scan the lockers. I find a stack of clothes with a note laying on top.

Wear them, Piper. I'm sorry.

My brows furrow together. I read the note two more times before I scramble to get dressed. I don't know who left these for me, but I'd bet it was Mac. He seems too sweet to go along with Connor and leave me stranded here. I have no doubt Gray was happy to help Connor humiliate me.

After I quickly put on the clothes, I grab my backpack out of my swim locker and head out to the parking lot. I'm not surprised when Connor's car is gone. He's such a prick. I guess I should just be happy he left my backpack and cell phone.

I tug my phone out the pocket and call the one person I know is solidly on my team.

"What's wrong, darling?" Fernando's Italian accent makes me smile.

"Could you send Roger to pick me up from school?"

"Connor left you there without a ride, huh?" I can hear him chopping things in the background.

"How'd you know?" I wrap my arms around myself, uncomfortable with being in clothes that aren't mine.

"Well, he walked through the kitchen twenty minutes ago and I didn't see you. I had Maria check to see if you were home and sent Roger to get you about ten minutes ago. He should be there any second."

No sooner are the words out of his mouth do I see Roger's SUV pull into the parking lot and slow. He's scanning the area for me. I wave him down and smile. I'm more than thankful for Fernando, Roger, and Maria. They've been one of the good things that's happened to me since I moved here.

"Thanks, Fernando. I'll see you soon." I end the call and slide my phone back into my pocket.

Roger steers the car over to me and pulls to a stop. He rolls the window down and flashes me a toothy smile.

"I've got some great candy in here."

"You better have strawberry Twizzlers," I mumble, making him chuckle. I climb into the front seat and buckle my seatbelt. When Roger doesn't say a word or move the car, I turn my attention back to him. "What?"

"Nothing... it's just I've never had anyone sit in the front seat with me. Mr. Ward and Connor always sit in the back."

"Do I have to sit back there?" I scrunch my nose with disgust. "I'd prefer the front, I'm not a toddler. I promise I even weigh enough to be up here."

"Fine, I won't even make you step on a scale. But if James asks, you insisted on sitting up here."

"Anything for you, Roger." I flash him a cheeky grin.

We pull into the long driveway a few minutes later. Roger tells me to hop out at the front door then he pulls the car around to wherever he keeps it parked. I've never seen it in the garage with Connor's car. I'm sure there's a separate garage I'm unaware of.

"There's my girl!" Fernando glances up at me and smirks when I enter the kitchen. "What happened to your other outfit? Did you do a wardrobe change at school?"

"Connor stole my clothes during swim class. A friend left these for me."

I'd love to know who this friend was. I'm still betting on Mac, but I'm not positive.

"That little shit. I swear one day I'm going to put laxatives in his pudding." Fernando tosses a bag of icing on the counter and folds his arms across his chest. A frown transforms his face, somehow making him more handsome.

"Why do you work here? You're an amazing chef. You could work anywhere." Sliding onto a stool, I squeeze a little bit of icing onto my finger and lick it off.

The cake Fernando was decorating is gorgeous. It has delicate lace work piped onto the sides and big roses on the top. It looks like something you'd see on the cover of a magazine or at a wedding, not for dessert on a random weeknight.

"I don't know. I've always dreamed of having my own restaurant, but I never had the money to invest in something like that. James has always been kind and pays me well. I enjoy getting to make something different every day and most of the time he gives me free reign over the menu. I get to try new recipes and I receive honest feedback on them." Fernando leans forward and whispers, "Lord knows Connor isn't going to keep his opinions to himself."

"I think you should do it. Start your own restaurant, I mean. If I had money, I'd invest in it. My dream has always been to have my own business. I want to work for myself rather than someone else."

"Smart girl. Maybe one day we can go into business together... but until then, I need to get started on dinner. James will have a cow if dinner isn't ready at six on the dot." He rolls his eyes.

I tell him I'll see him later and hop down from my stool. I'm on my way up to my room when Mac steps out of Connor's room.

"Hey, Piper... how was school?"

"Oh, just great. Swim class was my favorite," I hiss, pushing past him.

The guilty look on his face speaks louder than words. Mac had a hand in this, and he definitely didn't leave the clothes for me. If he did, he wouldn't look nearly as ashamed as he does.

"Pipe..." He reaches out a hand to grab my wrist.

"No, Mac. I never asked for your friendship, but I expected more from you. From Connor or Gray, it wouldn't surprise me... but from you... it hurts a little more."

"Piper," he groans, following me down the hall.

I don't turn around. I don't speak to him again. Instead, I slam the door shut in his face and flick the lock. I don't want to hear his excuses. I knew I'd never be able to trust him, but I didn't expect he'd be an enemy.

Chapter 11
Grayson

The first time I see Piper today, she's standing in the hall, talking to Will. I walk past her, knocking my shoulder into hers. She loses her balance and tumbles into Will. Her books fly out of her hands and scatter all over the ground. I spin on my heels and watch her with a smirk. She glares up at me, but doesn't say a word. Will doesn't have the same control.

"Do you always have to be such an ass, Gray?" He hands her the math and English books she dropped and helps her stand. I've never wanted to punch someone as much as I want to punch him right now.

"Maybe Piper should move out of my way." I shrug and continue on my way.

I need to keep my distance from Piper. I have to make sure she doesn't suspect I helped her. The last thing I need is her thinking I'm her hero.

I'm nobody's hero.

No matter how hard Hadley finds it to believe, I'll never be anyone's price charming either. I'm never going to ride in on my white horse and change a woman's entire world with a dazzling smile on my face.

I quickly move through the cafeteria and grab something for lunch before dropping into a seat next to Mac.

"Her legs are so long. I've never seen someone so fit." Mac stares across the room, his gaze locked on the table Piper, Hadley and Will are sharing. She must've come in right after me.

"You better be talking about Will," I grumble under my breath.

"Why would I be talking about Will's body? It's not even nice. I have a much better body than him. We both do." Mac lifts up the hem of his shirt and checks out his own abs, almost like he's confirming what he just said.

"Drop your damn shirt! I don't need to see that when I'm trying to eat."

"Are you worried I'll make you horny?" Mac rubs his nipples, letting out a fake moan. He gains the attention of all of the tables around us.

The girls stare at him, wishing they were the ones rubbing his chest. They'd stab each other in the back to gain his attention. The guys glare, hating how they don't have a body like his. They hate how every female in the school flocks to Connor, Mac, and me.

"Shut up, Mac. I don't want a bunch of desperate girls coming over here." I shove him away from me, grinning when he almost falls off his seat.

"I wasn't talking about Will," he urges, dropping the hem of his shirt. He knows how much I hate dealing with the girls in this school.

It's not that I don't want attention from them, it's just that most of the ones who fight for our attention are the ones I'd never date. I don't want to date someone who thinks they can change their social standings with my help. I want someone real. Honest. Genuine.

"Well, you better not be talking about Hadley. I'll kill you if you are," I growl.

"I wouldn't touch Hadley with a hundred-foot pole." He chuckles under his breath.

"What the fuck's wrong with my sister?" I slap a hand across the back of his head.

"Ouch! Fuck, dude! Nothing's wrong with her! She's gorgeous, but she's your sister and I'd like to live past my nineteenth birthday so I've placed her solidly in the friend zone. She's more like a little sister to me than an actual woman."

"You better think of her like that." I glare at him for a few moments before I relax. "Connor's going to kill you if he thinks you have a thing for Piper."

"How can you not have a thing for Piper? She's like this little box of perfection. She's hot and knows how to banter like it's her favorite thing in the world. I think she's the perfect woman for me."

"Who's the perfect woman for you?" Connor drops into the seat across from us.

"Presley," I blurt out before Mac can do something stupid like tell Connor he has a thing for his stepsister. That wouldn't end well at all.

"Presley would be great if she knew how to use her mouth for more than just talking. I swear she never shuts up." Connor takes a big bite of his pizza and chews slowly.

"What's your next evil plan to upset the Pretty Princess today?" Mac mumbles around his food. The two of them have taken to referring to Piper as the Pretty Princess.

They both think she acts like royalty. Like she thinks she's better than everyone else and is using Papa Ward to get what she wants.

I think she just doesn't give a fuck and does whatever she wants. She isn't looking for validation or approval. She's happy just being herself and saying screw everyone else.

"Oh, I have a few things planned. The first one should go into effect any minute..." He stares at the door and smirks when the school counselor comes into the cafeteria. She scans the area, her gaze landing on us.

Connor's expression drops and he almost looks worried. He flashes her a sad smile and points in the direction of Piper. Mrs. Gowen wastes no time. She hurries over to Piper and whispers something in her ear before leading her towards the doors.

Piper peeks over her shoulder at us and glares at Connor. When she doesn't move quickly enough, Mrs. Gowen grabs her arm and tugs on it.

"What'd you do?" I sigh, more than done with the day. My sister's scowl is already pointed at our table and I know I'm going to get a ton of crap about this at home.

"Nothing really. I just told Mrs. Gowen how I'm so worried about my new stepsister." Connor goes on to explain what he did and I have to say, it's a stroke of genius on his part. It's definitely going to bite me in the ass though. I can't wait to go home and deal with the after effects.

On the bright side, Hadley isn't going to look at me like a hero any longer. She might finally see me as the villain I am.

When I get to science later in the day, Piper scowls at me. She turns her body just enough away from me that I can't see her face.

"You must work together to figure out what the different properties are within your cup of mud. Do the necessary tests until you figure out each one and write them down. Once you're done, give me your report and I'll tell you if you're right. If you're not, I'm going to give you a different cup and you'll have to start all over. The first two groups who get it right don't have to take midterms or finals this year." Mr. Murphy smiles at us like this is the coolest thing in the world. "Read over the instructions, then we're going to watch a movie for the remainder of the class. We'll start the project on Monday. You should think about your plan over the weekend so you're ready to begin right away."

"Just great," Piper groans.

"What's wrong with you?" I snap. I spent the last two classes dealing with annoying classmates who thought they're funny and kept making comments about my sister. They'll all be getting black eyes at the end of the day. To say my patience is gone is an understatement.

"You! You're what's wrong with me! Out of all the partners I could've had in this class, I got stuck with you! You're grumpy and moody. I don't know how to deal with you!" Piper keeps her voice low so those around us don't hear what she's saying, but she doesn't keep her feelings to herself one bit.

"Wow, did the shy girl finally grow a pair of balls?" I stare at her with a bored expression.

"I'm not shy at all. And I've always had balls, they're just located on my chest instead of between my legs." She folds her arms across her chest, pushing her 'balls' up higher, giving me an even better view.

"I'm surprised you don't have more facial hair with all that testosterone flowing through your veins."

Her brows form a deep V as she glares at me. I turn my attention back to our project and read through the instructions. The faster we get through this, the faster I can be done working with her.

I have to bite my cheek to keep from laughing when I catch her running her fingers over the skin above her upper lip from the corner of my eye. Apparently, I got to her. I can't believe she thinks she has facial hair.

We spend the remainder of the class lost in thought and barely acknowledging each other. I have no clue what's playing on the TV, but it really doesn't matter. As long as we can get this correct, we won't have to take our midterm or finals.

Hopefully we don't kill each other before we can accomplish that.

"You fuckers know why you're here and you know what you did. I'm not going to take it easy on you." I thrust my fist into the first asshole's stomach, smiling when he falls to the ground with a low moan.

The other four stare at me with various expressions. Two look scared, one seems pissed, and one looks bored. He's going to fight back. I have no doubt.

Mac and Connor are blocking the exits, but I told them I don't want them touching a hair on these idiot's heads. This is my fight. I'm going to make sure they all know I don't need my friends' help to beat their asses.

They'll never speak badly about my sister again. She doesn't deserve their asshole remarks or sleezy attention. No matter what they do in life, they'll never be good enough for Hadley Young.

"Are you all just going to stand around and watch me beat the shit out of him? You're awful friends." I bring my fist down into the nose of the guy on the floor and clench my teeth when I hear bone crack. It's a nauseating sound. One I plan to hear four more times before I leave this room.

The two scared guys, I don't waste my time with them. They're not going to fight back and I guarantee they have zero pain tolerance. Breaking their noses will be more than enough punishment for them.

If they don't learn their lessons from today, I'll make sure to break multiple bones next time.

They collapse to the ground as soon as the awful sound echoes around the room. The pissed off kid has had enough. He attacks me, throwing wild punches. One hits me in the mouth and stuns me for a moment, but I don't let it stop me from hitting back. He's going to get a hell of a lot more than just a broken nose.

He's on the baseball team. I know he's the star pitcher, but it's going to be awfully hard to pitch when he has a few broken bones in his pitching hand. If only I knew which hand that was.

"Say goodbye to pitching this year," I growl, bending both of his middle fingers back until he howls in pain and the bones break.

I know all about how pitchers need their index and middle fingers to throw the ball properly. Sure, I could've done the index fingers and it probably would've affected his day-to-day life a little more, but it seemed a bit more poetic to break the middle finger. A little fuck you for him every time he stares at his hands.

Once he's on the ground, holding his left hand against his chest – I guess the left was his throwing hand – I punch him in the nose, smiling when blood spills down his shirt.

It feels good to let the little monster inside of me out to play every once in a while. Being able to fight five guys in one afternoon really helps.

Where most people would be flooded with adrenaline right now, I actually feel calmer. A sense of serene bliss floods my body as I step up to the last fucker. This one isn't going to be as easy.

Chapter 12
Piper

I can't believe him. I can't fucking believe Connor would stoop this low! I squeeze my eyes shut, willing for patience I don't possess. I'm going to kill him.

I'm going to stab him and let him bleed out all over the plush white rug in the living room. I have no doubt Fernando will hold him still and Maria would probably happily clean up the mess. He treats both of them worse than he treats me and that's saying a hell of a lot after today.

It was one thing to stuff my locker full of condoms and steal my clothing, but this? This is a little excessive.

"Miss Lawson, are you even listening to me?" Mrs. Gowen raises a brow.

"Honestly?"

"All I ask in this office is that you give me honesty."

"No, I'm not listening to a damn thing you're saying because Connor's lying." I fold my arms over my chest and stare her down.

"That's quite the accusation."

"And telling people I'm trying to kill myself isn't?" I ask in disbelief. She can't be serious right now.

"Piper," she sighs, setting her glasses and clipboard on the little coffee table separating us. "I understand moving and changing your life so drastically is hard. There's no shame in the adjustment being difficult on you. Many people deal with anxiety and depression."

"You're right, Mrs. Gowen. There is no shame in having anxiety or depression. There's no shame in admitting you need help or that you're overwhelmed. We completely agree there. What we're clearly *not* agreeing on is the fact I'm not struggling!"

"This is a safe space, Piper-"

"I get that! But I don't need to talk about anything! I'm fine!" I slide my long sleeves up my arm and flash my forearms to her. "There are no marks, no scars! I have never cut myself!"

"People cut in other places than their arms." She sighs again like I'm being ridiculous.

"Do you want me to strip down to nothing? Because I will if that will get me out of this damn office and back into class." I begin working the button on my jeans. The overwhelming desire to strangle Connor increases with every second.

"Stop. There's no need for that. Connor was worried. He must have been mistaken. Mistakes happen, Piper. I'd rather he come to me with wrong information than him to keep it to himself and something happen to you."

"Well, I'm glad you care so much. I'd much rather he didn't spread rumors about me, though." I snatch my backpack off the floor and throw it over my shoulder. There's only a little over two periods left of school now.

I've been stuck in this damn office for two hours trying to convince Mrs. Gowen I'm not hurting myself and I don't plan on starting to.

"You may go back to class, but I'll be checking in with you every so often."

"Oh, I'm so glad," I mutter sarcastically.

I stomp down the hallway, trying to release some of the anger pumping through me. There's so much rage begging to break free. If Connor was in front of me right now, I have no doubt I'd attack him and I wouldn't stop.

Handing my teacher the note, I take my seat and try to pay attention to what they're teaching, but it's impossible. My blood is still boiling and I'm itching to ram my fist into Connor's face. Maybe I can find an excuse for him to meet me at the pool after school and I can drown him.

I'm sure I could make it look like an accident or self-defense. It can't be that hard, right? Anyone who knows Connor would believe it or look the other way because they too wanted to kill him multiple times in their lives.

Throughout science class, I have my fists clenched at my sides and I ignore Gray the best I can. As much as I hate him and want nothing to do with him, I don't think this was his doing. He doesn't try to get other people to do his dirty work. He's happy to roll up his sleeves and get dirty by himself.

As soon as the bell rings after my last class, I'm out the door and yanking open my locker. I toss my textbooks inside, not really giving a shit what happens to them.

"Hey, are you ready to go?" Hadley leans against the locker next to mine. The owner of said locker looks slightly annoyed, but I'm fairly certain he has a crush on her so he doesn't say a word. I caught him staring at Hadley a few times this week during English.

"Yeah. I'm not taking any textbooks home this weekend. I'm so done with everything right now." I slam the locker closed and shrug my backpack over my shoulder.

"Did you pack clothes to sleep over?" Hadley falls in step beside me as we walk out to the parking lot.

"Yup. Are you sure it's ok for me to stay over?"

"Of course! My mom hasn't shut up about how excited she is. She's probably going to try to hang out with us, but I promise she's cool. She tells my brother what a shithead he is all the time. She holds nothing back."

"Sounds like we'll get along great then." We share a smirk.

As soon as we met, I knew I'd be great friends with Hadley. She's laid-back and so easy to get along with. My blunt personality didn't upset her one bit. She just smiled and retorted with great one-liners. She doesn't seem nearly as concerned with who's cool and who's not at our school and it's refreshing.

"Thanks for this. I could really use a weekend away from Connor." I glance around the parking lot like Satan himself is going to appear because I dared to utter his name.

"Has it even been that long since you moved in?" She chuckles.

"Nope. We moved in last Sunday and I'm already to my boiling point with him."

"Well, I'll make sure you have a great relaxing weekend. Maybe we can think of ways to get him off your back."

Hadley leads me over to her black Jeep. We toss our bag in the back and hop in.

"I just have to text my brother and see if I'm giving him a ride home. Most of the time he gets a ride with someone else, but I always have to check."

Her fingers dance over the screen of her smartphone. I swear she's texting faster than anyone I've ever seen. She turns her key and busies herself with finding something good to listen to while we wait for her brother's reply.

My thoughts drift to her family. I wonder what her brother is like. I'm assuming he's younger than us since she drives him and we're seniors. I hope he's as nice as Hadley is. That would make this weekend so much nicer.

"Ugh, he wants us to wait. He's walking out now... I hate waiting for him. I don't understand why it takes him forever to get out here. Like we get it, all the girls fling themselves in his direction, but just act like a snow plow and push them all away!"

I chuckle at her and watch everyone exit the school. The number of students leaving dwindles until only a few are coming out at a time.

"Finally! There he is!" Hadley drums her fingers on the steering wheel.

Gray's rushing down the steps towards Mac and Connor. A few other students file out and I figure they must be freshmen. They don't look very old.

"Which one is he?"

"The tall one with dark hair."

I scan the small group of kids, but they're all short and have lighter hair. I furrow my brows and glance all around, wondering where he is.

"I don't see anyone with dark hair."

"Right there, Piper!" Hadley giggles and points right at the guys.

"Are you kidding me? Gray's your brother?"

"Ugh, I hate when people call him Gray." She rolls her eyes. "His name is Grayson. Yes, Grayson's my brother."

"But you're both in the same grade."

"We're even the same age. That's how twins work. We have the same birthday and everything." She smirks.

"Hadley, I can't stay at your house this weekend! Grayson hates me!"

"Oh please, he hates everyone. He won't screw with you at our house though. My mom would kill him and he knows it. Trust me, you're safe with me. He's really not as bad at home as he is at school."

Grayson turns in our direction and climbs into the backseat without a word. He keeps his head down the entire time.

"What took you so long?" Hadley glances in the rear view mirror at him.

"I had to handle shit. Don't worry about it," he mumbles under his breath.

"Fucking hell. Grayson! Look at me!" Hadley slams her hands on the steering wheel, accidentally blaring her horn.

I glance over my shoulder right as Grayson raises his chin and meets Hadley's gaze in the mirror. She gasps and covers her mouth with her hand. He has a split lip and his right eye is already starting to swell and bruise.

"I knew it! What the hell, Grayson! Mom's going to kill you."

"I'm fine. Don't worry about it. I'll deal with Mom," he grumbles under his breath.

"Yeah, and how's the other guy?" She raises a knowing brow.

"There were five of them. They all have broken noses, maybe a few black eyes and a couple of broken fingers." Grayson dabs at his lip with the back of his hand. Blood smears over his skin, but he doesn't seem to care.

"You're going to get suspended." She shifts the car into gear and exits the parking lot.

"I will not. They're not gonna say a damn word. They wouldn't have the balls to."

"Did they breathe in your presence funny?"

"Don't worry about it, Hads. They deserved what they got and so much more. They got off easy, but they won't if they do it again. I'll fucking kill them."

Sure, Hadley, he doesn't seem bad at all. I don't know what I was thinking.

Chapter 13
Grayson

I was really hoping Hadley and Piper wouldn't hit it off. Sure, she was talking about becoming friends with her, but I didn't think she'd actually do it.

The last thing I want is for Connor's focus to move from Piper to my sister. I won't let him near her. I'd kill him before I let him hurt Hadley.

"Are we dropping her off?" I nod to Piper, completely ignoring the fact she's in the car with us. I need to maintain this attitude of indifference towards her, if not hatred.

"No, we're not dropping *her* off. Jeez, Grayson, she has a name." Hadley's brows draw low. She keeps her gaze on the road and refuses to glance in the mirror at me. I've officially been added to her shit list.

"Then where are you two going? I would've just gotten a ride with Connor."

"We're going home. Piper's coming over."

"Why?" I frown, staring out the window at the beach rolling by. Maybe I can make it out to surf tonight. The waves are perfect right now.

"Because we're friends! What the hell is wrong with you? I swear by the end of the year you're going to become just like him!" Hadley slaps her hand on the steering wheel again. She doesn't have to say who she's talking about. We both know. She hates Connor more than Dad does, and that's saying a lot.

"I'm nothing like him," I grumble under my breath.

"When you watch him screw with people's lives and do nothing to stop it, you're part of the problem, Grayson." She lets out a long sigh.

Piper remains silent. If I keep my focus out the window, I can almost pretend she isn't even here. It's just me and Hadley coasting down the highway.

"What do you expect me to do, Hads? Do you want me to throw away an eighteen-year long friendship?"

"Yeah, I do! I want you to be smart about this. He's going to get you into trouble time and time again. But one day, you won't be able to get out of it. You'll be the one to take the fall because Connor Ward doesn't give a shit about anyone except himself."

The second Connor's name falls from Hadley's lips, Piper tenses in the front seat. I know things are bad between them, but I'm not exactly sure how bad. I'm not sure if he's doing even worse things to her at home than he is at school.

"The sad part is you're smarter than this. You know what he's doing is wrong. The person who will pay the most because of Connor is going to be Mac. He sees everyone in a good light and doesn't realize when Connor's manipulating him into doing shit," Hadley adds with a shake of her head.

"I won't let Mac get hurt," I growl.

"No, you'd take the fall to save him. Get away now. Save both of you."

Hadley pulls her Jeep into the garage and hops out before I can say a word. She's not wrong and this little twin heart to heart hit a little too close for my liking. I have no doubt Connor's going to push too hard one day. I feel like that day is creeping up on us. Piper's presence is making Connor even more unstable. He's willing to do just about anything to get rid of her.

Running a rough hand through my hair, I tug on the ends. I need to figure out how to handle all of this. It takes me a few minutes before I climb out of Hadley's Jeep and step through the door to the kitchen. My backpack is carefully hung on the hook in the mudroom and my shoes are kicked off below it. Hadley's and Piper's are right next to mine. It's weird to see her things in my space.

I'm not the same person at home as I am at school. At home I can shed the asshole persona and just relax and be myself.

The issue is, with Piper here, I don't know how to act. Mom and Dad won't put up with me being an ass. They'll call me out on it immediately and hound me about why I'm behaving like that. It's not worth it.

"There's my favorite son!" Mom holds out a plate of snacks and presses a kiss to my cheek. She ignores the busted lip and swollen eye, but I know I'll get questioned about it later.

"I'm your only son," I mumble, wrapping an arm around her to give her a hug.

"Thank God, because if I had another son, you'd have some competition. I don't think you'd win, Gray." Mom shrugs with a smirk on her lips.

I love this woman to death. I hope whoever I marry is just like her. I want the sass, the smartass responses, and the love she shows to us every day in my life forever.

"Nah, I'd kick his ass."

"Well, that's no way to earn a mother's love."

"Touché. But should someone really have to *earn* their mother's love?" I arch a brow, taking a seat at the island next to Hadley.

"I liked you so much more when you were nine and stupid." Mom rolls her eyes.

"I'm still her favorite twin." Hadley flashes me a big grin.

"How? You don't do anything."

"Exactly. She doesn't have to go to stupid games for me. She can live her life however she wants. No parental obligations for me."

"She has an excellent point." Mom nods her head. "Speaking of parental obligations, what time is your game next Friday?"

"Seven. I don't know if I'll come home or if I'll just pick up something to eat and go back. I think I need to be there at six."

"You're not just picking something up. I'll have dinner ready at five. Dad's taking off that day. You know he'll never make it if he's working." The door to the kitchen opens and shuts. A big smile spreads across Mom's face. "Speak of the devil!" She hurries over to the door and flings herself into his arms. Dad chuckles and presses a kiss to her forehead.

"I'll never get tired of how excited you get when I come home." Dad lifts Mom into his arms and carries her into the kitchen. "Oh, a new person!" He flashes Piper a big grin. "I'm Gray, you must be Piper. I swear Hadley hasn't stopped talking about you."

She hasn't? Sure, Hadley's talked about Piper, but not that often. I know Dad wouldn't say something like that unless it was true, though. How much of Hadley's life am I missing?

"It's nice to meet you. You have a beautiful home." Piper shakes Dad's outstretched hand. I'm surprised once again at how quiet she's been since she walked into science class. I wonder if she's mad at me. But of course she's mad at me. I purposely ran into her this morning and sent her books flying, then I was a total ass in science.

The only reason I've been doing any of this is because of Connor. He wants revenge and I'm the idiot who's more than willing to carry it out for him. That's exactly what Hadley was talking about in the car. Connor says jump and we say how high. Mac and I are always the ones who carry out his plans. We're the ones who get in trouble while he stands by with an innocent smile. I won't let that happen anymore.

It's time for things to change.

———

"So, Piper, how are you enjoying Prescott High so far?" Dad smiles at our guest.

Mom and Dad are loving Piper. I think they're just happy Hadley has someone like her as a friend. Someone who doesn't seem to be sticking around for what they can gain from the relationship. Someone who genuinely likes Hadley and wants to get to know her.

Piper's genuine and she doesn't strike me as someone who wants to gain a social status.

She doesn't care about any of it. She just wants to be treated with respect and interact with friendly people.

"It's an adjustment for sure. My last high school was a lot different. Hadley's making the change a little easier to deal with." She smiles at my sister.

"I hope my son is helping too, or at least not making it worse." Dad eyes me with a raised brow. "How's Connor with all of this?"

"Connor's been nice. He's been welcoming me into my new life." She looks like she's in pain having to utter that lie.

Mom snorts with laughter and Dad joins her. They know there's no way Connor's being nice.

"I'm sorry, did I say something?" Piper glances at Hadley, who's trying her hardest not to laugh.

"Oh, sweetie! You don't need to lie in this house. Connor's fucking awful! He's the furthest thing from nice there is." Mom dabs a napkin under her eyes.

"Whenever you want to escape that little shit, you're more than welcome in our home. I can't even imagine how horrible it must be to live with that abomination of a man." Dad shakes his head.

"You know how horrible Connor is?" Piper's brows draw together in confusion.

"Of course we do. Everyone does. Grayson's forbidden to speak to him after they graduate or he won't be working for me." Dad shrugs unapologetically.

"And Connor's not allowed in this house. I have more important things to do than play babysitter to Satan." Mom giggles.

"Why don't you tell us how you really feel?" I roll my eyes.

"Oh hush. You know exactly how horrible he is. I don't know how you've been friends with him for so long."

"He changed after his mom died," I whisper. "I couldn't exactly walk away from him then."

"I guess not, but that doesn't mean you need to entertain or assist with his personal vendettas." Dad pins me with a look.

No matter how much I want to squirm under his attention, I keep my back straight and my chin held high. He knows I'm helping Connor with whatever he's doing to Piper. He doesn't know I'm also trying to help Piper. I'm going to make sure she doesn't get hurt nearly as much as Connor wants her to.

Chapter 14
Piper

Tugging the outfit out of my backpack, I tiptoe down the hall and knock on Grayson's door. I twist my toes in the plush cream carpet and wait for him to open his door.

My heart hammers against my ribs as anxiety fills me. I know it was Grayson. There isn't a doubt in my mind anymore, but to actually call him out on it is different. I want to know why he stepped in to help me. What benefit could he possibly get from saving me from humiliation?

"What do you want?" He mumbles, rubbing sleep from his eyes. His shaggy hair is a wild mess. I want nothing more than to run my fingers through it.

"Sorry, I didn't expect you to be asleep. I heard the music..."

"I always sleep with music on. What do you want, Piper?"

Butterflies erupt through my stomach. This is the first time he's ever called me Piper. Normally it's Princess or something equivalent to 'hey you'. With how deep his voice is and the gravely tone he has from sleeping, I can't respond.

"Piper?" Grayson arches a brow, waiting for me to speak.

"I think you left something in the girl's locker room." I thrust my hand in his direction and wait.

We both stare down at the clothes, but neither of us say a word. It feels like an eternity of silence between us.

"I don't know what you're talking about. I think those are a little small for me."

"I know it was you, Grayson." I drop my arm to my side, Hadley's clothes still fisted in my hand.

"You know what was me?"

"Are you really going to play stupid?" I stare at him, a little surprised with his reaction.

"It's not playing if I have no clue what you're talking about." He folds his arms over his chest. His biceps bulge, drawing my attention.

"Fine, I'll tell Hadley she can have her clothes back."

I turn and make it a whole two steps before fingers wrap around my wrist and halt me from moving further.

The front of his body molds to my back, his warmth seeps through my clothes overheating me almost instantly.

"I'm only going to say this once, so listen and listen well." His lips brush against my ear as his warm breath fans across my neck. "You shouldn't trust my words, but you can trust my actions."

I suck in a deep breath as my eyelids slide closed. I'm savoring the feel of him pressed against me, letting his words sink in. All too soon, Grayson slips away, taking the clothes I was just clutching in my hand and his door closes softly behind him. I'm blanketed in silence. A shiver runs through me at the loss of his heat.

What the fuck was that?

You shouldn't trust my words, but you can trust my actions.

What does he mean by that? Is he talking about the clothes he left for me? It had to have been him. Mac feels too guilty about what happened, but Grayson? He feels nothing. His conscience is clear.

I stumble back into Hadley's room, but I know I won't be sleeping well tonight.

Every interaction I've had with Grayson plays on repeat in my head. He doesn't hate me. He wants to, but he doesn't. He's just following what Connor wants him to do.

I'm not sure if that makes it better or worse. People need to stop being scared of Connor and just tell him to fuck off. He's only going to get worse until someone stands up to him.

Chapter 15
Grayson

I barely slept after Piper paid me a visit. I couldn't get her out of my head. I don't know how she figured out it was me who left those clothes, but I'm not admitting to anything. I'm going to feign innocence for as long as I can.

I know I got to her last night, though. When I stepped closer and pressed myself against her, I felt her body shudder against mine. This attraction I feel for her is like nothing I've ever felt before.

I need to shut this shit down. Nothing good can come from me being drawn to her. Being attracted to her. I can't save Piper from Connor. The best I can do is lessen his blows.

I stumble down the stairs, searching for coffee to help wake me up. I need that liquid gold to make it through this day. I don't do well with lack of sleep. I'll be grumpy as can be and Mom won't put up with that shit. I turned eighteen last month, but that won't stop her from sending me to my room.

"Morning, handsome." Mom's leaning against the counter with a mug in hand. She takes one look at me and holds it out for me to take.

"Thanks," I mumble, barely aware of my surroundings.

"I'd ask how you slept, but I think I can figure it out just from that grumpy face."

"I'm exhausted. I'm hoping this shit is strong enough to give me some energy." I take a greedy sip before mimicking her position against the counter. Mom chuckles. We're pressed hip to hip, shoulder to shoulder, but I tower over her.

"When I brought your tiny body home from the hospital, I never imagined you'd tower over me one day."

"What can I say? I'm a growing boy."

"Why is my growth stunted?" Hadley pouts from the island. I don't know how I didn't realize she was there.

"It's not, you're just mini sized." I smirk over the rim of my coffee when she sticks her tongue out at me.

Piper saunters into the room like this is her house. She hops up on the stool next to my sister and picks up the mug in front of her. She takes a healthy sip before placing it back on the counter. She keeps her hands wrapped around the mug like she's absorbing all of her heat from it. When she glances up, our gazes collide and I can't look away.

Piper's eyes travel down my body and it's only then I remember I didn't wear a shirt down here. All I have on is a pair of dark gray sweats that hang dangerously low on my hips. I take another sip of my coffee to hide my chuckle. I've heard what women say about gray sweatpants, this is basically lingerie to them.

I wait for Piper to meet my gaze again. When she does, I raise my brow, silently calling her out on checking me out. She rolls her eyes and brings her coffee to her lips. I love how she isn't embarrassed that I caught her. Most girls would be blushing and more than embarrassed, but not her.

Because I'm an asshole, I return the favor and let my attention fall south. I take in her tiny tank top that hugs every curve. I don't miss the fact she's not wearing a bra. Instead, my attention lingers a little too long on that. I slowly lift my eyes back to hers, finding a light blush staining her cheeks. Ah, so she does blush.

I expect Piper to cross her arms over her chest to hide, but she doesn't. She leans back in her chair, letting me see the smooth skin her tank top doesn't cover. Her belly button ring is almost the same color as her eyes and I can't pull my focus away from her body.

"Grayson!" Hadley claps her hands several times with an annoyed look on her face.

"What?" I widen my eyes like she's the crazy one.

"I've called your name like five times."

"Sorry, I'm still waking up. I didn't sleep most of the night."

"Why? What were you doing?... actually, don't. I don't wanna know. I think we're beyond the sharing is caring point." She holds up a hand to stop me. I let out a deep chuckle, drawing Piper's attention immediately.

"I wasn't jerking off, Hads. I just couldn't turn off my brain." I shrug it off like it's no big deal. It's not, this happens to me more than I care to admit.

"First off, ew. I don't need to know if you were or weren't. Second, I wanted to know if you wanted to go to the movies with us today." She's so hopeful, I'm tempted to go.

Hadley's my weakness. I'd do just about anything to make her happy. The guys are constantly razzing me about it. I'd move Heaven and Earth for my sister and I'm not ashamed of it. If Piper weren't here, I'd jump at the movie idea, but I know Piper will be going too and that makes me hesitate.

"I don't know, Hads."

"Please! We're going to see that new horror movie and you know how I get. Piper isn't going to want to be my friend if I break her hand." The most adorable pout settles over Hadley's face as she stares up at me with puppy eyes.

"I don't understand why you insist on going to every horror movie when you're scared to death of them." I shake my head. Sometimes I don't understand her.

"Because Mac said I'm too much of a baby to see them. I'm proving him wrong, Grayson!"

"Are you though? You still need your big brother to go with you." I wrinkle my nose as I call her out on it.

"I hope you're talking about size because I'm three minutes older than you." She points a tiny finger in my direction.

"Fine. When are you going?" I sigh, rubbing a hand over my chest. Piper follows the motion, watching me closely.

"Six fifteen?"

"You're going to make me spend my Saturday night with you?" I groan like I'm annoyed. I'm not. I'd rather hang out with her and Piper than Connor and Mac. That should tell me something, but I stuff that thought down as deep as I can.

"Please?"

"You owe me." I arch a brow at her. Hadley leaps off her chair and rushes around the island to throw her arms around me.

"You're the best brother in the world! Thank you, Grayson." She squeezes me as tight as she can. We used to do this to each other to see who could squeeze the other a little too tight. Hadley stopped winning years ago.

"Don't forget it." I press a kiss to the top of her head.

"Now that that's out of the way, let's discuss the busted lip and swollen eyes you came home with yesterday." Mom crosses her arms over her chest and levels me with a look that says I'm not leaving this room without explaining myself.

"Let's go, Piper. They'll be here forever discussing this. I'd rather go shopping for a little bit." Hadley rolls her eyes, dragging Piper off the stool.

My attention is solely focused on them as they walk out of the room. Piper's wearing the tiniest pair of black shorts I've ever seen and her shirt doesn't even reach her belly button. Was she wearing that last night when she came to my room? I can't remember. I was still trying to wake up.

"Grayson, spill it. And don't you dare try to lie to me." She pokes me in the chest.

"Ow, Mom." I pout and rub at where she just poked me. She rolls her eyes and motions for me to continue. "A bunch of guys were talking about Hadley inappropriately. I taught them a lesson, but it was five against one. They got a few lucky shots in before I dropped them to the ground," I say emotionlessly.

"I hope you broke their fucking noses... was any of it true? What they said?"

"Nah, Mom. Hadley doesn't do that shit. She's a good girl. Which is why they deserved what I did to them. I won't let them spread rumors about her. She doesn't deserve that. But yes, they'll be seeing plastic surgeons for sure and one of them might've lost his chance of playing college baseball."

"You really are the world's greatest brother. Thank you for protecting her." She stands on her toes and presses a kiss to my cheek.

"Always," I whisper. She pats my chest twice then disappears upstairs.

I'm let in silence, wondering if I'm really a good brother. So many times, I feel like I'm missing more in Hadley's life than I'm present for. I could attempt to be home more. To spend more nights and weekends with her rather than the guys.

"You should tell her." I glance up to find Piper standing in the doorway.

"I thought you were upstairs. Are you eavesdropping on me?"

"Nah, I needed to grab something out of my backpack. But you should tell her why you beat the shit out of those guys. She doesn't think it was to protect her." Piper takes a few steps towards me.

"No. If I told her, she'd want to know what they were saying about her... she'd be horrified. She doesn't need to hear that shit."

"Doesn't she deserve to know?" She takes a few more slow steps towards me, making me feel like I'm losing control. I'm so focused on her that I can barely think straight. If someone asked me what my birthday was right now, I'd probably get it wrong.

"Why does she need to know the fake shit people are saying about her?"

"How do you know it was fake?"

"Because I know my sister wasn't on her knees begging to suck those pieces of shit off. I'm not saying she's a virgin because I don't know if she is... but she's not begging for someone like them. She doesn't even like them."

"You're right. I know who she likes."

"You don't even know who I fought." I roll my eyes, trying to keep these high walls up as a barrier between us.

"It doesn't matter, I know which guy she does like and he wasn't on the other side of your fist... does it hurt?" Piper hesitates before she trails her finger across the bruised flesh of my lip.

"I'll be fine," I murmur. I don't know when I moved, but my hands are on her waist, holding her in place.

"You're nothing like Connor." Piper's gaze stays on my mouth, and she refuses to meet my gaze.

"No, I'm not." My thumbs move back and forth, finding her skin just as smooth as I thought it would be.

"Why do you hide this side of you? You're kind and loving, nothing like the image you present at school." Her fingers trail down my neck, stopping briefly on my collarbone.

"I don't hide it, I'm only this way with my family. I'm every bit of the dickhead you see at school." My eyes slowly slide shut when her touch moves to my chest.

"I don't believe you. You saved me from a world of humiliation. You didn't have to do that."

"You don't deserve his wrath, Piper. He's only trying to get rid of you and your mom." I don't know why I'm spilling any of this to her. It's like I'm under a spell and telling her any secret I have. No matter how much I want to walk away, I'm rooted in my place. I might as well be a statue.

"He's not going to stop until I make him," her whispered confession makes my eyes fly open. She's staring at my chest, still avoiding me. I lift her chin with my thumb and index finger, forcing her to meet my gaze.

"You can't go after him. He'll stop at nothing to make you suffer if he thinks you'll fight back."

"I'm not going to let him ruin this for my mom. She deserves so much more than what she's been given. I've stood by and let him think he's winning, but I'm done with that."

"Let me take care of it. I'll deal with Connor. You stay as far away from him as you can." My hand slips from her chin along the side of her jaw until I'm threading my fingers through her hair.

"I don't need you to fight my battles."

"I never said you did. I won't let you get hurt, though."

"Why?" Piper tilts her head to the side, daring me to tell her the truth.

She wants to know she means something to me. She wants to know I'm at least intrigued by her. I give her none of that. Instead, I hide behind the one innocent truth I have.

"Hadley would kill me if I let something happen to you at the hand of Connor."

Her lips pinch into a thin line and she takes a step back, severing the connection between us. My hands fall to my sides and reality comes crashing down around me.

"I better get back up to Hadley or she'll come looking for me." There's something in her tone I can't quite place, but if I were a betting man, I'd say she's hurt. She wanted more from me and instead of stepping up and admitting how I feel to her, I'm hiding behind my sister.

"Piper..."

"No, Grayson. Don't. Just... don't let him ruin the person you really are. I caught a glimpse of that guy and he's pretty awesome. I'd hate to see him disappear."

"Just remember what I said..." I'm grasping at anything to keep her here. I don't want her to leave yet. I don't want her to turn her back on me. "You shouldn't trust my words, but you can trust my actions."

"Maybe your words should match your actions." Piper gives me a tight smile before she disappears out of the kitchen.

I'm left trying to figure out what the fuck just happened. I can't be falling for my sister's best friend. My best friend's stepsister. This would be a bad idea on so many levels... then why do I feel myself stepping closer and closer to the edge. More than willing to take that leap and fall into the unknown.

Chapter 16
Piper

I stop outside of Hadley's room and suck in a deep breath. I don't know what the hell just happened. I was touching him before I could stop myself and then his hands were on me. And holy shit did it feel amazing.

But when he said he was only protecting me because of Hadley, it was like a bucket of cold water being poured over my head. He doesn't give a shit about me. He only cares about himself and the wrath he'll get from Hadley.

Part of me wonders if getting me to fall for him is part of Connor's plan. From the way Hadley talks, it sounds like Grayson and Mac do whatever Connor asks of them. They're like his little minions.

I need to remember who the enemy is. No matter how drool worthy he looks without a shirt on. No matter how much I want to run my fingers over each hard muscle covered in soft skin. I need to remember who Grayson is and where his loyalties lie.

"What took you so long? I'm almost ready to go!" Hadley tugs the door open and frowns at me. She spins on her heels and rushes into the bathroom, shutting the door before I can respond.

A creak on the stairs has me practically leaping into Hadley's room and shutting the door before Grayson can see me again. Tugging on a pair of black leggings, I pair it with a loose blue crop top and pile my hair in a messy bun on the top of my head. If I'm going shopping, I want to be comfortable.

I swipe on some mascara and carefully outline my eyes in black liner. I don't put any other makeup on. I hate having a ton of stuff on my face. I prefer to have clean skin and just accentuate my eyes.

"Well, that's just not fair," Hadley groans from the doorway.

"What?"

"You look like that in less than five minutes and it took me twenty minutes to look like this." She motions to her body.

She's wearing a cute pair of skinny jeans and a flowy black shirt. Her hair is curled into loose waves and she has on a little bit more makeup than I do. She's gorgeous. Flawless and perfect.

"You're beautiful. Let's go." I usher her to her door, trying to escape before we run into Grayson again.

As usual, luck is not on my side. I swear it hasn't been since I stepped foot in this stupid town.

Grayson's door opens right as we try to walk past it. He steps out into the hallway, blocking our path.

"Can I go to the mall with you? I need to get another pair of sweats." He keeps his attention on Hadley, but I can tell it's taking so much effort for him not to glance at me.

"I guess. You can be our bag holder when we try on clothes." She smirks and continues on her way down the steps, leaving Grayson and me behind.

"I'm sorry-"

"For someone who tells me not to trust their words, you sure say you're sorry a lot. Am I supposed to believe it?"

"Piper."

"Just quit while you're ahead, Grayson. I got the memo. We're not friends. In fact, we're enemies and the only reason you're playing nice is to stay in your sister's good graces. I heard you loud and clear." I march past him and continue all the way out to the garage where I slip into the front seat of the Jeep and stare out the windshield at the solid white garage door.

Hadley eyes me with interest, but she doesn't say a word. As soon as Grayson's in the car, we're driving down the driveway and out onto the road.

"What do you think about this one?" Hadley peeks out of the dressing room before opening the door all the way and showing us the dress she's trying on for the homecoming dance.

"It's perfect!" I say at the same time Grayson says, "It's too short. Try something else."

"Ignore him. You look gorgeous in it." I plant my hand over Grayson's mouth to keep him from denying it.

His tongue peeks out and swipes across my palm. My eyes widen, but I show no other acknowledgement of what he just did. As soon as the door to the dressing room shuts with Hadley inside, I spin to face him.

"What the hell is wrong with you?"

"I don't like people putting their hands over my mouth." He shrugs, sinking a little deeper into the comfy couch.

"So you thought 'hey, let's lick her'?"

"It was that or swat your hand away. I have to admit, I expected more of a reaction from you." He shrugs and turns his attention back to his phone.

"Can you stop?"

"Stop what?"

"Stop acting like we're friends. We aren't. Not even close."

"Yet we're spending the day shopping together and going to the movies. You're even sleeping over at my house the whole weekend." He leans in close and whispers in my ear. "That kinda sounds like we're friends."

"Let's see how friendly we are on Monday." I arch a brow, daring him to argue.

Grayson's jaw clenches and I know I hit the nail on the head. He's going to be all buddy-buddy with me when he can blame it on Hadley, but the second we step through the doors of Prescott High on Monday, he's going to go back to his normal hateful self.

"It's your turn!" Hadley singsongs, handing me a pile of dresses she wants me to try on.

"Hads, I'm not going to homecoming. I don't need any of these."

"Why not?" She frowns at me. "It's our senior year, you have to come!"

"Because I don't know many people and I doubt I'll have a date."

"I'll find you the perfect date! I promise! Please?" She gives me the same look I saw her giving Grayson earlier and I totally get it. It's so hard saying no to Hadley Young.

"I'll try on the damn things, but I still don't guarantee I'm going to the dance," I grumble, locking myself into a changing room.

The first dress is so uncomfortable I don't even exit the room to show her. The next is a little too small in the chest for me.

"Come out here!" Hadley calls.

"I will when I find something I like."

"No! Whatever you have on right now, get out here."

"Fine, but it's awful." I unlock the door and step out.

Grayson's staring at his phone, completely ignoring us. Hadley bursts out laughing as soon as she sees me.

"Oh my gosh! No... just no!"

I catch the second Grayson looks up. His eyes nearly bulge out of his head as he stares at my chest.

"I told you it was awful. One wrong sneeze and I'll be flashing the entire school."

"Try on the blue one next. I think it will look amazing." Hadley shoves me back into the dressing room.

I struggle to get this dress off. Once I accomplish that, I slip the soft blue one over my head and look in the mirror. It's darker, more of a royal blue, and I love it.

It hugs every curve without looking like I was poured into the fabric. It shows off my cleavage without looking slutty and even makes it look like I have a great ass. Which I don't.

I don't hesitate to show Hadley this one. I know I'm going to buy it before she says a word, but I'm still not sure I'm going to homecoming. It really doesn't seem like something I want to do.

"It's perfect!" Hadley leaps off the couch and claps her hands. "You have to get it."

"Fine, but only because I really like it. This isn't me agreeing to homecoming." I point a finger in her direction, wanting to make it clear to her that I'm not promising anything.

"You will when the perfect guy asks you to be his date." She wiggles her eyebrows.

I quickly change back into my clothes and we both pay for our dresses. I even use my new credit card from James. It feels weird to use his money, but I can't afford this dress without it. He seemed very insistent too. I'm sure he checks the bills constantly and he'll get offended if I don't use it every once in a while.

Hadley and I end up buying shoes and accessories to match our dresses and when we're done, Grayson runs all the bags out to the car for us.

We pick a little restaurant in the mall to eat at before the movie and settle into a booth. Grayson's sitting directly across from me, making it impossible to ignore him.

"What up, fuckers?" Mac stops at the end of our table. "What are you doing here?" He asks Grayson.

"Hadley wants to go to that new horror movie."

"Ahh, so you have to go and protect her from the big scary monsters?" Mac coos like he's talking to a baby.

"Shut up!" Hadley tosses a wadded-up napkin at him, making him chuckle.

"Slide over, home fry." Mac nudges me until I move far enough into the booth for him to sit next to me. "What time are we going?"

"*We* are going at six fifteen. *You* aren't coming with us." Hadley pins him with a glare.

"C'mon, Hads. Let me come with you. I have nothing to do tonight. Connor's busy and I'm between girls at the moment." He winks at her, flashing his panty-melting smile.

"Excuse me while I puke…" Hadley buries her face in her purse and fake dry heaves. "How'd you even know we were here?"

"Find a friend app." He shrugs. "I figured I'd stop by and see what Gray was up to. I didn't expect to get so lucky to find you and Piper here too."

"Oh please," I groan with an eyeroll.

"What's wrong, Princess?" Mac flashes me a knowing smirk.

"You hate me."

"What are you talking about? I don't hate you at all." Mac frowns and it almost seems genuine.

"If you don't hate me, why'd you help Connor steal my clothes, bathing suit, and towel?" I cross my arms over my chest and wait for him to answer.

Hadley's eyes narrow and she turns her angry gaze on her brother. He fidgets under her inspection, but neither of them says a word. Hadley knows better than to call him out in front of Mac, but she knows. I'm sure she's going to question him on the way home tonight.

"Piper, it's not personal," Mac groans.

"It's not personal to leave me naked in a high school? Are you kidding me?"

"Well, I didn't hear about the naked new girl, so I guess you figured something out. Clearly you were fine." He tries to appear nonchalant, but I can see the tension filling his body from a mile away. "In my defense, I didn't know he was having someone take your bathing suit or towel until after we took your clothes. Connor kept those little details to himself."

"Oh, so that makes you completely faultless. What about telling the school counselor I was harming myself? Whose idea was that?"

"What the fuck?" Grayson stares up at the ceiling, anger radiates off of him. "Connor said he was telling the counselor you were having a hard time with all the changes. He never mentioned anything else."

"Sounds like your homeboy only gives you enough information to get you to do his bidding. What a surprise?" I roll my eyes and pop another fry into my mouth.

I'm done with this conversation and with them. It eases the hurt just a tiny bit knowing they're never fully aware of what they're doing, but they're far from innocent. They both know how bad Connor is and they're doing nothing to stop him.

Chapter 17
Grayson

When we get to the movies, I pay for everyone. Mac and Hadley volunteer to grab drinks and snacks while I lead Piper into the theater. We find our seats and she enters the aisle first. I quickly take the spot next to her and bite the inside of my cheek to keep from laughing when she groans.

She was right when she said Connor only tells us enough to get us to do what he wants. He used to spill his whole plan to us, but he's being more careful when it comes to Piper and that worries me even more.

"Listen, I really am sorry about my hand in what Connor's doing. I'm going to figure out a way to end all of this, but I need time. I can't let him know what I'm doing until I decide how I'm going to handle it."

"Whatever, Grayson. I'm done with whatever this is we're doing. I told you, we're not friends and I don't plan on changing that."

Piper tugs her phone out of her pocket and soon her fingers are flying across the screen. Her lips tip up at the corners and at one point she lets out a little laugh. It's a full five minutes of this before I snap.

"What are you doing?"

"Not that it's any of your business, but I'm texting someone."

"Who? You're only friends with Hadley."

"Not true," she singsongs. "I'm friends with Will too."

"Will's a piece of shit who just wants in your pants," I growl.

"Probably, but he's still my friend." She shrugs, turning her attention away from me. "I'm not texting him either. You know, before I moved here, I actually lived in an entire world where you didn't exist. I had friends and everything. There was even a boyfriend or two. I know that's super hard for you to believe that things exist outside of you, but it's true. I have pictures and scars to prove it."

"Has anyone ever told you you're a smartass?"

"Yup. Plenty of times. Pretty sure I even got sent to the principal's office a few times because of it." She smiles again at her phone and starts responding to whoever she's texting.

"So, are you texting a boyfriend?" I inch a little closer, trying to see her phone.

"Nope. I'm talking to my best friend. He's filling me in on all the drama I'm missing."

"He? Your best friend is a guy?" My brows reach for my hairline. I never imagined Piper having a male best friend. I don't think I've ever been close enough to a girl to call them my friend, let alone my best friend.

"Yup. Tim's awesome. He's the greatest. He's been there for me through everything. The only reason I didn't want to leave my old life was because of him."

"If you're so close, why hasn't he come to see you since you moved?" I smirk to myself, thinking I caught her in a lie.

"Easy, I don't want Connor anywhere near Tim. He's too sweet for someone like Connor to sink his claws into."

"You're in my seat." Hadley kicks my calf with her foot.

"Nah, you can sit there." I point to the seat to my left.

"Piper doesn't want to sit next to you, Grayson. She doesn't even like you." Hadley rolls her eyes.

"Yeah, but then you'll be between Mac and me. You can squeeze the shit out of our hands and not wound your friend."

Hadley hands Piper a tub of popcorn and taps her chin a few times. She thinks it over before she gives me a single nod.

"He's not wrong, Piper. I think it'd be better if I crush their hands instead of yours." Hadley shrugs before dropping into the seat between Mac and me.

She bought two buckets of popcorn and two large sodas. Because of where we're sitting, that makes Hadley and Mac share one, while Piper and I share the other.

The movie starts and we're plunged into darkness for several seconds before the screen lights up the theater the smallest amount. From what I read online, there are quite a few jumpy moments in this one. I know Hadley's going to be clutching my arm in a death grip in no time.

"Do you like scary movies?" I whisper to Piper as I grab a handful of popcorn.

"They don't bother me. I'm not a fan of gore though."

No sooner are the words out of her mouth do we enter a particularly gory scene. Piper stares at my shoulder rather than the screen, trying her hardest to ignore what's playing in front of her.

"You can try to break my throwing hand if it will make you feel better." I hold my hand out to her, not surprised at all when she turns me down.

"I'm sure I'll be fine."

Her rejection hurts more than I ever imagined it could. It's like a knife straight into my chest. I want her to trust me, even though I understand why she doesn't.

I turn my attention back to the movie and try my hardest to ignore the blue-eyed goddess sitting next to me. She jumps several times when something or someone pops out, but other than that, she's fine.

We're about half way through the movie when Piper leans on my arm. I smile to myself before I glance down at her. She's sound asleep, resting her head on my bicep. There's a small pang to my ego knowing she's not willingly leaning on me, but I still take it as a win that she trusts me enough to fall asleep next to me.

I lift the armrest separating our seats and slide my arm out from under her head. I place it around her shoulders and let her cheek rest against my chest.

"Stop making a move on my friend!" Hadley hisses from her spot beneath Mac's protective arm. I raise an eyebrow, flickering my gaze to Mac's arm before bringing it back up to her. I swear her cheeks redden, but it's too hard to tell in the dim light. "Touché... just don't make her hate me."

"She's asleep, Hads. I'm just making sure she's comfortable."

She nods her head, turning her attention back to the screen. I don't miss the way she snuggles a little deeper into Mac or how his arm tightens even more around her. I never imagined my best friend would fall for my sister, yet it's hard to explain what I'm seeing as anything else.

Running my hand up and down Piper's side, I settle back into my seat and try to enjoy the movie. I don't particularly like horror movies. There's nothing wrong with them, it's just not my preferred choice of genres. I'd much rather watch something action or adventure filled. I want more of a story line than someone targeting a vulnerable female, or the victim making countless stupid mistakes while trying to escape whatever threat is after them.

Piper shifts in my arms, moving even closer to me. The next time my hand runs up her side, her shirt comes with it. My fingers glide over her smooth skin, warming me to my core. Her curves are in all the right places. That much was proven with the first dress she showed us at the store. I've never seen someone's breasts spill out of a dress like hers did. I actually wiped my chin, expecting to find a trail of drool running down it.

The second dress was even better. The royal blue fabric draped over her body like it was made for her. The color made her light blue eyes seem even brighter. I swear I could stare into them forever.

Resting my head against Piper's, I let my eyes close and enjoy the feel of her in my arms. I know she's never going to let me hold her like this when she's awake. This will probably be the last time I ever get to be like this with her. I better memorize every single detail before she wakes up.

Chapter 18
Piper

I can't believe I fell asleep on Grayson. Who does that?

I woke up minutes before the credits started rolling with Grayson's head on mine. His arms caged me against his hard body. I tried to move, but his grip tightened. I planned on yelling at him, maybe even pinching him a time or two, but then I realized he was asleep, too.

Now, I don't really know what to do. Do I cough really loud and hope the noise and jostling of my body wakes him? Do I try to get Hadley's attention and demand her help? Purple nurpling him is always a good option.

I'm just about to clamp my thumb and forefinger around his nipple, planning to squeeze and twist with all my might when Grayson moves. He covers my hand with his and settles them both on his thigh.

"Please tell me you weren't about to do what I think you were going to do." He stares down at me.

"I wasn't about to do what you thought I was gonna do." I blink up at him innocently.

"Is that the truth?" He arches a brow.

"Who's to say what the truth really is?"

"Piper…"

"Fine! Yes, I was going to purple nurple you. What else was I supposed to do?"

A snort of laughter erupts from Grayson. He's so carefree when Connor isn't around. It's crazy how one person can change his mood so drastically.

"I don't know, carefully shake me? Say my name? Tap my leg? You had plenty of other options."

"I'm not sorry." I shrug my shoulder.

"I wouldn't expect you to be." He chuckles softly.

When the lights come on, we all start filing out of the aisle and through the parking lot to Hadley's Jeep.

"What are you doing the rest of the night?" Mac works hard to act like he doesn't care, but he does. He wants to be included in whatever we're doing.

"Piper's sleeping over. We're probably going to chill in the den until we get tired." Hadley stares up at Mac.

"Do you wanna come over?" Grayson runs a hand through his hair. He looks like the last thing in the world he wants is to have Mac over. "I don't have any plans."

"Sure, I'm free. This entire weekend has been empty. I don't know what Connor's up to, but he hasn't been answering me." Mac tries to act nonchalant.

He's like a little puppy. He wants someone to pat him on the head and tell him what a good boy he is. He's begging for attention, but everyone's just pushing him out of the way. I almost feel bad for him... that's not true, I do feel bad. But I shouldn't.

"I want cookies. Do you know how to make cookies, Piper?" Hadley opens her door and climbs behind the wheel.

"Depends. What kind do you want?"

"What kinds can you make?" She smirks.

"S'mores, turtle pecan, or peanut butter blossoms. I don't know any of the other ones by heart."

"Oh damn, those sound so good," Grayson groans from behind me.

"I guess we're stopping at the store on the way home." Hadley flashes me a grin before pulling out of the parking lot. "Text Mac and let him know. If he shows up at the house and we're not there he's going to pout and think we stood him up."

"Already did. He said he's stopping at the store with us."

"That man has a severe case of FOMO," Hadley giggles.

"What the hell is FOMO?" Grayson frowns.

"Fear of missing out." I laugh at the accurate description of Mac. "He really does. Let's hurry, now I want cookies too."

As soon as we pull into the parking lot of the grocery store, Mac's car slides into the space next to ours. As we walk into the store, he hurries to grab a cart and starts pushing it down an aisle.

"Where are you going?" I chuckle, grabbing his arm and leading him to the correct aisle.

"How the hell would I know? You know I've never been in a grocery store, right? You're lucky I even knew where it was."

"How... you know what, never mind. I know how. I guess it's just weird to me. I've never had a Fernando, Maria, or Roger. It's always been me and my mom doing everything for ourselves."

I stop in front of the baking supplies and start loading up the cart. I have no clue what they might have in their kitchen, so I'm making sure I get everything I could possibly need.

I glance over my shoulder when I hear Hadley say something, but her and Grayson are at least twenty feet away from Mac and me. She's glaring at him and he's trying to smooth over whatever she's mad about.

It's cute how much Grayson loves his sister. I didn't expect that from him. At least not from the version of him I met at school. But this version... I could fall too easily for this man.

Hadley's brow smooths out and Grayson pulls her into a tight hug. I wish Connor and I could have a relationship like that. I know it's never going to happen, but having a friend and ally at home would be nice.

Once I've gathered all of the ingredients, we move to the checkout line. Mac and Grayson place everything on the conveyor belt and smile like they helped so much.

The cashier tells us the total and before I can respond, Grayson inserts his credit card and pays while Mac loads the cart up with our groceries. I could get used to shopping with them.

Chapter 19
Grayson

That was the fastest shopping trip ever. Grocery shopping isn't something I normally do. I have no clue where anything is in the store so when I have to stop for something, it takes me forever to find it. Piper seems right at home in the store. I'm surprised since the Ward's have Fernando. He does all the grocery shopping. If you want something special, you just have to add it to the list on the refrigerator.

We don't have a chef. Mom likes cooking too much to step aside and let someone else do it. She refuses to take us grocery shopping though. She claims when we come with her, the bill almost doubles and she doesn't get any of the stuff she needs. I'm not sure if that's true or not, but we stay home anyway.

Hadley cornered me at the grocery store and demanded to know what Piper was talking about with

Connor stealing her clothes. I assured her I was taking care of everything and I made sure Piper wasn't stranded naked. She asked me if that was why I needed her locker combination and I considered lying, but there's no point. I'd rather my sister realize I'm not a monster. So, I told her the truth and I think she's forgiven me, but she said I need to make it up to Piper.

"Can I help?" Hadley hops onto the counter as soon as we get home.

"Have you ever made cookies?" Piper peeks up at her through her lashes.

"The kinds that come from a bag or box." She giggles.

"You can if you want, but I don't mind doing it all myself." Piper turns back to the flour, carefully measuring it. "I love baking and I don't get to do it anymore. Fernando says that's what he's paid for."

"You can take over our kitchen whenever you want," I offer.

Everyone's gaze snaps to me. I try to brush it off like it's not a big deal, but it is. I hate having strangers in my space, in my home. Even Mac and Connor rarely get invited over. I normally just hang out with them at their houses, so this is shocking for everyone. Even me.

I can't take my attention off Piper. The way she moves around the kitchen is mesmerizing. She's so comfortable. So carefree.

She makes sure all of the cookies are evenly spread out before she opens the door and places the first tray in the oven.

Mom insisted she needed two ovens when we remodeled the kitchen last year and Piper's thrilled with it. She claims our kitchen is her dream. She wants something just like this when she has a home of her own. She sets a timer on her phone and starts working on the next batch of dough.

"How about I find something for us to watch and grab drinks? That way we can dig in as soon as the cookies are done?" Hadley snatches a bag of chips before she heads out of the kitchen.

"I'll help you. I'm useless in the kitchen anyway." Mac follows after her like a lovesick boy.

I'm going to have to have a talk with him. I don't particularly care if he has a crush on my sister, but I won't let him treat her the way he treats some women. I want to make it painfully clear that he better place her on a damn pedestal and keep her there. There will be no hitting it and quitting it where my sister is concerned.

"You should go help them. I'm fine here." Piper mixes the next dough up and forms little balls. She dips each one into sugar before she places them on the cookie sheet.

"I'm sure between the two of them they can find drinks and something to watch. I'd rather stay here with you."

"So, you can make sure I don't steal something?"

"What the hell? No. Why would you think that?"

"Connor follows me around the house all the time saying he's making sure I'm not stealing the crystal or some shit like that." She waves a hand in the air like that explains everything.

"I don't think we even have crystal." I rub a hand along my jaw. The rough texture that meets my skin reminds me I never shaved today. "I just like watching you bake."

"That's not creepy at all. Should I lock Hadley's door tonight? 'I just like to watch you sleep'." She mimics my voice, doing better than I care to admit.

"How do you know I didn't watch you sleep last night?" I quirk a brow.

"I don't. For all I know you could've snuck into the bathroom while I was showering, too. Nothing would surprise me at this point."

The timer for Piper's cookies goes off and she spins around to get them. She hits a cup with her elbow in the process and it tumbles to the ground, shattering all over the floor.

"Don't move!" I jump out of my chair and grab a pair of sneakers from the mud room. I slip them on and find Piper crouched on the ground, picking up glass. "Piper, stop." I move to her side and pick her up, placing her on the counter.

Lifting the trash can, I help her dump what she picked up into it and place it on the floor. Scanning her body, I look for any sort of injury. I take her hands in mine, running my rough fingertips over her smooth palms. I want to make sure she didn't get cut. It wasn't very smart to start picking up the glass like that.

"Grayson, I'm fine. Those cookies are going to burn." She tries to jump back down, but she's barefoot. She'll get all cut up.

"Stay. I'll get it." I plant my hands on her hips and hold her in place until she nods.

Slipping my hands into the oven mitts, I set the hot trays on trivets and put the new batches in the oven.

"Can you bring those over here? I need to get the chocolate and marshmallows in them before they cool."

I do as I'm told, moving them so they're on the counter next to her. Grabbing the chocolate kisses and marshmallows, I hand them over before gathering a broom and dustpan.

"I'm sorry. I didn't mean to knock it over. Your Mom's going to be so upset."

"Piper, it's fine. I'm just glad you didn't get hurt. Mom won't care. She bought three extra sets of those glasses because of how often Hads and I break them. She told us she's hoping by the time we move out, she has at least the number of glasses she initially wanted."

"That's ingenious. Ugh, I think I have glass in my hand," Piper groans.

"Let me see... where do you think it is?" I take her hand in mine and run my finger gently over the spot she thinks there's glass. I can feel a small bump. "I'll be right back."

I return a few seconds later with a first aid kit and get to work. It only takes me a few moments to get the glass out and to cover the wound with a Band-Aid.

"I think you're good to go." I lift her palm to my mouth and press a soft kiss to it. I peek up at her through my lashes when she makes a soft gasp.

Slowly lowering her hand, I keep my attention locked on her. Neither of us break the silence between us.

I lean in, intending to kiss Piper, when she places a hand on my chest to keep a little bit of distance between us. I could push harder and eliminate the space between us. She couldn't keep me away if I tried to move closer, but I freeze.

"What are you doing, Grayson?" Her voice is barely a whisper. Her gaze flickers between my eyes.

I don't know what the hell I'm doing. I'm drawn to her. I'm like a moth to a flame. I can't resist her even though I know she'll be my downfall in the end.

I place a hand over hers that's still on my chest and squeeze my eyes shut for a moment. Do I want to take this step? Once I do, there's no going back.

I peel my eyes open and stare into her bright blue ones. I don't think I've ever seen anyone with eyes this blue.

"I can't stay away from you," I murmur softly. "I'm not sure I even want to anymore."

"But Connor-"

"Connor can go fuck himself. You don't deserve his wrath. You deserve to be placed on a throne and showered with affection." I tuck a strand of hair behind her ear, never breaking eye contact.

"You told me not to trust your words. How do I know this isn't all a ploy Connor's come up with? Make me fall for his best friend? Sounds like a pretty easy way to bring my world crashing down around me." She shrugs.

I can't blame her for not trusting me. She shouldn't. Not at school. But here? At home? I'm real. I'm honest. I'm myself.

"From this moment on, inside these walls, you can trust anything that comes out of my mouth."

"Unless Mac's here, right?" She arches her brow.

"Even with Mac here. He wouldn't dare say a word to Connor. He hates him more than I do."

"Then why are you friends with him?" She blinks up at me with innocent eyes.

"Because high school is all a game and we're just the players. I need to be smart, bide my time, and only show my cards when the time comes."

I move in closer and this time I don't try to kiss her lips. I lean in until my mouth is touching the shell of her ear. My hands find her hips and I wait a moment, letting myself collect my thoughts. It's hard to think with her this close.

"I won't kiss you. Not tonight. Not because I don't want to... but because I want you to know where you stand with me before I make that move. Just know, I want you more than anything."

I take her hand in mine and rub it over the bulge in my pants. I want her to know exactly what she does to me. Piper stares at me with wide eyes, but she doesn't say a word.

I hear footsteps coming down the hall and take a step back right before Mac and Hadley step through the door.

"Stay over there. There's glass on the floor. I knocked a cup over." I meet Piper's gaze and catch a twitch of her lip when I take responsibility for her clumsiness.

"Dammit, Gray! That's the third one this month! Mom's going to kill us. I think she bought another three sets. She said something about stocking up even more before they stop making them." Hadley rolls her eyes.

I quickly finish cleaning up the glass, but I still don't want Piper jumping down. There's no telling if I missed a few tiny pieces.

I snatch my phone off the counter and text the cleaning service to come tomorrow and do a thorough cleaning in the kitchen. I don't want anyone else getting glass stuck in their skin or getting cut.

As soon as all the cookies are finished baking, I hand the plate over to Hadley and chuckle when she lifts it to her nose and sucks in a deep breath.

"These smell so good! We might have to kidnap you every weekend!"

"We need milk!" Mac motions to the fridge. I roll my eyes, but grab the gallon and a few glasses before handing it all over to him.

As soon as they disappear back into the den, the room Mom and Dad deemed the kid's hangout space years ago, I turn my attention to Piper. She's about to lower herself onto the floor and I'm not letting that happen.

"Don't you dare. You already got hurt." I plant myself between her legs, not letting her get down.

"I'm not going to sit on the counter all night, Grayson!"

"You're right. I'm going to carry you to the den."

"You're not carrying me." Her gaze flickers to my dick then back to my face.

"Then I guess you'll be sitting on the counter all night. I'm not letting you touch this floor."

Piper glares at me. She doesn't want to give in and let me win. She's not used to folding at other people's wills, but I'm not budging on this. I'm not going to risk her getting a piece of glass stuck in her foot.

"Fine!" She throws her hands up in the air. "Turn around and you can give me a piggyback ride."

"Nah. I don't think I want to do that." I shake my head with a predatory smile.

"Wha-" The word dies on her tongue when I slide my hands under her ass and lift her body against mine. She lets out a little shriek and wraps her arms and legs around my body, holding on for dear life.

We move down the hall to where the den is, but I stop outside the door. I push her against the wall, my body pressing into hers. Her eyes snap to mine, trying to figure out what's going on. Her chest rises and falls a little faster with every passing second as she anticipates what I'm going to do next.

"I told you, I'm not going to let you get hurt. Trust me to keep you safe." I bury my face in her neck and place a gentle kiss against her warm skin.

I take another second to breathe in her scent and memorize the feel of her body against mine. When I pull back, I don't let her down. Instead, I spin around and carry her into the den. I collapse onto the couch with her on my lap and sigh.

"What are we watching?" My tone is bored, like I couldn't give a shit about anything happening tonight. It's a total lie. I'm barely able to control myself. All I want to do is pin Piper against the wall again. I want to make her mine and erase any doubt she has about my intentions.

My voice breaks Piper out of her shock. She scrambles off of my lap and onto the couch next to me. Mac and Hadley are curled up on one side of the L-shaped couch. I guess we get the other side. Am I really expected to sit here and pretend I don't know my best friend and sister have something going on between them?

I guess I am. After all, aren't I expecting the same thing from them when it comes to Piper and me?

Chapter 20
Piper

I'm going to get whiplash. There's no other way to explain what being around Grayson Young is like. He's so hot and cold. I don't know what version I'm going to get of him every time we encounter each other.

Hadley presses play on the TV and another horror movie fills the screen. I can't resist rolling my eyes. She hates these movies!

"Why does she keep watching horror movies if she hates them?" I whisper only loud enough for Grayson to hear me.

"Because she wants an excuse for Mac to hold her."

"She likes Mac?" I feign innocence. I know all too well how much she likes Mac. She never stops talking about him.

"I'm fairly certain they like each other. They both think I'm too stupid to realize there's something going on between my best friend and my twin. It's kinda insulting."

"They're cute together." I smile over at my new best friend.

Mac's carefree surfer boy appearance is a complete contrast to Hadley's perfectly put together image. Her dark hair is always styled like she just stepped out of a salon. Her make-up is kept light and mature. There are no wild colors on her eyelids or bright lipstick to gain attention. She's the girl next door personified.

She doesn't dress to make guys drool over her body, though I know she has a nice figure. She blends into the crowd when she could easily stand out. But that's not who she is.

"Cute? They're not cute together."

"Who would you consider cute together then?" I roll my eyes. "Blake Lively and Ryan Reynolds?"

Grayson stares down at me for a few moments before he responds. He's searching for something, but I'm not sure what. I don't think he's going to find whatever it is in me.

"Us. I think we'd be cute together."

"Yeah, ok." I snort with laughter. The thought of Grayson and me together is ridiculous.

He doesn't like me. He just likes the idea of me being forbidden. Connor's an idiot for telling his friends I'm off limits. It's just going to make them want me more.

"What's that supposed to mean?" Grayson frowns at me.

"You just want what you can't have. Connor said no, so you want to claim me to piss him off."

"Do you really think I'm that immature?" His forehead creases even more.

"I think it's human nature. Even if we won't conquer the entire world, we want to know it's a possibility." I shrug, leaning back into the couch cushion.

I turn my attention to the TV, trying to signal this conversation is over. Grayson and I would be awful together. I wouldn't be able to handle not knowing which version of him I was going to get. I need a dependable boyfriend, not one who's going to slip behind a mask every time someone's there to witness his words and actions. No thank you.

The first half of the movie, Grayson's practically pouting in the corner of the couch. He's not happy I turned him down. I'm not going to date a guy just to piss off my stepbrother though. Connor's already impossible to deal with, I can't imagine how much worse he'd get if I were dating his best friend. I'm fairly certain his head might explode.

Grayson sighs for the third time in a row, pulling my attention away from the killer stalking its prey and back to him.

"What's wrong?"

"I'm uncomfortable." He's wiggling a little in his seat like a toddler.

"So, get comfortable!"

"I want to lay down."

"Then lay. I'll sit on the floor." I glance around to make sure there isn't another spot to sit. There's not.

Mac and Hadley are covering the other half of the couch and I'm positive Grayson will take up this half. He's well over six foot tall.

I go to move onto the floor, but Grayson stops me. He shakes his head and pulls me back down to the cushion.

"You're not sitting on the floor. Lay with me."

"Why?" I furrow my brows.

"Because there's nowhere else to sit and I'll feel like an ass if you sit on the floor. Please?"

"Grayson," I sigh. I don't want to be that close to him. I know I could easily fall for this side of him. The sweet, loving brother he is when he's in this house.

"Then I'll just go upstairs and let the three of you finish the movie. Goodnight." He rises to his full height before I can stop him.

"Stop it! You're not leaving. I'm a little worried if you do, Mac might start making out with Hadley and I don't want to be stuck here to witness that. Just lay down." I motion to the couch.

"Will you lay with me?" He arches a brow knowing I have no choice.

"You can put your feet on my lap."

"Nope. Try again." Grayson folds his arms over his chest, drawing my attention to his bulging biceps.

"You can put your head on my lap?"

"Nope. One more chance. If it's not good, I'm leaving."

"Fine! I'll lay with you."

"Deal." A mischievous grin spreads over his face. The asshole is so used to getting his way.

I move from the couch and let him get comfortable. As soon as he's lying down, I try to figure out how I'm going to fit on this thing with him. Grayson's massive.

Wide shoulders tapper into a narrow waist, but he's still a big guy.

"What are you waiting for?" An amused smirk spreads over his lips.

"I'm trying to figure out where I'll fit! You're huge."

"I'm glad you noticed." He glances down at his crotch and back up at me. I roll my eyes so hard I'm worried I might hurt myself.

I peek over at Mac and Hadley hoping they can't hear us. They're whispering to each other, completely ignoring us.

"Lay between me and the couch. I'm worried if you lay on the edge, you might fall off."

Very ungracefully, I climb over Grayson and wedge myself between him and the cushions. I wiggle down until my head is even with his chest, there's no other place for me to put it.

Grayson slips his arm under my head and around my back. He pulls me flush against him and lets out a little sigh of contentment.

"Are you comfortable?" He whispers a few minutes later.

"Surprisingly, I am. Your fat pecs are oddly comfortable." I'm lying – about the fat, not the comfort level – doing my best to upset him.

"My pecs aren't fat. It's called muscle. I know that's hard for you to understand given the fact you don't have any."

"Are you saying all I have is fat?" My brows skyrocket up my forehead as I stare up at him in shock.

"Not at all." He chuckles under his breath. "I saw you in your itty-bitty pajamas, I know there's no fat."

We both turn our attention back to the movie. I'm just getting lost in the story when Grayson murmurs under his breath, "There was also no bra."

"Oh my gosh! What is wrong with you!" I swat at his chest, my flesh hitting against what feels like solid rock.

Grayson grabs my hand in his huge ones. His deep chuckles shake my entire body, making my head bounce on his chest and I glare at him. He lifts my hand to his mouth and presses a soft kiss to my palm. He's gentler than I expect.

The first time I met Grayson, I figured he was all hard edges and hostility. He came across worse than Connor. My brain is still having trouble accepting this is the same guy.

Grayson intertwines our fingers and lays them on his stomach. His hand resting on my back, runs in slow strokes back and forth. Each time he moves up my back, he takes my shirt a little bit higher with it. After a few minutes he's touching my bare skin. I don't want to admit – even to myself – how good it feels.

He grabs a blanket off the back of the couch and spreads it over us. I snuggle deeper into him, laying a little bit more on my stomach.

"Do you like to sleep on your stomach?" Grayson asks after the third yawn escapes from me.

"Yeah."

"Lay on top of me on your stomach."

"Yeah, I'm sure you'd love that."

"I told you, I won't make a move until you understand where you stand with me."

He scoots down the couch a little bit until his head is flat on the cushion. He stuffs a throw pillow under his head and shifts me until I'm lying on top of him. I really don't want to acknowledge how comfortable he is to lay on.

My face is tucked into the crook of his neck, letting me breathe in his glorious scent. There's a hint of something woodsy, but the rest is all man. All Grayson.

My eyelids close on their own and soon I'm drifting off to sleep.

Chapter 21

Grayson

"You better be fully clothed under there." Dad nudges me awake and pins me with a look.

"Wanna check?" I roll my eyes.

"Nah, I've seen your dick more than I care to admit. I don't want to chance seeing it again." Dad grimaces as he glances down at me.

"Are you afraid you'll feel inadequate?" I smirk.

"You're a little shit," Mom chuckles, stepping up next to him. Dad wraps an arm around her waist and tugs her into his embrace. "What's going on with them?" She motions to Mac and Hadley, who are sound asleep, wrapped up in each other just like Piper and I are.

"I'm fairly certain they have a thing for each other," I whisper.

"Dammit, now I'm going to have to threaten Mac's life. I liked that one. He's just stupid." Dad sighs.

"He won't hurt her. He knows I'd kill him," I glance at Piper to make sure she isn't waking up from us talking. She lets out a soft snore and I can't help but smile.

Mom's smirking when I meet her gaze again. I frown when she doesn't say a word. Mom doesn't know how to keep her nose out of our business. Normally she'd be asking a hundred questions, why not now?

"You're not going to ask?" I arch a brow.

"I don't need to. I already know."

"I'm sure." I roll my eyes.

"I can tell when my son is falling, I don't need you to admit anything. I doubt you would anyway." She doesn't smirk or tease me, she's being serious.

"I'm not falling," I grumble under my breath.

"You are, but it's ok. You're happy. Don't let Connor ruin this for you. I have no doubt he'll try... and don't hurt her. She's pretty great and your sister will stab you if you cost her a friend." Dad presses a kiss to Mom's head. "We should let them sleep, sweetheart. Grayson, if I become a grandpa in nine months, I'm going to hold you responsible."

"What if it's them?" I motion to my sister and best friend.

"You're still responsible. I'm adding it to my calendar! Nine months from now if there's a new baby in this family, I'm holding you responsible!"

"Mom! Keep your legs shut!" I call to them as they start to leave the room. They both laugh and shut the door behind them.

"Grayson? What's going on?" Piper lifts her head off my shoulder and rubs at her eyes.

"Nothing, baby. Go back to sleep."

"I should wake up Hadley and we can go upstairs." She starts to push off of me, but I hold her in place.

"Stay, Piper. I like having you in my arms."

She stares sleepily at me before nodding her head and laying back down. Placing my hands on her lower back, I slip them under her shirt and slowly stroke her bare skin. I could become addicted to Piper. I don't know how Hadley would feel about us though.

Hadley's never been close to many people. She's popular and friendly with everyone at school, but she's never had her own group of friends. I haven't heard anyone say anything negative about her, just guys claiming she did things she didn't. But she doesn't have a close friend to talk to. I never really understood why she keeps people at a distance, yet I'm the same way.

I don't let Mac or Connor fully see who I am. I keep certain parts of myself hidden and I barely invite them into my home or my life away from school. Hadley's right, I'm a completely different person when I'm at home. I'm not jaded or cruel, I'm a nice person. I don't scowl and I help whenever I can.

I fall asleep thinking about what I can do to help Piper. She doesn't deserve to be on the receiving end of Connor's wrath. She didn't do anything wrong. I just don't know how I can stop him. But I will. I'll stop Connor Ward from going after Piper if it's the last thing I do.

I blink my eyes open and the scent of pancakes fills the air. A hand pushes into my chest and I let out a low moan.

"Sorry, I didn't mean to wake you up." Piper winces at me.

"It's ok... but maybe don't try to impale my chest with your bony hands next time."

"Oh, I did not!"

"Tell that to my bruised sternum." I rub at my chest.

"I'm sure you're fine." She rolls her eyes.

"Look at this bruise!" I lift my shirt up to my shoulders and point to the center of my chest.

"There's no bruise! There's barely even a red mark."

"Which means there's at least a little bit of a mark." I stick out my bottom lip in a pout.

"Oh my gosh! You're such a baby!" She leans down and presses a lingering kiss to my chest. "It's all better."

"No, it's not. It still hurts." I stick my bottom lip out in a pout and give her my best puppy eyes.

"I kissed it and made it better. That's how it works." She places her hands on her hips and scowls at me.

"Maybe it needs more than one kiss. Maybe you hurt me so deeply I'll need multiple kisses to heal properly." I flash her a lopsided grin.

"Grayson," she groans, letting her head fall back until she's staring up at the ceiling. "Are you going to tell me I hurt other spots while sleeping on you too? Make me kiss all over the place?"

"Now that you mention it... my cock kinda hurts, too."

"Oh, fuck off!" She laughs softly. I love the sound more than anything I've ever heard.

She's so much different when she doesn't have her guard up. She seems relaxed here, a complete contrast to how she is at school. She's just Piper here.

"Breakfast is ready, sleepyheads." Mom pokes her head into the den with a big smile on her face.

"We'll be right in." Hadley stretches her arms over her head and yawns from her spot next to Mac. I don't miss how Mac's gaze snaps to where her shirt has risen up or how he stares at her like she's his whole world. We're going to have to have a talk, the sooner the better.

"I can't believe we fell asleep last night. This couch is way too comfortable." Mac stands to his full height and holds out a hand to help Hadley to her feet. She gazes up at him like she wants to wrap her arms around his waist and I have to refrain from placing my body between them.

I understand my sister is the same age as me and therefore probably wants to date Mac just as much as I want to date Piper. But I also know what type of thoughts are going through Mac's head and I don't like that one bit.

Mac wouldn't be a bad boyfriend if he could refrain from flirting with every girl he meets. He loves pulling them into his arms and kissing their necks or making them squirm by whispering dirty things in their ear.

It doesn't matter if he's dating them or not, he doesn't care because he loves the attention. I don't want that for my sister. I want her to find a man who will treat her like she's the only woman in the world. One she won't have to worry about being faithful to her.

We spend the rest of the day hanging out with each other and after Piper leaves, Hadley goes up to her room. I'm sure it's because she doesn't want me to know she likes Mac. She'd never hang out with us if Connor was here, so she's not going to now.

"I guess I'll get out of your hair. I know you don't like people in your space." Mac runs a hand through his hair and stares where Hadley just disappeared.

"I wanted to talk to you about something." I drop onto the couch and motion for him to take a seat. This isn't going to be a quick talk.

"What's going on?" He rubs the back of his neck, more than uncomfortable. I'm sure he's worried I want to talk to him about Hadley, and I do, but not today.

"It's not that I don't like you in my space, I just don't want Connor here. I'm cutting ties with him when we graduate. It's the only way my dad will give me a place in the company."

"Seriously? I didn't know there were conditions for you getting the job."

"Not only the job, but also for them paying for college, too. I have to leave Connor behind."

"Shit... what about me? Do we have to stop being friends, too?" He looks a little scared, like his whole world is about to crash down around him. I get it. If I'm not allowed to be friends with him, Hadley definitely can't date him.

"Nah, my parents love you. They think you're stupid, but they love you anyway."

"I'm not stupid! I get good grades." He folds his arms over his chest and glares at me.

"Yeah, but you also do Connor's bidding, just like I do... that's what I wanted to talk to you about. I'm done. I'm not going to allow Conner to hurt her anymore. She doesn't deserve it and I kinda like her."

"I figured, especially when I woke up and found her laying on top of you." He smirks. "I'm not going to tell Connor if that's what you're worried about... I haven't really wanted to be friends with him for a while, but you know he'll make our lives hell if we try to break up with him."

"Don't say break up with him. You make it sound like we're dating." I roll my eyes.

"You know what I mean." He chuckles. "He's all about his personal vendettas and I don't want to be his next target. We have less than a year left until we scatter for college."

"I agree. I don't want his sights turned on me either. So, I have a plan..."

Chapter 22
Piper

I hate Mondays. I know, I know, everyone does. But this is different. Monday is the start of a new week of school. One I know will be full of Connor trying his hardest to torture me. I don't know how much more I can take before I stab him and leave him lying on the carpet to bleed out.

For the most part, Connor leaves me alone at home. Sure, he's put fake spiders in my bed and somehow took all of the toothpaste out of my tube and replaced it with mayo. It was gross, but it wasn't a big deal.

"Mornin', Piper." Fernando smiles at me as he sets a plate full of waffles in front of me.

"What if I didn't like waffles?" I arch a brow.

"You do. Your mom filled out a little questionnaire when you both moved in. I know you hate seafood and avocados. You only like chunky peanut butter and raspberry jelly. Seedless." He places his hands on his hips and stares down at me with a smirk.

"Do you know how I like my coffee?" I smile innocently, knowing Mom always gets it wrong.

"Black, just like your step brother's heart."

"How'd you-"

"I watch everything going on in this house. Do you really believe I let you into my kitchen without tracking your every movement? No one steps foot in there without me knowing what you're doing. I even have cameras in there. I wouldn't put it past that asshole to screw with something I've made. He hates me. I'm waiting for him to try to set me up and get me fired."

"You're so trusting." I chuckle, taking my first bite of food.

James strolls into the room with a genuine smile on his face. He's dressed in a navy suit with a crisp white shirt and red tie. He's handsome, confident, and someone I've come to actually like.

"Looking good, Stepdaddy." I smile when he rolls his eyes. I've taken to calling him Stepdaddy because it annoys Connor and amuses James and me.

"Thanks, Princess. Do you want to go car shopping today? We could go right after school."

"Are you sure you want to buy me a car? I really don't need one and I'll be going away to college next year..." I trail off not knowing what else to say. I'd love to have my own car so I can avoid Connor more, but Hadley's going to pick me up today. It will be nice to ride to school with her instead of the boys.

I wouldn't mind seeing Grayson though. He was so sweet this weekend. Taking care of the glass in my hand, carrying me into the den so I didn't get any glass in my foot, letting me sleep on top of him.

But I know when I see him today, he could be a completely different person and that hurts. I can't look forward to being around him. I can't let my guard down with him no matter how much I want to. I need to keep the walls carefully constructed around my heart. There's no other way for me to survive Grayson Young.

"Of course I want to buy you one. Let me spoil you, Piper. I know a car was never an option for you before I married your mother, but you deserve to be treated equal to Connor." He glances around before leaning in and whispering in my ear, "Maybe even better." He stands back to his full height and takes a seat at the head of the table.

Connor stomps into the room a few seconds later with a scowl on his face. He flops into the chair across from me and angrily cuts up his waffle before stuffing it into his face.

"Connor, you have a football game on Friday, correct?" James peeks up at his son before turning his attention back to his food.

I feel bad for James. I think he wants a relationship with his son, but he doesn't know how to get one. And Connor definitely doesn't make it easy.

"Yeah. You don't have to come. There's no reason for you to act like a doting parent just because you have some woman to impress."

"That *woman* is your stepmother and you'll treat her with respect. Lauren has been nothing but kind to you and you've been rude every step of the way. I didn't raise you to be like this."

"You didn't raise me at all." Connor snorts with laughter. "Who raised me? Connie? Was that her name? I remember her sticking around until I was in middle school. I'm pretty sure you were fucking her. Then you lost interest and she left and was replaced with... Sharon? She lasted a while before she too couldn't hold your attention. I wonder exactly how long Lauren will be able to." Connor flashes an evil smirk at James.

I glance up to find Mom standing in the doorway to the dining room. I have no doubt Connor said all of that to try to upset her, knowing she was there.

"Sweetheart..." James stands from the table, glaring at his son.

"Don't worry about it, James. Connor has made it well known he doesn't want me or Piper here. But as he likes to remind us daily, he won't be here much longer anyway. After all, he can't wait to move out of this *hell hole*, as he likes to call it." Mom folds her arms over her chest and pins Connor with a look I know all too well. The disapproving mom look.

She doesn't like him and she doesn't care how he feels about us. She's not going to bend or break because of him. She's going to ignore his tantrums and keep living her life. He won't win, he won't get her to run away like the rest of them. Mom is stronger than that.

And so am I.

The tension in the room grows to suffocating proportions. Connor's sitting back in his chair with an emotionless expression while Mom stares at him in disappointment. James won't remove his gaze from Mom. He's silently begging her with his eyes to not walk away.

I feel sorry for James. He didn't ask to have Satan as his one and only spawn. It must suck knowing he's all yours and no one else has to take responsibility for him.

My phone vibrates on the table and flashes a picture of Hadley and me from this weekend.

"I gotta go, my ride's here." I stand from the table and give Mom a hug before I kiss James's cheek.

I'm showering James with attention and acting like the daughter he so desperately wants because I think he deserves to have one kid who cares about him. Connor treats him terribly and I don't think it's fair. Plus, if my actions piss off Connor, it sounds like a win-win situation to me.

I snatch my backpack from beside the door and leave. Racing down the stairs to the driveway, I count each one. It's become a habit of mine. There are exactly twenty-seven steps from the house to the driveway.

Hadley's drumming her hands against the steering wheel in beat with the music blaring from her stereo. As soon as I climb in and shut the door, she moves down the driveway and away from the house.

"How's Prince Douchebag?"

"He's such an asshole. I swear James is counting the days until he moves out." I sigh as I buckle my seatbelt.

"Can you imagine having to live with him for eighteen years? That sounds like a prison sentence." Hadley cringes.

"He wasn't always this bad. He used to be nice... it's only been since his mom died," a deep voice rumbles from the backseat.

I spin around, coming face to face with the boy I can't get out of my mind. Except he's not a boy. He's all man. A slow smile curls up the corner of his lips.

"Shouldn't you be riding with Connor?"

"Oh, I'm sorry, I didn't realize this was a girl's only club." Grayson rolls his eyes.

"Well, it can't be now!" Hadley groans. "Are we picking up Mac?"

"No. Connor can get him."

"Why do you and Mac not drive? You're always riding with Hadley or Connor."

"Mac does drive." Grayson frowns at me. "Remember, he drove to our house over the weekend."

"But neither of you drive to school." I give him a *duh* look.

"Grayson's not allowed to drive until after we graduate. He totaled his car last year because they were racing and he lost control on the ice." Hadley keeps her eyes on the road. She doesn't see the glare Grayson has pointed at her.

"Thanks, Hads," he hisses.

"What? I'm not the idiot who decided to drive like you have a death wish." She peeks at her brother in the rear-view mirror. She turns her attention to the road before glancing at me. "He almost died. He was in the hospital for two weeks."

"Enough. Piper doesn't give a shit about any of this," Grayson growls.

He's wrong. I have so many questions. I want to know if it was Connor's fault. Did he push Grayson to do something he wasn't comfortable with? It would make sense. That could be why Mr. and Mrs. Young want Grayson to cut ties with Connor. I would too if he was the cause of them almost losing their son.

"Mac gets rides to school because of the umbilical cord attached to Grayson and Connor, plus his FOMO." Hadley rolls her eyes.

We pull into the school parking lot and Hadley parks in her normal space. I've noticed no one ever parks here or in the one Connor uses. I don't think they're assigned since they're not numbered. I'm pretty sure people wouldn't dare park in the kings' of Prescott High's spots.

Hadley gets out right away and shrugs her bag over her shoulder. She stops at the front of the car and pulls her phone out of her pocket, checking something.

"Hey, are you ok?" Grayson stops me from opening the door.

"Yeah, why wouldn't I be?" I turn to face him.

"I don't know. You got kinda quiet after Hadley blabbed about the accident."

"You almost died, Grayson," I say softly.

"Before you even met me." He rolls his eyes. "You wouldn't have missed me."

"But now I've met you," I whisper.

"Are you saying you'd miss me?" His intense gaze is locked on me. I swear the world around us could disappear and he wouldn't even notice.

My heart pounds against my ribs. I want to tell him I'd miss him so much. That it would kill me to lose him, but I can't.

As soon as we climb out of this car, he's going to treat me like the dirt on the bottom of his boots. I can't let myself get attached to someone like that.

"I'm not sure yet. I guess that depends on which version of you I get." I press my lips into a hard line and open the door. Grayson follows my lead and presses his chest against my back when we're both standing outside of the car.

"Don't give up on me yet," he whispers, his lips grazing over the shell of my ear. "I'm protecting you the best I can."

"You're protecting yourself and your reputation."

"That's where you're wrong, baby. Sometimes you need to sleep in the wolf's den to protect the ones you care about." He places a hand on my hip, slipping it under my shirt and squeezing my body gently.

I suck in a sharp breath. I'm not sure if it's from the term of endearment or from the unexpected physical contact. Grayson's so hot and cold. I feel like I'm constantly off balance around him.

"Maybe you should be a mountain lion and eat the damn wolf." I step away from him, letting his hand fall back to his side.

I don't look back at him, I keep my head held high and slip my arm through Hadley's. We climb the steps to school together, never once looking behind us.

Chapter 23
Grayson

She's going to be the death of me. All I want to do is tell her how I feel. I see the way these fuckers keep their eyes locked on her. They all want her. It's only a matter of time before one of them grows the balls to ask her out. And what will she do? There's no reason she has to say no. I have no claim on her, not officially.

Do I mean enough to Piper for her to turn them all down? Does she feel this thing growing between us?

"Dude, you look like someone just stole your candy and teddy bear." Mac clamps a hand down on my shoulder.

"Drop it before Connor hears," I growl. The last thing I need is Connor getting involved in my shit.

"My lips are sealed where the girls are concerned," he says seriously, dropping the act. We stare at the girls' retreating backs, both of us obsessed with one of them and no one knowing.

Piper's long brown hair is twisted into French braids today. She has a red plaid mini skirt on and it makes her long legs look even longer. She has on her little ankle boots that I swear she wears everywhere and a long sleeve black shirt. She looks so innocent and tempting. It's taking everything in me not to chase after her and lock her in an empty classroom with me.

"What the hell were you talking to the Princess about?" Connor folds his arms over his chest and glares at me.

"I'm reminding her where she belongs and warning her that Hadley can't save her." I turn an emotionless gaze to Connor. "My sister doesn't get touched."

"I guess that depends on who's side she's on."

I move before Connor can react. Gripping him by the neck, I slam his body against Hadley's Jeep and place my forearm over his neck. I press down hard, knowing he can barely breathe.

Connor's trying to seem calm. He doesn't attempt to remove my arm or beg for me to let him go, but I can see the fear in his eyes. He's not used to me turning on him, but he knows the monster I keep hidden inside could kill him in a second.

"If you touch a fucking hair on my sister's head, I'll kill you. Do you understand me? Hadley doesn't get pulled into your little bullshit. She's innocent in all of this." I push harder on his neck as his face begins to turn a little purple, but I don't give a shit. He's not going to die, but he needs to know I'm not joking.

"We're gaining an audience," Mac hisses under his breath. "Let him go, Gray."

"Do you fucking understand me?" I roar, releasing a little bit of pressure so he can talk.

"Yes! Fuck! I won't touch Hadley."

"You won't involve her in any of this? I don't trust your twisted words. She's not your target and you better remember that."

"I won't do a damn thing to her," he hisses, pushing at my chest.

"Good. I'll be watching, asshole." I step back and let him go.

To his credit, he doesn't fall to the ground, gasp for air, or touch his neck. Nope, Connor Ward doesn't want a single person to think he's weak. He glares at me, keeping his head held high.

I briefly wonder if he's going to have a bruise, but I shake the thought away. I really don't give a shit either way. My focus is on the girls and nothing else.

"Let's go, Mac," I growl, pushing past Connor, making sure my shoulder knocks into him.

Mac's at my side like an obedient dog. He knows Connor's not going to be by our sides for long, I'm the dependable and sane friend.

"What the hell are you going to do? He's going to hit them hard. I don't believe for a second he's going to leave Hadley alone." I can hear the worry in his voice and I feel the same way.

As soon as we're in the school and away from Connor, I tug Mac into an empty classroom. I didn't want to have this heart to heart with him yet, but I don't have a choice anymore.

"Listen, I'm fairly certain you have a thing for my sister so I know you don't want anything to happen to her either."

Mac opens his mouth to respond, but I hold up a hand and stop him.

"I don't want you to confirm or deny my assumptions. I just want you to keep an eye on her and protect her from Connor."

"I can do that. How are you going to protect Piper? He's not going to back down. He saw you talking to her and he wasn't happy."

"He doesn't know what I was saying and Piper marched off all pissed off. He won't suspect a single thing."

"I think he's about to lose it, Gray. He wasn't in a good headspace on the way to school. Apparently, there was a big blow up at breakfast and basically Lauren called him out on his bullshit. James jumped to her rescue and Piper kissed daddy dearest on the cheek before she left. He's spiraling. I'm afraid he's going to do something we can't save her from."

"Then I'll just have to get closer."

"He's going to turn his sights on you if he thinks you like her."

"Not if I offer to take Piper down in exchange for him leaving Hadley alone," I say as an idea takes root.

"What are you going to do when you don't succeed in pulling off whatever he wants?"

"I don't know. I'm fucked no matter what I do."

The bell rings, pulling me from my misery. I need to figure this out and fast. Connor's going to strike soon. I need to figure out his plan and interfere before anything happens.

"So, what are we doing to her next?" I drop my lunch tray onto the table in front of Connor and give him a bored look.

"I have a few ideas up my sleeve." He flashes me a sinister smile.

I'm not even comfortable being friends with him anymore, but it's what I have to do to protect Piper and Hadley. And I'll do anything for the two of them.

"Care to share with the class?" I arch a brow. I can't let him think I'm too interested in what he has planned.

Connor's not an idiot. He'll see right through me if I push too hard. He'll realize something more is going on and he'll stop trusting me. The only thing I have going for me is I can blame it on my love for Hadley.

"I'm going to humiliate her at the football game on Friday. She'll be the laughing stock of this school." He folds his arms over his chest with a pleased grin.

"How are you going to pull that off?" Mac leans in like he's interested.

It's almost disturbing how easily the two of us can hide behind these masks. We're completely different people when Connor isn't around.

"Don't worry about it, I'm going to have the cheerleaders help me." Connor leans back with a smirk.

"How do you know she's going to be at the game?"

Shit. I know she'll be there. She's planning on sitting with my parents and sister. They were talking about it all weekend. I'm sure James and Lauren will be sitting with them too. This isn't going to end well.

"Her and my father were talking about it last night." He shrugs like he doesn't care.

Connor stopped calling James dad when Piper moved in. Since then, he's been referred to as father. Connor's jealous and hurt, but he'll never admit that to anyone.

"Don't you think they'll be sitting together?" Mac voices my concern.

"Mac, my old man hasn't come to a game in years. I doubt he's going to start now. And even if he does, I don't really care if he witnesses this." He looks away and takes a big bite of his sandwich. "Oh! I'm also paying Cherie to steal her clothes after swimming again, but this time she's going to snap a photo of her naked and spread it around the school," he says it so casually, like he's talking about the weather or what he's having for dinner.

"Dude, are you sure that's a good idea?" Mac glances at me, but I keep my expression blank.

I want to pin Connor against the wall and strangle him. This time I don't want to stop. I want to squeeze the air out of him and watch his lifeless body drop to the floor. He's a destructive person who doesn't care what carnage he leaves in his wake.

"I'm untouchable, Macky. Don't you know that by now?" He smiles triumphantly.

I want to erase the smile from his lips and give him a lesson about just how easily someone can get behind his defenses and take him down.

"Here comes the Princess now. I hope she enjoys her time here at Prescott High while she can. I have a feeling she's going to be running for the hills by next week... and if she's not. I'm going to up my game." The grin that spreads over his face makes me nauseous. Even in my wildest dreams, I couldn't treat someone the way he treats Piper.

As soon as the bell rings, I'm racing out of the cafeteria and to my next class. I want to talk to Cherie before anyone gets to our class. I don't need witnesses who could report back to Connor. People are always looking for ways to get on his good side in hopes that he'll befriend them.

When Cherie walks into the room, I drag her to the back and push her up against the wall. Anyone who walks in will think I'm trying to make a move on her, not that I'm threatening her within an inch of her life.

"What are you doing, Gray?" She blinks up at me, a slow smile spreading across her lips. She's stupid enough to think I want her. I don't. I'd like to stay STD free.

"Whatever Connor's planning for you to do to Piper, I don't want you to do it."

"Aww, does someone have a crush?" She coos, running a long nail over my chest.

"No. I love Hadley and they're friends. Anything bad that happens to Piper will upset my sister and make my life hell." The lies fall so easily from my lips.

"What do I get out of it?" She folds her arms across her chest and raises a brow.

Cherie doesn't come from a wealthy family. At least not as wealthy as the rest of the people in the school. The only reason she's popular is because she's the captain of the cheerleading squad. And because she's a bitch. She knows exactly how to manipulate people into doing what she wants. She's very easily convinced to do something if you flash some money in front of her face though.

"I'll pay you double whatever Connor is."

"Triple." Her grin widens and I know if I don't give in, she'll go back to Connor, hoping he'll give her more for snitching.

"Fine! Just leave Piper alone no matter what Connor asks and don't mention this conversation or I'll destroy you," I growl.

"What am I supposed to tell him? I can't just not do it. He'll suspect something."

"Tell him she didn't take a shower after class. If he wants you to do something else, come to me. I'll make it worth your while."

"Fine. But I expect something every time I come to you with information."

"You'll get it."

"What about a date?" She smirks.

"We both know you care more about the money than you do about my dick. Plus, you couldn't handle me, sweetheart," I lean down and growl in her ear.

"Grayson, Cherie, take your seats so we can begin class," our teacher sighs.

I do as I'm told, slipping into my seat and tugging my phone out of my pocket. I shoot off a single text before I stare at the teacher and attempt to pay attention for the remainder of class.

Chapter 24
Piper

"How's Connor torturing you this week?" Will peeks at me over the rim of his coffee.

My old school didn't have a barista or a coffee machine, unless you're talking about the old one in the teacher's lounge. But Prescott High has it all. Anything to make their spoiled students happy.

"He hasn't done anything yet, but I'm sure the temporary peace will come to an end today." I sigh, glancing over at my stepbrother and his friends.

"We should figure out a way to get even with him." Will smirks.

"I'd love to, but I have a feeling he'll come back harder. I'm not sure I can outdo Connor Ward." I toss a fry into my mouth and chew slowly.

This weekend the thought really took root and I'm beginning to wonder if I can outdo him. He's always going to push things further and won't be afraid of the consequences. He has no morals or conscience. I can't compete with that.

"There's got to be some way to get him to stop," Hadley murmurs, barely glancing up from studying for a test next period.

"That's going to be hard. I have to go give Mrs. Peters a late assignment, I'll catch up with you guys later. I'll see if I can come up with any plans for Connor." Will gathers his things and rushes out of the cafeteria like his ass is on fire.

"What's going on with you? You're awfully quiet." I lower my voice so only Hadley can hear me.

"I don't know. I just hate how things are so weird right now. They treat us so differently outside of school and it's starting to piss me off." She glances over her shoulder at Connor's table, which now only consists of Grayson and Mac.

I find it interesting how Connor doesn't let anyone else near him. He clearly rules this school, he's made that painfully clear multiple times. Yet he's never surrounded by his fan group. It's only ever Grayson and Mac.

"I know. It's annoying."

"My brother likes you. He hasn't said it, but I can tell. He doesn't treat girls the way he treats you... at least when we're not here." She motions around us. "He's himself when you're around our house and that's rare... I was actually kinda shocked he let Mac come over. He hasn't let him or Connor come over in years."

I frown at that. If Connor and Mac are his best friends, why wouldn't he let them come over? I could understand if Mr. and Mrs. Young don't want Connor over, but they seemed to like Mac.

"I think Mac likes you." I grin, thinking about how cute they were together this weekend. They looked like a real couple and it was adorable.

"It doesn't matter. Grayson would never let us be together." She sighs, resting her chin in her hand.

"And you think Connor would allow me and Grayson to be together?" I pin her with a disbelieving look.

"Brothers are stupid," she mutters under her breath.

"Stepbrothers are worse."

Unknown: Don't shower after swimming.

I stare down at the text from an unknown number and frown. Who is this and why do they care if I take a shower after swimming?

Piper: Who is this?

I type out the message without looking away from the board. They're stricter on cell phone use here than they were at my old school. If I get caught, I'll lose my phone for the rest of the day.

Unknown: The man you want to kiss.

Piper: I think you have the wrong number.

Nausea fills me. What could possibly happen if I shower? I got a lock for my locker. There's no way for anyone to get my clothes anymore. And I've started keeping my bathing suit on while I shower. I don't trust that someone won't try to steal it again.

Unknown: Piper, you know who this is. There's only one man you want to kiss and you were laying on top of him Saturday night.

Piper: Grayson?

Unknown: Don't shower, sweetheart.

I wish this was the Grayson I always got. I hate how there's two of them. I never know who to expect or how to act.

Piper: Why?

Unknown: Just trust me.

I drop the subject, knowing Grayson isn't trying to mess with me... I don't think. He seemed really genuine this weekend. I can't imagine he'd do all of this just to get me to relax around him... unless that's the plan. Connor uses his best friend to get close to me and when I drop my defenses, he strikes.

Fuck.

I make it through the rest of the day without running into Connor or any of his minions. Cherie scowls at me throughout our entire time in the pool, but she doesn't say a word to me. I guess I should consider myself lucky.

While the rest of the girls shower, I take my clothes into a bathroom stall and change. I'm not risking anything at this point.

I'm shocked when I make it through another day without Connor trying anything new on me. My only concern is am I experiencing the calm before the storm?

"Which one do you want, Princess?" James smiles at me.

"You really don't need to do this, it's too much."

"Piper," he sighs. "I know you're not used to having a father figure and I'm not used to having a daughter, but I truly love your mom. I want us to be a real family."

"I'm fairly certain Connor isn't on the same page as you."

"He's awful. I love him because he's my son, but I don't understand him. He just kinda fell off the deep end when his mom died. I don't know how to fix him and I'm not sure it's even possible anymore... Connor's taken it as his own personal mission to run off every woman I've ever dated. He's left your mom alone which makes me think he's going after you... I need you to tell me if he's doing anything."

"I'm fine. He's not doing anything I can't handle." I wave him off. I know the only reason I'm surviving Connor is because of Grayson. He's doing something to protect me.

"But he won't stop. Not until he gets what he wants. Please don't hesitate to come to me. My son doesn't have boundaries... or a conscience. I'm terrified of what he might do one day."

I wrap my arms around James' waist and squeeze him tightly. I think he needs this more than he'll ever admit.

James has been nothing but kind to me since we moved in. He treats Mom like she's his queen and I'm his princess. He's gotten over the mini shorts and crop tops, finally accepting Mom's rules and not fighting them.

"I think you should get an SUV. They're bigger and you'll be safer in it." James leads me over to something similar to Connor's car.

It takes us a little over an hour to pick out the perfect car and to get all the paperwork done. It's so much faster when you're paying out of pocket and not taking out a loan.

Soon James is handing me the keys to my very own car. He smiles from ear to ear. It's adorable how happy he is to give me such a lavish gift.

"Why don't you go visit Hadley and show her your new car." He presses a soft kiss to my forehead. "Be careful driving. I'll let your mom know where you're going."

"Thank you, James." I wrap him in another hug.

"You're welcome. You deserve it."

I climb in the car and run my hands over the soft leather. I wanted a used car, but James insisted on something new. He said a used car could have problems we don't know about and he's not going to risk the safety of his daughter to save a few dollars.

I never imagined a stepdad treating me like his real child, but James does. He makes sure I'm taken care of and that I'm happy all the time. He's the perfect husband for Mom and I'm so happy she gets to experience love once again.

I smile the entire way to Hadley's. If it weren't for Connor, this new life would be pretty perfect. Almost like a dream.

Soon I'm pulling into Hadley's long driveway and hopping out of the car. I knock on the door and am surprised when a shirtless Grayson opens the door.

"Hey, I didn't know you were coming over." He grips the doorframe and smiles at me.

"I-I didn't... I mean I didn't know either... I got a car..." I point over my shoulder like an idiot. Squeezing my eyes shut, I try to regain my composure and clear my throat. "Let me start again," I whisper, not opening my eyes. "I got a new car and wanted to show it to Hadley."

"Open your eyes, baby," Grayson murmurs, lifting my chin.

"No. I don't want to."

"It's not my fault you malfunction every time you see me without a shirt on." I can hear the smirk in his voice.

My eyes fly open so I can scowl at him. I don't like him thinking he has any sort of power over me. Grayson's too powerful on his own, he doesn't need me inflating his ego any more.

"I do not!"

"Sure you do, but it's ok. It's kinda cute and I like it."

"Should I take my shirt off and see if you malfunction?" I arch a brow, planting my hands on my hips.

"I'd do more than malfunction," he grumbles under his breath as Hadley pushes past him.

"Thanks for letting me know Piper's here." Hadley rolls her eyes before turning her attention to me. "Is that yours?" She points to the SUV excitedly.

"Yup! James is so sweet. I can't believe he got me a brand-new car. I was expecting a used one at best."

"Pfft, Daddy Ward would never allow his little princess to drive a used car." Grayson snorts and shakes his head.

"Stop calling me that." I fold my arms over my chest and glare at him.

"Oh, c'mon, Piper. That man adores you."

"You've never even seen us together. You have no clue. You only know what Connor's told you." I open the door so Hadley can climb inside and take a look inside my new car.

"Well, I guess that will change tomorrow when I come over to hang out with Connor."

"Why are you coming over?" I pin him with a look.

He takes two steps in my direction and shuts the door, closing Hadley inside. He leans against the door so she can't get out through this side.

"Connor wants to plan a way to get to you since you somehow avoided being photographed naked today. He planned to plaster those photos all over town."

"That's why you didn't want me to shower?" I whisper, my brows pulling together.

I can't believe Connor hates me so much he's willing to spread nude photos of me around the school. I haven't done a thing to him.

"I told you I'd protect you." Grayson runs a gentle hand down my cheek. "Don't trust anyone that doesn't have my last name, Piper."

"What about Mac?"

"Connor's always been able to easily manipulate Mac and get him to do what he wants. Mac isn't a fan of Connor right now and he has a soft spot for you. He's probably safe, but..."

"What about Will?"

"I wouldn't trust him. I'm not exactly sure where he sits with Connor. They seem a little too friendly lately."

I stare down at my feet. I'm tired of constantly fighting Connor and having to worry about who I can trust. Life wasn't like this before I moved. Life was easy, predictable, and fun.

"Hey, come here." Grayson tugs on my hand and pulls me into his embrace. "It's going to be fine, baby. Don't worry about anything."

My body melts into his, but I keep my walls up around my heart. Grayson's too easy to fall for and I'm still not sure I trust him. What if this is all a ruse for me to fall in love with him? What if this is all part of Connor's master plan and I'm playing right into it?

Chapter 25
Grayson

Piper stiffens in my arms and I can guess what she's thinking. How can she really trust me to have her best interest at heart? If she's smart, and I know she is, she should be wondering if I'm trying to trick her into trusting me.

Fuck. How did I get myself mixed up in all of this?

I've never had a girlfriend. Not because I didn't want one or because I wasn't interested in one, they just weren't worth it. Connor's always needy. Demanding I drop everything to come help him with something. I didn't want to ignore a girlfriend because of him.

I know I should've just stopped being friends with Connor, but that felt like such a shitty thing to do. He changed after his mom died. James didn't handle things well and he immersed himself in work. He practically ignored Connor's existence. I understand where both of them are coming from, but they needed each other.

I stayed by Connor's side, just like Mac did, and he's only gotten worse. I think we're both still friends with him because we don't trust him. It's easier to keep an eye on what a friend is doing rather than what an enemy is scheming.

"Let me out of here!" Hadley's muffled voice is accompanied by her tiny fists pounding on the window.

I take a few steps away from the door, taking Piper with me. I'm not letting her go, not yet anyway.

I hate acting like I feel nothing towards her at school. It's all a lie, a way to keep Connor off my scent and the only way to keep her safe. If Connor didn't trust me, I never would've found out about his plans for Cherie to take photos of her. I need to stay in his good graces.

"Sometimes you're a real asshole, Grayson!" Hadley crosses her arms over her chest and glares at me.

"I keep trying to tell you that." I shrug, it's not my fault if she doesn't want to see the bad in me.

"Let go of Piper. We're going to hang out."

"See, that's why I barricaded you in the car, you don't like to share your toys." I glance down at Piper. "She never was good at sharing."

"Grayson!" Hadley stomps her foot. She gets so mad when I act like this. It's entertaining. She's so tiny, she looks like a little pixie. "Piper's not a damn toy!"

"Fine! I'm letting go of her." I unwrap my arms from around her, but I grab for her hand and intertwine our fingers.

Piper stifles a laugh and peeks over at Hadley. She doesn't find this nearly as entertaining.

"Grayson," she groans. "Piper's staying for dinner. Can't you just stare at her longingly across the table like a normal person?"

"Only if she'll play footsie with me." I arch a brow at Piper.

"I don't know. I don't play footsie with just anyone. I need to be in a committed relationship for that and I don't think that's what you're looking for. Sorry, handsome" Piper pats me on the chest and takes a step away from me.

She drops my hand and it falls to my side. I watch in shock as her and Hadley walk into the house and leave me dumbfounded in the driveway. What the hell?

"I'm thinking we can go to the game together." Mom smiles from the head of the table.

Dad's on the other end with Hadley and Piper sitting on one side and I'm stuck all by myself on the other side.

"Are you going to wait until I'm done to go home then?" I arch a brow. They never want to wait that late. It's almost eleven by the time I get out of the locker room.

"Ugh, I forgot about that. Hads, you can drive so you can give him a ride home." Mom waves her hand in my sister's direction.

"I can just get Mac or Connor to give me a ride. It's fine." I shove another bite of mashed potatoes into my mouth. Mom's an amazing cook, but her mashed potatoes are my favorite.

"No. Hadley can wait for you." Dad pins me with a look and I know there's no arguing.

"Mac isn't like Connor, Dad," I whisper, wanting to make sure he doesn't view Mac wrong.

If he and Hadley ever start dating, I want him to know Mac's not a bad guy. I don't think he'd intentionally hurt Hadley, but that's what I'm afraid of. That's the only thing keeping me from being their biggest cheerleader.

"I know he isn't. He's a good kid, but still dumb as a doorknob. Mac rarely drives though. Which means you'd be getting in the car with Connor and I don't like that idea. I gave you until the end of the year, but that doesn't mean I'm going to push you towards him until then. I'm tugging on that damn leash, trying to pull you away from him, you're just too stubborn to come willingly... I'm sorry, Piper, I shouldn't be talking about your family like this... at least not in front of you." He flashes her a cheeky grin.

"It's ok, Mr. Young. I know exactly who Connor is and I don't blame you. I don't like living in the same house as him." She shrugs, taking a bite of her food. "If I could get away from him I would."

"Well, you're always welcome here, sweetie. We love having you visit. If you ever need to get away for a few days, weeks, or months, our door is always open." Mom smiles.

"Months?" Hadley falls into a fit of laughter. "Should we just give Piper her own room now?"

"Nope. I'm not sure I'd be able to keep boys out of it." Dad raises a brow and stares directly at me. I chuckle and shake my head. What else am I supposed to do? Everyone at this table knows I'd be sneaking in there every night and they wouldn't be able to stop me.

"I hear the blue bedroom has a tree branch leading to the window." I smirk, stealing a glance at Piper.

"Oh, you mean the room right next to yours and furthest from the rest of the bedrooms?" Mom asks with an amused grin.

"Exactly. It would be a great place for her. You know, if there's a fire, that branch could save her life."

"Placing Piper in the blue room might save her life, but it might end someone else's. I'm not sure I want to be down to one kid. I put so much time and effort into two. The return on my investments would be split in half." Dad strokes his chin like he's actually thinking about it. "Plus, I don't think Hadley wants to run the company, so I'd have to work longer."

"So... the blue room is out! I'm tired of being the only one at home. I have things that need to be handled and I can't do them alone." Mom places her hands on the table and wiggles her eyebrows at Dad.

"Oh, gross. I'm done. I've lost my appetite." I shake my head with my lips pinched together. "Shit, I might vomit. I think you've ruined mashed potatoes for me."

Piper and Hadley giggle from across the table, bright smiles lighting up their features.

"Does anyone want to slam my head against the wall until I can't remember what I just witnessed?" I fake dry heave, making the girls laugh even harder.

"How do you think you got here? A stork didn't drop your ass at the door." Dad chuckles.

"I know that. But in my head, you've fucked once in your life and that's it. It was a one and done deal. You made us and you called it quits." I shake my head, squeezing my eyes shut.

"I think it was twice today alone, right, honey?" Mom snorts with laughter.

"Yup. Three times yesterday."

"Lord, couldn't you just kill me? It would be less painful." I stare up at the ceiling and spread my arms wide.

"I thought the girls were supposed to be the dramatic ones." Dad rolls his eyes.

"Clearly your sperm screwed up." Mom leans back in her chair with an amused grin.

"Ugh, Mom! You can't say sperm!"

Chapter 26
Grayson

"Grayson!" Mac hisses, shoving me into an empty room as soon as I walk through the front door of school the next morning.

"What?"

"Connor put a huge bag of cocaine in Piper's locker. It's all divided into tiny bags so she looks like she's dealing. He's paying a student to report it anonymously. If the cops show up and they search the lockers, she'll not only get suspended, she'll probably get arrested." Mac paces up and down the length of the room.

I wrack my brain trying to come up with the best solution to save her. This is so much further than I thought Connor would ever take things.

"Was anyone else around when he did it?" I thrust my hand through my hair in frustration. I'm not letting her go down for this, even if it means showing Connor my hand before I'm ready.

"There were a few kids in the hallway, but no teachers, why?"

"Because then one of them could've witnessed it and told Piper. Give me whatever money you have in your wallet." I hold a hand out and wait for him to hand over whatever he has. I'm shocked when he hands over three hundred fifty dollars. "I'll take care of it, Mac. Don't worry about a thing. Go to class and I'll make sure Piper doesn't get in trouble."

"Thanks, Gray."

I shove him out the door and fire off a few quick text messages. I shake my head, unable to believe this is what I'm doing at seven o'clock in the morning.

Grayson: Can you call the school and say I'm going to be late?

Mom: Why would you be late? You should be there already. Is everything ok?

Grayson: I am here. I'm saving Piper from Connor. Please, Mom?

Mom: Always the knight in shining armor. I'll cover for you.

The next one is a message I dread sending. I know she's going to ask questions and I don't want to give her answers, not yet.

Grayson: What's your combination to your locker?

Piper: I'm not stupid, Grayson. I'm not telling you my combination.

Frustration rolls through me at her distrust. I understand why she doesn't trust me, but that doesn't mean it doesn't bother me.

Grayson: Piper, I'm not joking. I need it now.

Piper: Why?

Grayson: If you don't want to go to jail for possession of drugs with the intent to sell, you'll tell me.

I'm quickly losing patience and know the clock is quickly ticking down. I don't have long before he's going to have someone call this in. If I get stuck with the drugs or don't get it out of her locker in time, we're fucked.

Piper: 5-26-18.

Grayson: Stay in class. I'll text you as soon as I can.

The last text is to the man who can save all of us. The only hope I have of making sure none of us get in trouble.

Grayson: Meet me in room 404 if you want a free bag of coke to sell. No strings attached.

Sean: Be there in five minutes.

I rush down the hall to Piper's locker and quickly twist the dial until the lock releases. I scramble to find the bag, surprised at how much Piper has in her locker when she's only been at this school for a few weeks.

I finally find the bag of white powder rolled up inside of one of her sweatshirts. I'm sure the drug sniffing dogs will be able to smell the drugs on the shirt so I take that too. Sorry, Piper, I'll buy you a new sweatshirt.

Connor was smart. She never would've found this when she went into her locker this morning. She would've been caught if Mac hadn't told me what was going on.

At least I know Mac is loyal to Hadley, Piper, and I, not Connor. It's one less thing I need to worry about.

I race to room 404 and slide to a stop right inside. Sean is already waiting for me. His face lights up when he sees the bundle in my arms. He doesn't give a shit where it came from, he's just happy to have more.

"And I don't owe you anything?" He glances up at me with a raised brow.

"I'll give you five hundred dollars if you get this out of the school before an anonymous tip goes to the cops about a student having drugs."

"You want to give me all of this, plus five hundred dollars?" Sean stares up at me like I'm crazy. "What's the catch? There has to be something I'm missing."

"The only catch is you can't tell a fucking person about this. If you do, I'll make sure you're beaten so badly your own mother won't recognize you," I growl, shoving Piper's sweatshirt into his hands.

"Dude, I'm not going to say shit! You know I'd never do you wrong, Gray. You've always been nice to me. Thank you. Seriously, man, I'm happy to help with whatever this is. I appreciate you coming to me. This is really going to help at home." Sean actually looks appreciative and it makes me wonder what his home life is like.

Sometimes I forget there's a small neighborhood that's poor within the school district. Not many kids come from there, but there's enough. I glance down at Sean's worn jeans and the holes in his shoes. I never really noticed it before, I wasn't raised that way.

I was taught to never look down on someone less fortunate than me. Money doesn't matter in the long run. Sure, it's nice to have, but you can lose it in an instant.

"Sean, let me know if your family needs more help." I clasp a hand on his shoulder and meet his eyes. "I'm serious, if I can help in any way, let me know."

"My little sister's sick. We can't afford her medicine. You might've just saved her life, Gray." Tears gather in his eyes, but he refuses to let them fall.

"Get these out of here before the cops come then. If they catch you with them, you're screwed." I tug my wallet out of my back pocket and hand over the five hundred dollars Mac and I were carrying this morning. I make a mental note to talk to my parents about taking care of Sean's sister's medical bills.

I might not know what it's like to have a sick sibling and not be able to pay for the medication that can help, but I can understand the responsibility he feels. If it were Hadley, I'd go to Hell and back to save her.

As soon as Sean's out the door and running to his car, I hurry to the bathroom and wash my hands before slowly walking to my locker. I open it and gather my books for the day before stopping in the office to let them know I'm here.

"Go straight to your first period class, Mr. Young." The secretary eyes me as the first police officer walks through the door with a K-9 trained to sniff out drugs.

"Of course. I wouldn't dare hang out in the hallways. I'm a model student." I flash her a smile and quickly get to my first class.

As soon as I'm in my seat and pretending to pay attention, I tug my phone out of my pocket and tell Mom I'm in class and everything is fine. I also ask her to look into Sean's family and tell her about his sister being sick.

Mom: I'll talk to Dad and take care of it. Thank you, sweetie. We raised you right. You make me proud.

I have to resist rolling my eyes at her text. I know I'm not a bad guy, but I'm not great either. I could be a lot better. I don't like my good deeds being rewarded or praised though.

Grayson: You're safe, baby.

Piper: Whatever you did, thank you. You're a lifesaver.

"I don't know how she didn't get caught!" Connor glares at Piper from across the lunch room.

"Dude, you weren't even secretive about it. You tossed that bag in her locker even though there were at least a dozen people in the hallway! Anyone could've told her. It's not like you keep your feelings hidden over your new step sister." Mac rolls his eyes, trying his hardest to convince Connor it might've been something he did.

"I thought you were doing some shit to her at the football game?" I take a bite of my food and chew slowly, swiping my phone screen.

"She didn't take a shower after swimming yesterday! By the end of the week, she'll be done swimming and be in gym class the rest of the year. I needed to take measures to get her out of here more quickly. I don't understand how she keeps getting off so easily." Connor slams his fist into the table.

Connor would never believe Mac and I are the reason Piper's remained practically untouchable. He'd never believe we'd go behind his back and help the enemy.

"I'll try to think of something else we can do to her. No one can avoid every disaster thrown their way. It's just not possible," I mumble.

I hate myself for each word flowing past my lips. I don't want Piper touched, but I need to play the game if I want her out of this safely. I just need to come up with a brilliant plan. One Connor would never expect and go along with easily.

Chapter 27
Piper

School was surprisingly uneventful today after Grayson texted me. Connor kept to himself which honestly worries me a little more than I care to admit. When he's quiet I know he's up to something.

I know Grayson saved my ass today and I appreciate it more than he'll ever know. If he weren't on my side, I'd be completely screwed. I'd never be able to avoid a single prank – if you can call any of these pranks – Connor's pulled on me.

Mac and Grayson have been at my house all afternoon and I can't help but wonder why they're here.

"You look sad. What's wrong, Piper?" Fernando places the last dish on the table and stares at me with his hands on his hips.

"I'm not sad, just tired. It's exhausting living here."

"That it is. I wish I could help. My offer of putting something in his food is always on the table," Fernando leans down and murmurs in my ear before moving away to finish getting ready for dinner.

"I'll keep that in mind." I chuckle, shaking my head. He's my favorite person here.

Fernando presses a hidden button on the wall that calls everyone for dinner. He stands in the corner of the room and clasps his hands together. He'll wait until everyone is seated before he'll tell us what's for dinner. Then he'll leave to eat dinner in the kitchen with Maria and Roger.

Mac slips into the chair across from me and flashes me a megawatt smile. He's adorable and I'll always have a soft spot for him, but I need to remember who he's friends with. I won't let my guard down until I'm positive I can trust him.

Connor drops onto the chair next to him like a sack of potatoes. The guy acts like he lives the worst life in history. He doesn't. His life is pretty damn cushy.

Someone settles into the spot next to me and I don't need to look to know it's Grayson. I can feel how close he is. I have this special superpower where he's concerned, I can tell where he is at all times.

James and Mom take their places a few moments later and Fernando tells us what we're having. It's all a jumbled mess of words I don't understand. He likes to use fancy words to make the meal sound better, but I'm fairly certain it's chicken, potatoes, and... something else. I'm not really sure what that orange blob is though.

Fernando scoops a little of everything on each plate and hands them out.

Meals are where the change to my life has been the most drastic. Everything is carefully planned, perfectly executed, and delicious. There are no last-minute meals or throwing something in the microwave. Hell, I don't think we've had takeout once since I moved in.

I do wonder what Fernando does with the leftovers though. He always makes too much food and I can't imagine he just throws it all away.

"How's school going for everyone?" Mom smiles at each of us.

Connor offers some sort of a mixture between a grunt and a groan, but nothing more. Mom glances at me, clearly wanting something so she doesn't feel stupid. I feel bad. She's been trying so hard to make the transition into this world easier and Connor never helps.

"It's good. We have a big project we just started in science. It's kinda interesting and fun to figure out what's in the sludge. If we get it right, we don't have to take midterms or finals. If we get it wrong, we have to start over with a different cup of sludge." I have to resist the urge to look at Grayson.

"I hope you have a good partner. That sounds like a lot of work," James says.

"She has the best partner in the class. I'll make sure we don't have to take any tests." Grayson gives Mom and James a small smile.

"Oh! I didn't know you two were partners. That's awesome!" Mom beams at us. "Mac, what about you? How's school?"

"It'd be a lot better if my teachers were as pretty as you." He winks at Mom, making her giggle. "I hate school, but I'm good at it so I might as well finish. It'd be a little weird if I dropped out with a perfect 4.0 GPA." He shrugs like that isn't a big deal.

My brows furrow as I stare at Mac. How does he have such high grades? He doesn't seem to care about anything.

"Wow, that's impressive, Mac!" Mom beams at him.

"I can show you something else-"

I brace myself for the inappropriate comment I know is coming. I have a feeling Mom is going to be horrified.

"Mac," Grayson growls, shaking his head. Mac clamps his mouth shut and doesn't finish his sentence.

I glance at Grayson, impressed at how easily he stepped in to stop Mac. I'm shocked he even cared enough to do it. Maybe he wants Mom to like him and see that he's a good guy, even if he is friends with Connor.

"You should finish school. I'd suggest going to college too. You'll regret not doing it later on in life." Mom either doesn't realize what Mac was about to say or she's choosing to ignore it. I'm guessing the latter.

Dinner continues with Mom asking questions and basically carrying the conversation. I'm not surprised. James and Connor seem to have this unspoken rule about not talking during dinner. Except James will talk if Connor isn't around. It's almost like he's uncomfortable around his own son. It's sad, really.

"I'm going to finish my homework then take a shower," I press a kiss to Mom's cheek before moving to James to do the same.

"Good idea, sweetie." James smiles up at me.

I can feel Connor's glare directed at me. I don't need to check to know it's him. It's always him. Instead of waiting around for the impending blow up, I choose to leave before anything bad can happen.

I don't have much homework, just a few pages of math. It takes me less than twenty minutes before I'm stepping under the warm spray in the oversized shower.

Going through my normal routine, I shampoo my hair before putting a deep conditioning mask on. While I let that sit, I shave my legs and wash my face before rinsing out the conditioner. Turning the water as hot as I can stand it, I drop my chin and just stand there.

It's something I've done for as long as I can remember. I close my eyes and wash away all the stress and anxiety from the day. I focus on the feel of the water running down my body and nothing else.

Turning off the water, I grab a fluffy towel and wrap it around my body. I twist a second one around my hair and open the door to my room. Having an en suite bathroom has to be my favorite part of my room. I would definitely be uncomfortable with the idea of sharing a bathroom with Connor.

After quickly getting dressed and brushing my hair, I climb into bed and find something to watch on one of the streaming platforms James has. I prop my phone against a pillow and snuggle under the covers. I barely slept last night. I don't know why, but I couldn't get my brain to shut down. I plan on making up for the lost sleep tonight.

I must've fallen asleep at some point, waking up when my door softly clicks shut. I do my best to remain calm and pretend I'm not awake. I have to pinch my lips shut to keep from gasping when someone crawls in bed behind me and wraps an arm around my body.

"I hate having to stay away from you," Grayson murmurs in my ear.

"That's your choice, I didn't tell you to stay away," I respond sleepily.

"This isn't my choice and you know it. If I had it my way, you'd be in my arms every single night."

"How are you here right now? Someone's going to see you."

"I pretended to leave with Mac and told my parents I'm staying at his house. Mac knows I'm here, but he won't say anything. I was thinking I'd sleep in your bed and sneak down to the garage before anyone wakes up. I'll lay in the backseat until you leave for school." He nuzzles his face into the crook of my neck.

"Grayson! That's crazy."

"Mac's waiting down the street until I text him. He doesn't think you'll let me stay." A soft smile spreads across his face, I can feel it against my neck.

"I wake up at five and everyone else wakes up right after me." I spin in his arms to face him.

"I'll wake up at four-thirty." He presses a kiss to my forehead.

I hate how there are two sides of him. How I never know who I'm going to run into and it's exhausting. I know he's doing what he has to do to keep me safe, but I don't like it one bit.

"Please, baby? I never get to spend any time with you alone." Grayson runs his knuckles down my cheek. I lean into his touch, knowing I should tell him no, but I won't.

"Four-thirty, not a second later."

"On the dot. I just want to be near you. I hate not being able to pull you into my arms whenever I want." Grayson smirks and tugs his phone out to send Mac a text. "I hate sitting next to you at dinner and not being able to hold your hand. It's torture... does your mom hate me?"

I take my time, really thinking about his question. I don't want to just brush him off, I want to give him an honest answer. I run my fingers up and down his arm while I think.

"My mom doesn't hate you, she doesn't really know you. But she doesn't like Connor, so you being attached to him is probably hard for her to understand."

"She shouldn't trust me. Do you trust me?" I can hear the vulnerability in his voice. He's struggling with being in the middle of this.

"Can you really trust anyone other than yourself? I mean, even the devil was once an angel... but I do trust you."

Grayson shifts until he's hovering over me, staring down at my body. He slowly lifts his gaze until our eyes lock and I swear all the oxygen in the room evaporates. I feel like he can see directly into my soul.

"What are you doing?" I whisper, barely able to find my voice.

"I... I don't know."

"This won't end well. We can't be together."

"It will blow up in our faces, but I can't stop myself." He lowers himself until my chest is pressed up against his. Each breath brings us even closer.

"What about Connor?"

"I don't know. Just be with me and we can figure out everything else later. I can't stay away any longer. Tell me you feel the same way."

I stare into the mossy green eyes I've come to love and know I can't deny him. Instead of saying a word, I slip my hand around to the back of his neck and pull his face to me. I press my lips to his and kiss him like I've been dying to do for the past few days.

Grayson braces himself with one arm and uses the other to run up and down my side. I've learned he loves to feel my bare skin. He craves that intimate connection more than anything else. But I want to touch him instead of him always touching me.

I slip my hands under his shirt and let them travel over the hard planes of his body. I don't know how much time he spends in the gym, but I'm sure it's more than I'd be willing to do.

Grayson sucks my bottom lip into his mouth and bites down gently. He presses his body into mine, still keeping most of his weight off of me. I groan, loving how he feels against me.

"I've been craving you since the first day I laid eyes on you," Grayson whispers. "I wanted to hate you so much. I wanted to feel nothing while I watched Connor go after you, but I couldn't. I wanted to know the girl who kept her head held high and told everyone to fuck off when most would've ran away crying."

I open my mouth to respond and he takes that as his chance to plunge his tongue in. He tastes like that stupid cinnamon gum he's always chewing and something sweet. It's an addicting combination.

Grayson moves his lips down my jaw and to my neck. He nips and sucks at my skin, making a groan rip free from me.

"If you don't be quiet, we're going to get caught. Everyone's going to think you're either playing with yourself or there's a guy in your room." Grayson smirks down at me, placing a few kisses on my lips before moving back to my neck.

"Don't you dare give me a hickey, Gray. It's picture day tomorrow."

He pauses his attack and stares down at me. He's searching my face, looking for something.

"What's wrong?"

"I don't like you calling me Gray. When you've been at my house, you've always called me Grayson. No one calls me that anymore, except my family. Everyone at school calls me Gray. I like you calling me Grayson."

"Hey, Grayson?" I smile up at him.

"Yeah?" He smirks.

"What are we doing? I hate not knowing exactly where I stand with you."

"Well, I'd love for you to be my girlfriend… but we'd have to keep it a secret until I can put Connor in his place."

"How are you going to do that?"

"I'm not sure yet."

"I don't know if I want to be your dirty little secret," I confess into the darkness.

"You shouldn't want to. I definitely don't like the idea. I want the whole world to know you're mine… can we just try?" He cups my cheek in his palm and presses a soft kiss to the tip of my nose.

"What if I don't like it?"

"Then I'll walk away."

"I don't believe you."

"You shouldn't." Grayson moves back to his spot next to me. He strips his shirt over his head and tosses it on the floor. "We need to get to sleep if I have to get up so early."

"Are you really going to sleep in jeans?" I eye the offending fabric with disgust. I hate sleeping in jeans. It's so uncomfortable.

"Miss Lawson, are you asking me to take off my pants?" Grayson quirks a brow and flashes me a cheeky grin.

"No... I'm saying I'd understand if you want to take them off." I shrug like I couldn't care less, but I do. I want to see all of Grayson even if we're not ready to take the physical things to the next level.

"I go commando, is the offer still available?"

"You do not!" I giggle, pointing at his waist band to his boxers sticking out above his jeans.

"Fine, I don't. But next time I sneak in here, I might." He slips his jeans off and drops them into a pile on the floor.

He's about to climb into bed when something occurs to him. Grayson tiptoes over to my door and flips the lock, then he stalks towards me like a hungry lion.

"Wouldn't want someone coming in here and finding us." He winks, climbing under the covers and pulling me against him. "You know, I'd understand if your tank top and shorts are uncomfortable and you want to take them off." He peeks over at me with a shit-eating grin.

"Grayson!" I swat at his chest, laughing at him.

"I'm just saying! It's your decision, I just wanted you to know I'd understand if you want to strip down."

He slips his hand under the waistband of my shorts and rests it on my hip. I contemplate telling him not to do that, but he doesn't move his hand. He just wants the physical contact.

Snuggling into his side, I rest my head on his chest and my hand on his stomach. He moves his hand over mine and intertwines our fingers. He presses a soft kiss to my forehead and lets out a little sigh of contentment.

He's quiet for a few minutes. His thumb strokes back and forth across my hip, soothing me into sleepiness. It's the only sign he's awake.

"This is perfect. Thank you."

"For what?" I peek up at him, but his eyes are closed and he looks adorable. So much more boyish than I've ever seen him before.

"For not kicking me out. For letting me keep my hand on your hip. For giving me a chance," he whispers the words into my hair right as I drift off to sleep.

I groan when the alarm goes off and swat at the air, attempting to turn it off.

"Shh, baby, go back to sleep." Grayson presses a gentle kiss to my head and holds me a little tighter.

"You said you'd leave at four-thirty on the dot," I mumble into his chest.

"I said I'd wake up at four-thirty. I never said when I'd get up."

"Grayson," I groan, throwing my leg over his waist. I don't want him to leave. I want to stay cuddled up with him for as long as possible, but he needs to go before anyone finds him here.

"Sweetheart, this isn't making me want to get up," Grayson growls, snaking both arms around me.

He moves me until I'm lying on top of him just like the other night at his house. Only this time, there's something hard poking against my inner thigh.

"Do you feel that?" Grayson cups my ass and presses down, rubbing me against his cock. "That's what you do to me."

I open my mouth to respond when there's a knock on my door. I freeze, unsure of what to do.

"Yeah?" I practically stutter out.

"Why's your alarm going off so early, Piper?" Mom's voice floats through the door.

"Oh, uh, I wanted to curl my hair for picture day."

"That will look beautiful, let me know if you need any help doing the back." Her footsteps move down the hall a few seconds later and I let out a groan.

"What's wrong?"

"Now I have to curl my hair and I hate doing that."

I'm almost late leaving the house for school. It took so much longer to curl my hair than I anticipated. That's why I never do it. I'd rather have flat hair and save an hour.

"Fernando, I don't have time to eat. Is there anything I can take with me?" I stop next to the dining room table where Mom and James are eating.

"Of course, Miss Lawson. Come with me." Fernando smiles, motioning towards the kitchen.

I hate when he calls me Miss Lawson, but he does it whenever James is around. I've begged him to call me Piper and he will, but only if it's just us.

"I made two breakfast sandwiches for you." He hands me a small bag.

"How'd you know I'd be late? Wait... why two?"

"Well, your mom asked me to make you something to go. She said it always takes you twice as long as you think to curl your hair." He smirks at me. "And the second sandwich is for Mr. Young. I saw him sneak through my kitchen and grab a banana on the way out. That won't be enough to sustain him until lunch," Fernando's voice is low enough that no one will hear him. I appreciate him keeping Grayson's presence a secret.

"Thank you, Fernando! I don't know how you knew he was in here, but I appreciate it!" I press a kiss to his cheek.

"Be careful with him, Piper. He's Connor's best friend." Fernando arches a brow.

"He's also the only person protecting me from Connor."

I don't need to ask Fernando to be quiet about this. I know he won't say a word to anyone. I grab the bag before hurrying out to my car before Fernando can say anything else.

As soon as I start the engine and pull out onto the street, Grayson sits up and climbs into the front seat.

"You took forever." He grabs his seat belt and buckles it across his lap before looking at me. "You look amazing, babe. Absolutely gorgeous."

"Thank you. There's a sandwich in here for you. Fernando saw you in his kitchen."

"How? No one was down there." He grabs a sandwich and takes a big bite.

"He has cameras in the kitchen. He said it's to make sure Connor doesn't screw with the food." I chuckle and motion for Grayson to give me my sandwich.

He carefully unwraps it and holds out the biscuit for me to take a bite.

"That's very helpful information," he says thoughtfully.

Grayson pulls some sort of Houdini act when we get to school and disappears before anyone notices he came to school in my car.

And so begins our secret relationship.

Chapter 28

Grayson

Friday night rolls around all too quickly. Soon the stands are full of people waiting to watch our first game of the season.

I pop a piece of cinnamon gum into my mouth and scan the crowds, looking for Piper and my family. They're sitting a few rows from the front. Mom hates when people walk in front of her and blocking her view, so she insists on sitting a few rows up. That way she's above them.

"Are you ready for this?" Mac slaps a hand on my shoulder.

"Yeah. I'm ready to tackle someone to the ground."

"One day that evil little monster that lives inside of you is going to break free and fuck shit up," Connor chuckles from beside Mac. He always refers to our dark sides as little monsters. I think it's how he copes with being so horrible. He blames it on the monster living inside of him. It's something his mom used to say when we were little.

Connor doesn't know the monster inside of me wants to break free every time I see him. Each time he glances in Piper's direction, anger rises up inside of me.

"I'd rather not be the target when it happens," Mac murmurs, staring at Hadley.

I wish he'd just grow the balls and go after her. They could be happy together, but I'm not going to make this easy on him. If he wants to date my sister, he needs to come out and tell me.

"What do I have to do to make Piper the target of your monster?" Connor leans in close like we're sharing a secret.

I glance at him, narrowing my gaze. There are so many ways I could respond to him. I could punch him in the face, knee him in the balls, or break his arm. Causing him to miss out on the rest of the season. Or…

"Can I do whatever I want to her? No limitations. You're not allowed to get involved?"

"Possibly…" Connor taps his chin, considering my offer. "What if I don't like your plans?"

"I don't really give a fuck. You either let me do this or I'm done helping you." I shrug and walk away.

I know Connor, he's going to take this opportunity and run with it. He's running out of options where Piper's concerned. She's avoided everything he's thrown at her and he's getting annoyed.

"Fine! But what are you going to do?" Connor catches up with me, grabbing my shoulder to stop me.

"I'm going to do what any smart man would do. The only way to make her truly want to leave."

"What's that?" Connor rolls his eyes. He likes to be the one in charge, the one making the plans. He wants to always be the smartest one in the room, but he's not anymore.

"I'm going to make her fall in love with me, then I'm going to shatter her heart."

I'm distracted. The entire first half of the game, I keep glancing up at the stands, waiting for something, but I'm not sure what. I have this bad feeling in the pit of my stomach like I'm missing something.

During half time, I convince Coach to let me and Mac stay on the field and throw the ball back and forth. Mac claimed his shoulder was stiff to back up my story. Afterall, we can't have a quarterback with a stiff shoulder.

"What's going on, Grayson?"

"I don't know. Something's about to happen. I can feel it."

I let the football sail through the air as my eyes scan the crowds once again. With each throw, I change positions on the side of the field until I'm facing my family and Piper. I keep my attention trained on them, catching and throwing purely out of instinct. As soon as I see the first cheerleader sneak onto the bleachers behind Piper, I know my gut was right. I completely forgot Connor planned something for tonight. He never told us what it was though.

"Hadley!" I yell and as soon as her and Piper glance up, I let the football fly towards them.

My sister yelps in surprise and ducks to get out of the way, but Piper shocks me. She reaches out and grabs the football like she's been playing her entire life.

I hop the fence separating the field from the spectators and jog up the steps to where they're sitting. The cheerleaders behind Hadley and Piper eye me, trying to figure out what they should do. I glare at them. It's a warning for them to back down. I drop down on the bench below Piper, making me only a few inches shorter than her.

"What the hell, Grayson!" Hadley scowls at me and I promptly ignore her.

"Hey," I murmur, staring at Piper with a lopsided grin.

"Hey yourself. Aren't you supposed to be down there?" She points to the field at my back.

"Probably, but I had something to ask you."

"Oh yeah? It couldn't wait until later?" Amusement lights up her features.

"I mean, sure, I could've waited. But where's the fun in that?"

"Are you going to ask me, or are you just going to sit there and stare at me?" She chuckles.

"I'm getting there, don't rush me." My smile is so wide I'm sure I look like I'm insane. "Will you go to homecoming with me?"

As soon as the words leave my lips, Piper glances around frantically like Connor's going to magically appear.

"Grayson," Piper hisses, scanning the faces around us.

"And will you be my girlfriend?" My smile stretches impossibly wider when her eyes nearly bug out of her head. "I need an answer, baby. They can't start the second half of the game without me." I motion to the field where the players have returned to the sidelines and Coach is frowning at me.

"We can't!" She leans in close so only I can hear her... and maybe Hadley.

"We can. I already talked to Connor. Obviously, he can see me talking to you too." I point to Connor and wave like an asshole. "Say yes, Piper."

"Yes," she whispers.

I take her hand in mine and press my lips to the back of it. I want to kiss her, but I'm certain that would be pushing things a little too far. No one's supposed to know we're already together.

"Wait for me after the game, girlfriend?" I scowl at the cheerleaders, making sure they realize Piper's off limits.

"Uhh, ok?"

I take the ball from her hands, race back down the steps, and hop over the fence once again. Coach gives me crap for being in the stands, but we both know it doesn't matter. If he wants to win this game, I need to be on the field. I'm the best wide receiver they have.

"What the hell was that?" Connor grumbles under his breath from next to me.

"The princess is now my girlfriend. Step one of the plan is done." I smirk. "I'll have fun with her, make her fall in love with me. Then I'll push her off that fancy pedestal Daddy Ward's placed her on, she'll fall and shatter into millions of pieces."

"I should've come to you earlier." Connor folds his arms over his chest with a satisfied smirk.

We take our spots on the field. The center snaps the ball to Mac. His gaze instantly finds me going down the sideline. I'm wide open and these guys won't be able to take me down. He launches the ball towards me and I take off down the field. I dodge and weave through the players from the opposing team, making it into the end zone without breaking a sweat.

We repeat the play three more times, each time scoring a touchdown. I don't know if this team is stupid or if they just can't catch me.

"Are you going to throw me the ball at all tonight?" Connor glares at Mac.

"Dude, we just got four touchdowns in less than ten minutes. Shouldn't we continue the play until it doesn't work anymore?" Mac folds his arms over his chest.

"No! Give me the damn ball!"

"Fine! I'll give it to you this time. You better be ready," Mac growls. He hates being told what to do on the field.

He's one of the best high school quarterbacks in the nation, he doesn't need to be told how to play the game.

We get back into position and the ball is snapped to Mac. He takes it and tosses it to Connor. He makes it a few yards before he's taken down.

Repeating the same play, not only does the other team take him down, but they push him back seven yards. I hate losing yardage.

Mac does it all over again and everyone can tell he doesn't want to give the ball to Connor. He's not going to get a touchdown, but he wants to be the best. He can't handle me scoring so many touchdowns. He's pissed.

The ball is barely in Connor's hands and he's tackled to the ground. I give Mac a look and he nods. Fuck Connor, we're going to win this game.

Fourth down, the ball is snapped and Mac whizzes it through the air and straight into my hands. I take off at a sprint and make it into the endzone easily. Every time I score a touchdown, I pound my fist over my heart and point at Piper.

She and Hadley have been on their feet the whole time. Screaming and cheering like they're being paid to do it.

By the end of the game, we've scored sixty-three points and the other team is pissed... so is Connor. None of the touchdowns were made by him and he's not happy. It's not my fault he couldn't run the damn ball tonight.

Chapter 29
Piper

"He was amazing tonight!" Hadley bounces on her toes and claps even louder.

The stadium is bursting with excited fans. The first game of the season was amazing. Grayson's ability to dodge and weave through players baffles me. It's like he knows where they're going to be and what they're going to do before they make a move.

"He really is."

"What's wrong with you?" Hadley scowls at me.

"I don't know. I just feel like something's going on. Earlier this week, Grayson and I agreed we couldn't date, then he made this public display to ask me out. In front of Connor no less. It just seems out of character."

"Maybe he finally told Connor to shove it up his ass." She shrugs.

"Sweetie, we're going to head home." Mom moves to my side and presses a kiss to my head.

"Ok. Is it ok if I hang out with Hadley for a while?"

"Actually, can Piper sleep over?" Hadley blinks up at Mom innocently.

"Of course. I'm so happy you've become such good friends." Mom smiles at us.

"We love having Piper over. We'd be happy to adopt her if you ever get bored of her." Mr. Young smirks. I roll my eyes at him and stick out my tongue. "Yup, she'd blend right in with the rest of my kids." He throws his head back and laughs.

"We'll see you tomorrow, Princess. Call us if you need anything." James kisses my head, just like he always does. He takes Mom's hand in his, leading her down the bleachers and out of sight.

"James is happier with your mom than he ever was with Connor's mom," Mrs. Young whispers softly. "He really loves you too. He couldn't stop talking about the two of you during the game.

"He's a great stepdad. We're lucky to have him." I smile at how drastically my life has changed since James bulldozed into it.

"Alright, we're going home. We're old, no one wants us to wait around for you guys." Mrs. Young stands and stretches her back. "I hate these damn seats. My back is killing me now."

"Let's go, old lady. I'll buy you a chair for the bleachers before the next game... Hey, Piper?" Mr. Young glances at me.

"Yes?"

"How much do I have to pay you to make some more cookies? They were so good." He pats his flat stomach.

"I'll make a few batches tomorrow. Free of charge." I grin up at them.

"Grayson better marry you, or I might have to adopt you," he mutters under his breath as they move past us and down the stairs.

"Let's wait by the gym, it's getting cold." Hadley rubs her arms, trying to get warmer.

"What are you doing here?" Connor steps out of the locker room first, followed closely by Mac and Grayson.

"It's a free country, Connor. We can wait for my brother wherever we want to." Hadley crosses her arms over her chest and stares him down.

His eyes roam her body, taking in her outfit and stopping at her chest for a little longer than I expect. Does Connor... like Hadley?

"Hey, baby." Grayson steps behind me and wraps his arms around my waist. He rests his chin on my shoulder and watches Connor.

I'm frozen in his arms, unsure of what's going to happen. Connor glares at us, clearly not one hundred percent on board with the two of us being together.

"Are you cold, Hads?" Mac tilts his head to the side, examining her.

"I'm freezing! Those bleachers are like sitting on ice. It's only September, how is it already this chilly?" She rubs her hands up and down her arms. Mac pulls her into his embrace and holds her tightly against him. "Open your sweatshirt, let me inside!" She tugs the zipper down his chest and makes him wrap it around her.

"Do you want to just crawl inside my skin?" He asks with amusement.

"If it keeps me warm, I'm not opposed to the idea. How are you so warm?"

"There's a special spot on me that's getting warmer by the second," Mac murmurs.

"Macalister!" Connor and Grayson hiss at the same time. My eyes widen at Mac's full name. I didn't expect that... I don't really know what I thought it was, but it wasn't Macalister

"What? I'm just telling the tru- Fuck! Your hands are so fucking cold!" Mac's body goes ramrod straight when Hadley slips her fingers under the hem of his shirt.

"Will you drive me home before you go home?" Grayson murmurs in my ear.

"I'm sleeping over. Hadley begged my mom to let me."

"Hmm, whose bed are you sleeping in? Mine or Hadley's?"

"Grayson..."

"If you sleep in hers, I might have to come join the sleepover."

"Sleepover? I want to come!" A smile spreads over Mac's face.

"No one invited you," Connor growls, his gaze focused on where Mac's hands are resting on Hadley's lower back.

It takes us nearly twenty minutes to convince Mac we're not doing anything fun during this sleepover. I'm shocked he keeps his mouth shut and doesn't tell Connor about our previous one.

Soon we're climbing into my car and pulling out of the parking lot. On the way to the Young's house, we stop at the grocery store to grab a few things.

"What are we getting?" Grayson follows me around the store.

"The ingredients to make cookies. I promised your dad."

"Whoa! You're making my dad cookies?" He arches a brow.

"Yup! He asked me what he had to do to get some."

"Then he went on to say you better marry her or he's going to adopt her." Hadley smirks at Grayson.

"Shouldn't you be making your boyfriend cookies? Not his dad?"

"Can't I make a few batches and the two of you share them?" I arch a brow.

"Will you make the s'mores ones?" He sticks out his bottom lip in a pout.

"I was already planning to."

"Best girlfriend ever!" Grayson lifts me into the air and spins me in a circle. He's so carefree tonight and I love it.

Chapter 30
Grayson

We don't make cookies tonight because we're all exhausted, but Piper promises to make them in the morning. Instead, I drag her into my room and shut the door. Within seconds, it's opened back up and Dad stares at me with a raised brow.

"Whatcha doing in here?" He folds his arms over his chest.

"He kidnapped me." Piper doesn't even try to get away from me. She giggles from her place in my arms.

"We're going to practice making you grandparents." I smirk.

"You're a little shit, you know that?" Dad shakes his head and chuckles. "Look, I know Piper's going to sleep over a lot. I'm not going to deny Hadley her best friend just because the two of you are dating now, but I also don't want grandkids yet. If Piper sleeps in here, the door stays open... and try to include Hads in any non-sexual things you do." Dad grimaces.

"I never exclude Hadley." I frown at him. He knows this. I love my sister and always want to hang out with her.

"You never mean to exclude her, Gray, but you do it all the time." Dad taps the doorframe and exits the room.

His words seep into my brain and run wild. Do I exclude her? I never meant to, but I guess I got closer to Mac and Connor, kinda leaving her behind.

"Would you mind..." I hesitate asking the question.

"Invite her to hang out with us. I don't mind at all. I love Hadley, she's the best friend I've ever had."

"Even better than Tim?" I growl, hating that she once had a best friend who had a dick.

"Yes." She giggles, ghosting her lips over mine.

"How would you feel about a three-some in my bed?" I wiggle my eyebrows.

"As long as we're talking about sleeping." She giggles.

"If it were a two-some, it could be more than sleeping?"

"Maybe one day, but not tonight. Go get your sister." She shoves me towards the door, but not until after I steal another quick kiss.

"C'mon, Hads. What's taking you so long?" I rest my shoulder against her threshold and fold my arms over my chest like I'm tired of waiting.

"What are you talking about?" Her brows furrow and I see just a bit of sadness that she isn't able to hide.

"Come sleep in my bed. We're waiting for you to watch a movie."

"Really?" Hope spreads across her features and I feel like a complete ass.

Piper's the first friend she's had in a long time. And I snatched that friend away almost immediately. I'm the worst brother in the world. I'll make sure we include her as much as we can. I don't want Hadley to feel like she's losing anything.

"Of course. I'm not stealing your best friend, Hads. I just want to hang out with you guys too... and maybe have some alone time with her every once in a while."

"Eww, I don't want to know about your alone time." She scrunches up her nose in disgust.

Hadley scurries down the hall ahead of me and when I enter my room, she's already making herself comfortable on my California king size bed. Piper's finding something to watch and the scene is perfect.

I take off running towards the bed and jump into the air, bouncing three times in the center of the mattress as the girls scream like someone's trying to kill them.

I tug both of them into my sides and press a kiss to each of their heads. Hadley pulls a blanket over the three of us and Piper presses play on whatever movie she picked.

"Wow, I never thought I'd see the day I'd let my teenage son have two women in his bed." Mom chuckles from the door.

"What can I say, I'm a ladies man." I smirk, tugging them closer to me.

"You are not. You hate most people." Mom rolls her eyes and laughs. "What do you guys want for breakfast in the morning?"

"Oh! We stopped at the store on the way home and I got stuff to make breakfast and cookies for Gray!" Piper grins from ear to ear.

"You better watch yourself, Grayson. If you don't hold on tight to this one, your dad might swoop in and steal her. He's already talking about giving Piper her own Easter basket."

"An Easter basket?" Hadley whispers like it's sacred and it kinda is.

Dad made these Easter baskets that are shaped like bunnies when we were younger. It took him forever to get them perfect and he only made four. Each one has our names printed across the front. He carefully painted the entire thing himself.

People have begged him over the years to make them some and he's always said no, it's too much work.

Hadley asked a few years ago what happens when we get married and have kids? She wants her husband and kids to have one too. He told her if we pick spouses he really likes, he'll make them a basket, but if he doesn't like them, they get a plastic one from the dollar store.

"Yup! And I don't think he's joking. Have a good night, kids." Mom blows us a kiss and heads down the hall to her room.

I smile to myself as I think about just how perfectly Piper fits into my family. I always wanted a woman who would be a best friend to my sister and my parents love like a third child. I think I finally found her.

———

Piper woke up at seven in the morning to make breakfast for everyone. I'm barely able to keep my eyes open, but

I'm slumped at the island, watching her move around the kitchen. My cheek rests against the cool granite countertop, the only thing keeping me from falling asleep.

"Why don't you go back to bed? You look exhausted. I'll wake you up when the food is ready." Piper moves around the island and stops next to me. She runs her nails up and down my back.

"That feels so good," I groan. "I don't want to go back to bed. I like watching you cook. Your ass looks amazing in those tiny shorts." I smirk when she swats at me.

"I want to curl up with you again. You're so warm and it's freezing this morning." She rubs her arms and frowns.

"I turned the heat down when we woke up," I murmur.

"Why would you do that?" Piper scowls at me.

"Oh, I have my reasons." I stare at her tits. Clearly, she isn't wearing a bra again.

"Are you kidding me?" She moves closer again, this time to smack me harder.

I grab both of her wrists before she gets a chance to hurt me and tug her into my arms. I slide a hand around to the nape of her neck and press a soft kiss to her lips.

Piper instantly melts into me. She gives up on her mission to hurt me and wraps her arms around my neck.

She plays with the strands of my hair and kisses me back with just as much passion as I'm giving her.

I slide my free hand between us and run my thumb over her pebbled nipple. She gasps into my mouth and the noise goes straight to my dick.

I want to throw her over my shoulder and carry her back up to my bed. I want to cross that line with her and never look back. But Hadley's still sound asleep in my room. Mom and Dad will be waking up any second. And I don't think Piper's ready for us to move forward.

A noise upstairs has Piper pulling away. She stares down at her chest and frowns.

"I need a sweatshirt. I don't want your parents coming down here when you can see my nipples!"

I chuckle as I reach a hand behind my neck and pull my long sleeve shirt over my head. I tug Piper closer to me and slip the fabric over her head. She looks adorable in my clothes. She's swimming in the fabric, but it screams *mine*.

"I look ridiculous." Piper motions to my shirt that's hanging down to just above her knees.

"You look like you're mine," I growl, my gaze skimming over her again. I can't get enough of this woman standing in front of me.

Piper places her hands on my bare stomach and lets one slide up to my chest. She runs a finger over my nipple and smirks up at me.

"That's not the only hard thing about me right now." I nip at her neck, making her giggle.

She lets her hand travel from my stomach down over my waistband and brushes my dick. It's already coming to life and jerking against her touch.

"You're killing me, baby."

"Morning, kids." Mom strolls into the kitchen with a big smile.

"Good morning, Mrs. Young." Piper grins, taking a step away from me.

I have to bite the inside of my cheek to hold my groan in. I'm going to have to find some way to get her alone for a night.

"Morning, Mom," I mumble back, dropping onto the stool and readjusting myself.

"Why's it so cold in here? Who turned the heat down?" Mom frowns at the thermostat.

"I was getting too warm. Apparently, I'm the only one." I shrug.

"I don't need to hear about you being all hot and bothered." Mom shakes her head with a grimace. "I miss when you and Hadley were younger and I could pretend you didn't have... desires."

"Eww, stop. It's too early to hear shit like this. I might actually puke."

"Here, babe." Piper places a plate of pancakes, bacon, and sausage in front of me. She places a scoop of eggs on the side and hands me a fork.

"Damn, look at the way she serves him! I swear, Grayson, if you don't marry her, I'm going to get adoption papers drawn up this week." Dad plops down on the stool next to me.

"Good morning, Mr. Young." Piper smirks.

"No, no. Mr. Young doesn't work for me. You should just get used to calling me Dad. I'm going to make it happen one way or another." He winks at her. Piper shakes her head and laughs. I love how well she gets along with my family.

"You want me to propose in high school?" I arch a brow.

"If the woman you're proposing to is Piper, then yes. Hell, I'll even buy you the biggest diamond ring we can find. But if you want to marry any other woman, no. Also, I might take away your trust fund and give it to Piper."

"What the hell?"

"Well, it's my money. If I disagree with your decisions, I can make it all disappear like that." He snaps his fingers in my face with a smug smile.

"Here ya go, *Dad*." Piper places a plate identical to mine in front of Dad. The smile spreading across his face is so big I'm worried he's going to hurt himself.

"Damn, that sounds good, doesn't it? So, what's it going to be, Grayson? Am I adopting a third kid or are you going to man up and take one for the team?" Dad elbows me in the side.

"I don't think it's considered taking one for the team if it's something good." Mom frowns at Dad from over the rim of her coffee cup.

"That's true." Dad shoves a fork full of pancakes into his mouth. "Oh, shit. These are amazing! How about I just pay you to be my own personal chef? You don't need to cook for any of these other people, just me."

Mom throws her head back and laughs. I was a little worried in the beginning. A lot of women would get upset if their son's girlfriend came in and took over. Especially when their husband raved about her cooking. But Mom doesn't seem to mind at all. She might even like it.

"Leave the poor girl alone and eat your food." Mom rolls her eyes.

Piper hands her a plate and Mom thanks her. I'm sure it's nice to not have to cook for a change.

A few minutes later, Hadley stumbles into the kitchen. Piper already has a plate ready for her and a cup of coffee.

"Seriously, best friend ever," Hadley mumbles, her eyes are barely even open.

"You're a mess." Piper uses her thumb to swipe at the corner of my mouth, leaving her with syrup on her thumb. Without a second thought, I suck her thumb into my mouth and run my tongue over her skin.

She stares at me, her blue eyes darkening until they look like stormy water. She's so addicting when she looks at me like this.

"Well, he could get her pregnant. That would save me paperwork and she'd be attached to us for life," Dad mutters loud enough for everyone to hear.

"Dad!" Hadley giggles.

"What? I'm determined to make her part of this family! Any chance you're batting for the other team?"

"No! I'm solidly into boys." Hadley laughs even harder. "Sorry to disappoint you."

"I'm not sure you'll find someone better than Piper."

Piper makes a plate for herself and stands next to me. I slide back and tug her onto my lap. I rest my chin on her shoulder and wrap my arms around her waist. I love having her in my arms. I love being able to touch her and know no one's going to say a thing about it.

"Thank you for making breakfast, it was delicious," I murmur in her ear.

"You're welcome. I'm glad you liked it."

"I like everything about you."

"You don't know everything about me." She chuckles, taking a bite of her food.

"Well, I guess we need to spend more time together then because I want to know all there is to know."

Chapter 31
Piper

Connor really seems to be calming down when it comes to me. He hasn't been pulling any shit at school this week and it's already Friday. It almost feels like he's given up, but I still don't trust him.

Mom and James are away for the next two weeks and Connor's decided we're having a party. I'm sure he's invited everyone from our school based on how many people are crowded into the first floor of the house.

I'm thankful he made the second floor off limits. If he finds anyone up there, they get kicked out and won't get an invite to future parties.

Normally, I wouldn't believe the threat would work, but coming from Connor, it does. No one wants to upset the self-proclaimed King of Prescott High. They know he's more than willing to make their lives miserable.

I look around the room and laugh at some of the outfits these girls are wearing. There's more skin on display than a Victoria's Secret runway. Glancing down at my outfit, I shrug and keep looking for my boyfriend.

I'm not changing out of my black skinny jeans and white fitted tee. If Grayson doesn't like it, oh well.

Two arms wrap around my waist from behind and tug me against a solid chest. I freeze for a split second, until Grayson's signature scent fills my senses.

"You look beautiful, baby," Grayson murmurs against the shell of my ear.

"You don't want me dressed like the rest of the girls?" I glance over my shoulder at him.

"Hell no! I want you just like this. They're so desperate for attention it's embarrassing... You could dress like that when it's only the two of us... maybe even less clothing."

Spinning around in his arms, I press a searing kiss to his lips. I've been waiting forever to be able to do this in front of people. Too many of the girls here flirt with my boyfriend on a daily basis. I'm ready to make our relationship more public. I want them all to realize he belongs to me and the rest of them better leave Grayson alone.

"Damn! I feel like I'm going to get pregnant just by watching you." Mac chuckles. His arm is wrapped around the waist of one of the barely dressed girls.

Grayson grips my hips and starts moving us to the music. He's a good dancer. He's definitely a natural and it shows.

"Where's Hadley?" I arch a brow, basically calling him out on his shit. We all know they like each other, yet his arm isn't around her.

"She's talking to some dork." Mac shrugs. "I'm not her keeper though. She can do whatever she wants."

"Good, I'll let her know she can use my room if she wants to get to know the guy better." I wiggle my eyebrows, making Mac glare at me.

His jaw clenches as his gaze flickers to Hadley and back to me. If he's not going to make his feelings towards her known, then he needs to face the reality that other guys are going to talk to her.

"Grayson would never let that happen," he hisses.

"She's a big girl, she can make her own decisions. Plus, my hands are full right now." Grayson smirks.

He turns me around, then slides his hands down to cup my ass. He tugs me flush against his body and grinds his cock into me.

Mac stomps his foot and pulls the girl behind him as he stalks over to where Hadley is. Mac inserts himself between her and the guy she was talking to.

"You're not actually going to let her do whatever she wants, right?" I peer up at Grayson.

"Nah, but Mac doesn't need to know that. I don't really want him to interrupt our night though." He spins me in a circle before pulling me flush against his body again.

"You're a good dancer."

"I'm good at a lot of things." He presses his lips to my neck, kissing up and down my exposed skin.

"You really are," I groan.

"I love everything about you... I love you, Piper." His voice is deep and raspy in my ear.

I suck in a deep breath and create enough space between us for me to meet his eyes. He nervously worries his lip between his teeth and doesn't look away.

"You love me?"

"Yeah, I do..." He's hesitating, vulnerable, and isn't comfortable. He runs a hand through his shaggy hair and glances around like he's noticing the crowd of people for the first time.

I can tell he's about to bolt. He doesn't think I feel the same way.

What a stupid boy.

Grabbing his hand, I tug Grayson in close and stand on my tippy toes.

"I love you too, Grayson Young," I whisper into his ear. I want to make sure he can hear me over everything happening around us.

"Really?" I don't need to look at him to know he's grinning.

"Really."

"Oh, thank fuck! I would've died if you said thanks or some shit like that." He grabs my waist and spins me in a circle again. He dips me low and presses a kiss to my lips.

When he pulls me back up to a standing position, Hadley appears at our sides with a sweet innocent smile.

"What? I know what the smile means and it never leaves me happy." Grayson tugs me back against his chest and we continue to dance.

"I wanted to dance with Piper. You can have her back in a little bit." She clasps her hands together under her chin and gives him the best puppy eyes I've ever seen. There's no way he's going to say no.

"Fine! But stay here so I can at least look at her," Grayson groans. He presses a quick kiss to my temple before he moves to where Mac is leaning against the wall with a girl hanging onto his arm.

"I'm not sure how I feel about you dating my brother." Hadley spins in a circle, moving her hips to the beat of the music.

"Shit. I didn't even think to ask you how you felt about it. I can end things between me and him. We haven't been dating for that long-"

"No! I don't want you to break up! He's in love with you and I think you're good for him... I just hate losing my best friend because of him."

"You're not losing me. In fact, you'll probably see me even more now."

"Yeah, but it's different. Now I'll have to share you with him. Don't I already share enough with him? I don't even get my own birthday."

"I promise you're going to get plenty of alone time with me. If we have to, I'll make a chart and divide my time between the two of you."

"Best friend ever!" Hadley throws herself in my arms and squeezes me tight.

"Girls, the party has arrived." Will inserts himself between the two of us and smirks.

"Hey... What the hell happened?" I stare at the blue and purple skin surrounding his eye.

"Oh, uh, got hit during practice. Nothing like an elbow to the eye to help you prepare for a game." He glances away and shifts uncomfortably on his feet.

"Don't you wear helmets during practice?" Hadley eyes him with suspicion.

"Yeah, but Josh is an idiot and tackled me on our way back into the locker rooms." He rolls his eyes. "Do you guys want something to drink? I'm headed to get something."

"Sure. I'll take whatever you're having." Hadley smiles as a guy from our grade comes up behind her and places his hands on her hips, moving with her.

"Piper?"

"I guess. Nothing strong though."

"Yeah, no problem." He swallows hard and a slight furrow settles between his brows. He quickly turns and walks into the kitchen before I can ask him what's going on.

"Oh my gosh! I love this song!" Hadley squeals, pushing the guy away from her and closes the space between us.

She takes my hands in hers and holds them over our heads. She grinds her hips into mine and I can't help but laugh. This is so unlike her.

Then I catch her looking over my shoulder and I know exactly what she's doing. She's trying to get Mac's attention without being as desperate as some of these other girls. She's putting on a show for him without anyone else knowing.

"Damn, can I get inside this sandwich?" Will stares at us with wide eyes and shakes his head. "I don't think I'll ever get this image out of my head."

"Oh whatever!" Hadley giggles and takes the drink Will offers to her. She takes a healthy gulp and lets out a sigh. "I haven't come to a party in forever. It's nice to just let loose for the night."

"Yeah. Parties at Prescott High are a lot better than anyone in my old school had." I swallow a mouth full of my drink and wince at the horrible taste. "What the hell is this? It's awful."

"Sorry, there wasn't much to choose from. The faster you drink it the faster you'll be too drunk to care what it tastes like though." Will nudges my hand holding the solo cup until I lift it to my mouth and drain half the cup.

"Seriously, you're fired from getting us drinks. This is the worst thing I've ever tasted!"

"Drink up, buttercup." Will nudges me again. "I'll happily never give you another drink," he mutters under his breath.

I finish the cup and drop the empty plastic on the coffee table. Hadley tugs me onto the make-shift dance floor and I get lost in the music. Within minutes I feel drunk and carefree. I'm having so much fun with Hadley, I couldn't care less about what's happening around me.

Chapter 32
Grayson

I can't take my eyes off of her. She's having so much fun with Hadley and I'm loving every second of it. I was always worried whatever woman I ended up with wouldn't get along with my sister. I'd never be happy if there was a wedge between me and my twin.

It never occurred to me how perfect it would be to date one of her friends. They're like sisters already and they've only known each other for such a short period of time.

Piper stumbles to the side and giggles, grabbing for Hadley's hand. She steadies herself and continues dancing like it never happened.

I'm talking to a few guys from school. Some are on the football team and some just want my attention. I couldn't care about any of them, my eyes are on my girl and nothing else.

"How many drinks has Piper had?" Mac moves closer, making sure no one except me can hear him.

I frown at my girl, she shouldn't be this drunk. She's barely had anything at all.

"She had one drink... something's wrong."

"Where'd she get it? Did you pour it?" Mac watches her every movement.

"No," I whisper. "Will got her a drink. He fucking drugged her, didn't he?"

"I think so. She's too sloppy for only one drink."

"I'm going to fucking kill him," I growl, scanning the area for the piece of shit. I haven't seen him in a while.

"Not tonight. Let's take care of Piper, we can worry about Cooper later... where did Hadley get her drink?"

"Fuck! You grab her and I'll get Piper." I push my way through my classmates. My deadly glare stops a few people from talking to me, they know better than to try when I'm this pissed off.

As soon as Piper sees me, her eyes widen and she sways on her feet. I don't waste a second, I snake an arm around her waist and pull her into me.

"What's going on, baby?"

"Grayson! Damn, you're so pretty." She runs a finger down my cheek, her gaze focused intently on her own movements.

"Thanks. How do you feel?"

"I'm really drunk. I don't think I've ever felt like this. Everything seems... smeared. Why are things smeared? And cloudy... I'm so tired, my body feels so heavy." She lays her head on my chest and I tighten my hold on her.

"You've only had one drink, right?"

"Yeah... it was really bad. Will's a horrible bartender."

"Can I take you home?"

"I ams homes, silly!" She throws her head back and giggles. She loses her balance and if I weren't holding onto her, she'd be on the ground right now.

"How about I take you to my home? You can sleep in my bed tonight and I'll take care of you."

"That sounds dirty." She smirks up at me. "What are we going to do in your bed?"

"Sleep. We're only going to sleep, babe." I brush some hair out of her face and kiss her temple. I wish I knew what Will put in her drink.

"What ifs I wanna do s'mores?" Her words slur together.

"Not tonight. Maybe sometime soon though."

"You're no fair!" Piper sticks out her bottom lip into a pout and I'd be lying if I said I didn't want to suck it into my mouth and do more than sleep next to her tonight. Nothing will ever happen between us when she's wasted though. I want her to remember every night we spend together.

"I'm not drunk, Mac! I don't need to leave!" Hadley folds her arms over her chest and glares at my best friend.

"Hadley, can you just come with us? For once in your fucking life don't give me a hard time and just listen to me." Mac reaches for her hand and she spins away from him, avoiding his touch entirely.

"I'm not your girlfriend. I don't need you to take care of me. Why don't you go back to whatever skank was hanging on your arm all night?" Her eyes flare with anger. I don't think I've ever seen her this upset.

We're drawing more and more attention with how loud Mac and Hadley are arguing. The last thing in the world I want is for someone to realize how fucked up Piper is.

"Hads, something's wrong with Piper. We need to leave now," I growl in a low tone so only she can hear.

Her eyes widen and flicker between me and Piper. She silently nods her head and takes Mac's still outstretched hand in hers.

He leads her to the front door and I follow. I'm trying to guide Piper, but she can barely stand at this point. Lifting her into my arms, I push past more people, coming closer and closer to the front door. We're only a few feet away when Connor stops in front of us.

"What's going on? Where are you guys going?" His gaze flickers to Piper and I swear I see a flicker of satisfaction cross his face before he can school his expression.

"Piper isn't feeling well and we all drove together." I shrug like this is the only reasonable explanation for all four of us to be leaving.

"Just throw her in her room and come back down to the party. She'll be fine up there all alone. No one's allowed up there, you know that."

There's something in his tone that makes me pause. Did he plan on me doing just that? I briefly wonder if Connor planned all of this. Does he want me to put her in her room and leave because he has something else planned?

I push the thought out of my head. There's no way he's really that deranged. Connor's done some really fucked up shit in his life, but drugging his own stepsister is a little insane even for him.

"Nah, that would make me look like a pretty shitty boyfriend. I have an image to uphold." I flash him a cocky smile. He won't see through my bullshit.

Connor would never suspect I actually love Piper. He trusts me more than anyone else in his life. By the time he realizes this is all real, it will be too late, and I'll already have him by the balls.

"Shit, I didn't think of that... yeah, get her outta here. Let me know if you need any help."

I push past him without another word. He doesn't give a shit about her and there's no way he'd actually do anything nice and help.

As soon as we get to the car, I place Piper in the backseat and glance at Mac.

"How much have you had to drink?"

"Three beers in the last hour. I can drive, I'll be fine."

"Fuck no! You're not driving with the two of them in this car if you've had a single sip. I'll drive. I didn't drink anything tonight. I was too busy watching them."

I climb into the front seat and start the engine. This is the first time I've been behind the wheel since the accident.

My hands shake as I place them on the steering wheel and take a deep breath.

"Gray…" Mac slowly climbs into the passenger's seat and shuts the door behind him. "I can drive. We'll be fine."

"I said I'd drive. Just keep an eye on them."

I'm about to shift the car into drive when someone in the backseat sniffles. I spin in my seat and find Hadley's cheeks covered in tears.

"What's wrong, Hads?"

"I didn't even know something was wrong with her. It's so obvious now. I'm such a horrible friend."

"You're not. You just thought she was having fun. It's all going to be ok. This is why I stayed sober, so you two could have fun and I could protect you."

"Thank you, Grayson. I don't know what I'd do without you." She buries her face in her hands and sobs.

"Get in the backseat, Mac," I whisper, barely able to hold in the anger flowing through my veins right now.

He holds my gaze for several long seconds before he climbs over the center console and into the back. He wedges himself between Hadley and Piper, checking on both of them. Hadley's in his arms seconds later, his chest muffling her cries.

"Are you guys good?" I glance in the rearview mirror.

"Yeah, we're good. Take your time, Gray." Mac eyes my hands. I'm holding the steering wheel so tightly my knuckles are turning white.

Fuck, how is this so hard? I've driven a car hundreds if not thousands of times. I've only been in one accident. This is crazy.

But I almost died the last time I climbed behind the wheel.

I shift into drive and suck in a deep breath. I'm the best option to get us all home safely.

***

"What's going on?" Dad arches a brow when I carry Piper into the house and Mac follows me with a crying Hadley in his arms.

"Can I talk to you in a few minutes? I want to get Piper to drink something and get her in bed."

Dad's brows furrow and he nods his head. I'm not surprised in the least to find him trailing behind us up the stairs and into my room.

Placing Piper in the center of my bed, I help her sit up and brush her hair out of her face. Dad hands me a water bottle without a word.

"Baby, I need you to take a sip of water." I have to sit behind her to keep her from falling over.

"No," she groans, trying to lay back down. "It's hard... I just need... sleep... later..."

"Gray, what happened?" Dad's worried gaze is focused only on Piper. "Is Hadley ok?"

"I think Hadley's fine. But... someone drugged Piper. She only had one drink. She shouldn't be this fucked up."

"Shit!" Dad paces up and down the length of my room, muttering more curse words under his breath.

"What's going on?" Mom yawns from the doorway.

"Piper was drugged at the party. Do you know who did this, Gray?"

"Yes," I whisper. "I'm going to fucking make him pay for it."

"I'm calling Jeremy. He's a doctor, he can come over and take a look at her. Make sure she doesn't need to go to the hospital." Mom already has the phone to her ear. She spins on her heels and leaves the room without another word.

"Who did it?" Dad sits on the edge of the bed and brushes Piper's hair over her shoulder.

"Will Cooper," Hadley whispers, stepping into the room with Mac standing behind her.

"I don't understand. He's a good kid. Why would he drug her? It makes no sense." Dad frowns at Piper with so much concern in his gaze. She means a lot to him already.

"It doesn't matter why he did it. All that matters is I'm going to make sure he never does it again."

Chapter 33
Grayson

It took my cousin, Jeremy, ten minutes to examine Piper and agree she was drugged. He said she'll be fine, but to let her sleep it off and to keep an eye on her. Fluids are her best friend right now. The drugs will be washed out of her system faster if we can get more water into her.

"I'm proud of you." Mom takes two steps into the room and stops.

I'm lying in my bed with my back propped up with pillows. Piper's asleep on her stomach with her head on my chest. I run a soothing hand up and down her back, though I think the movement is calming me more than her.

"For letting my girlfriend get roofied?" I deadpan.

"No, for protecting her from what could've been the worst night of her life. You have no idea what he had planned for her or if he had friends waiting to do something to her. Hell, for all you know, Hadley might've been his target. You protected them, Grayson."

"Mac realized she was acting weird first. Once he said something I realized he was right and I got them out of there. I might not have noticed anything was wrong if he hadn't questioned how much she drank." I shake my head, staring down at the woman who owns my heart and soul.

"Mac's a good kid. Don't let Connor pull him down, I'd hate to see that kid crash and burn because of his huge heart."

"I won't let anything happen to him. I'm handling all of it."

"I know you have broad shoulders, but that doesn't mean you have to carry the world on them, Grayson. It's ok to admit you need help. It's ok to *need* help." She stares at me for several long seconds. "I'm going back to bed. If you need anything at all, come get me."

"Thanks, Mom."

"I'm always here for you, honey. Anything you could possibly need, I'm here."

"Do you have a good hitman?" I smirk.

"I could find one easily enough. At this point, your father might even volunteer for the position. He's livid."

"He's upset because it could've been Hadley."

"No, Gray. He's livid that anyone would dare touch one of his girls. Piper has quickly become part of this family... I just hope she stays part of it... try to get some sleep."

She taps the doorframe twice before disappearing down the hallway. The house is quiet for a few minutes and I let my eyes close. There's no way I'm going to get any sleep, but it's nice to just close them for a little bit.

Piper's phone vibrates on the nightstand and I pick it up without thinking about it. There's a text there and I debate on what I should do.

Tim: Why aren't you answering me? I'm starting to get worried, Pipe.

I scroll through the message thread and see that Tim's been messaging her since the party started and she hasn't answered a single one.

Piper: Tim, it's Grayson. Someone drugged Piper at a party. She's ok, but she's sleeping it off. I was able to get her out of there before anything happened.

Tim: Can I come see her? I'm worried about her.

I quickly give Tim my address and close my eyes again. I'm exhausted, I need at least a little bit of rest, but I doubt that's going to happen.

Footsteps move down the hall and stop at my door and I peek one eye open to see who it is. Mac stands there, looking paler than he did earlier.

"You can come in."

"How is she?" He sits on the end of the bed and stares at us.

"She's barely woken up since Jeremy left. She was able to answer a few of his questions, but then she fell asleep again. I didn't know you were still here. I thought you left."

"I don't have a car." Mac shrugs, never letting his gaze stray from Piper.

"My dad would've driven you home, you know that."

"Hadley was freaking out. It took me a while to get her to calm down. She just fell asleep and I figured I'd check on you and Piper... She asked me to stay the night."

"Do it."

"Gray... I like her," he whispers. His attention is focused on his hands and his brows draw low.

"I know you do. I'm not an idiot, Mac. I see the way you look at her."

"But what about us? Where do you stand in this situation?" He peeks up at me and I can see the torment he's dealing with.

"I don't want you dating my sister." I keep my voice even and emotionless.

Mac lets out a ragged breath and runs a rough hand through his hair. His jaw clenches and he refuses to look at me.

"I knew it! You don't think I'm good enough for her!" His hands ball into fists. He wants to fight me and normally I'd let him, but right now I need to focus on Piper.

"Right now? No. But I think you could be good enough," I say softly.

Mac's gaze snaps to me and he furrows his brow. Good, I have his attention. I want to make sure he really understands what I'm saying and takes it to heart.

"I don't want you with my sister until you make it clear to every other girl around you that you don't want them. I don't want Hadley to have to worry you're cheating on her when she isn't around. Make her realize she's important to you. Show her she's different to you than the rest of the girls who follow you around. If you can do all of that, we can talk about this again and see if my opinion has changed. I won't let my sister worry if she's good enough for you because she sees you flirting with someone else or kissing their neck."

"I can't walk away from her."

"I don't want you to. I think the two of you could be perfect for each other, but I'm not going to let my sister shrink into herself because she's not as confident as the other girls who surround you on a daily basis. You can't hurt her, Mac. She wouldn't survive it."

"I think Hadley's a hell of a lot stronger than you think she is." He folds his arms over his chest and glares at me.

"Probably, but I'm not willing to risk her to find out."

"Should I just go home?" His focus is completely on his shoes. He's terrified I'm going to tell him to leave. I won't. She needs him just as much as Piper needs me. Hell, he needs her just as much as I need Piper. I see it, I'm not blind.

Hadley deserves to be happy and I'm fairly certain Mac's the person who can do that. Is it so bad that I don't want to see my sister get her heart broken? I've seen the way she gets when girls drape themselves over Mac.

He's the only one who will tolerate that behavior. Connor and I will shove them off of us and keep walking, but Mac's too nice for that.

He entertains them just enough to not hurt their feelings. Then they think he's interested and they keep coming back for more. Sometimes I think he flirts just because he doesn't know how not to.

I know exactly how the girls are going to react if he suddenly started dating Hadley. They're going to look down at her. They'll ask why he's babysitting my sister for me. They're going to belittle her and make her feel like she doesn't deserve a damn thing in life. I've seen them do it countless times and I'm not subjecting my sister to that. Not if I can help it.

"You should get back in Hadley's room and show her how much you care... just don't kiss her... or touch her anywhere you wouldn't touch her if my dad were in the room."

Mac hesitates and just when I think he isn't going to leave the room, he lifts his chin and stares directly at me.

"I'm going to do whatever I have to do to make her mine."

Chapter 34
Piper

Voices come and go around me, but I'm too tired to open my eyes. Something's wrong. I've been drunk before, yet this is different. I usually get clumsy but it takes at least three or four drinks. Last night I drank one and I can't remember *ever* feeling like this.

"Grayson," I mumble into a hard body. I know it's him, his scent is surrounding me like a warm hug.

I know he'll keep me safe and I think that's the only reason I'm not freaking out right now.

"What's wrong, baby?" He strokes a hand up and down my back. It feels so good. I just want to drift back off to sleep.

"What happened?" My words sound jumbled and slurred even to my own ears. I'm not sure Grayson can understand a single noise coming out of me.

"Someone drugged you at the party. They slipped something in your drink."

"I... I don't remember a party."

"Go back to sleep, babe. You're really hard to understand and the best thing you can do is sleep off the drugs." He presses a gentle kiss to my temple and rubs my back until I drift off to sleep again.

I'm not sure how long I have been asleep, but the next time I wake up I'm able to open my eyes and focus slightly. The edges of my vision are still a little blurry, but it's getting better.

Grayson helps me drink some water before I lay back down. I can't go to sleep though. I just watch my boyfriend. His eyes are closed, but I know he's still awake.

"You should sleep. I'm ok, just really tired and nauseous."

"Do you want me to get you something to eat?"

"No, I just want to stay in your arms. I know you'll protect me... can we turn off the light? It's making my head hurt."

"Of course."

"Can you help me up? I need to use the bathroom first." I try to push off of him, but it's like I can't control my own muscles. Everything hurts.

"Let me get Hadley so she can help you while you're in there, then I'll carry you into the bathroom."

Grayson slides out from under me and leaves the room. He reappears a few minutes later with Hadley. He tries to lift me into his arms, but I stop him.

"I want to do it myself. I *need* to do it myself."

I can't explain my stubbornness, other than my need to know exactly how fucked up I am. What if Grayson hadn't been there? What if he hadn't realized something was wrong?

The first step is harder than I expected. My legs feel like they're going to give out on me as my vision spins.

"Baby, please. Let me carry you," Grayson practically begs. It's killing him to see me like this.

I nod my head and lean against his body when he lifts me into the air. I don't know what I'd do without him.

As soon as the bathroom door is shut with Hadley in here with me, I peek at her for the first time. Her eyes are red rimmed and swollen. She looks like hell. I briefly wonder what I look like, but I push the thought aside, I'm not sure I want to know.

"Who did it?"

"Piper... I'm not sure-"

"I deserve to know who fucking drugged me, Hadley. I know Grayson's not going to tell me. At least not until he beats the shit out of the guy. I want to know."

"It was Will," she whispers.

A chill rolls through my body. Grayson told me not to trust him and I didn't listen. I thought Will was a real friend. How could I be so stupid?

Hadley has to help me unbutton my jeans and pull them down. I take care of my business and the thought of pulling those back on is too much.

"Can you ask Grayson if I can have a pair of sweats and a shirt?"

"Yeah. I can get you one of mine if you'd prefer it."

"I kinda want to be wrapped in his scent." I scrunch up my nose.

"I get it. Let me tell him to grab you something." Hadley flashes me a smile full of understanding.

She moves away from me and I have to lean on the counter to keep from falling over. My legs start feeling weaker and weaker. I'm not sure how much longer I'll be able to keep myself standing.

"Grayson!" I cry out, as my body gives out on me.

Grayson runs into the bathroom and catches me just as I'm going down. He carries me to his bed and lays me down. Hadley appears at the edge of the bed with Grayson's sweats in her hands.

"Are you ok?"

"I just feel so weak," I whisper as the first tear slips down my cheek and onto my shirt.

"It's ok, I've got you. Nothing bad can happen to you now." Grayson buries his face in my neck and holds me against him.

He gives me a few minutes to collect myself before he pulls away and stares down at me. There's so much care and worry in his emerald eyes.

"Can you help me get dressed?"

"Would you rather Hadley help?" Grayson whispers only loud enough for me to hear.

"No. I kinda want some privacy."

"Hads, I can handle it from here. Thank you."

"Let me know if you need anything else." Hadley ducks out of the room without another word.

Grayson quickly shuts the door and returns to my side. He helps me slip my legs into his sweatpants and tugs them over my hips when I lift up from the bed. He supports me when I try to sit up and takes my shirt off.

"I don't want my bra on either. It's uncomfortable."

"Ok. I can do that too." Grayson's warm fingers drift over my back and work the clasp quickly. He tugs the bra away from my body. When I peek up at him, I'm surprised to find him staring at the ceiling.

"What are you doing?" I chuckle.

"I'm not going to let the first time I see you naked be after you were roofied. I want to see all of you, but only when you want me to see you."

Grayson blindly grabs for the long sleeve shirt and slips it over my head. I slide my arms into the sleeves and he helps me slowly lay back down.

As soon as I'm comfortable, he walks over to his dresser and tugs out another pair of sweats. I watch as he lets his jeans drop to the floor, leaving him in only a pair of tight boxer briefs. He slips into the gray pants and tugs his shirt over his head.

I couldn't look away if you paid me to. Though to be completely honest, I'm not sure I'll even remember any of this once the drugs are out of my system.

Grayson spins around and catches me watching him. A slow smirk spreads over his lips. I want to kiss those lips so bad.

He opens the bedroom door, then climbs into the bed and slides under the covers next to me.

"Let's sleep for a little bit. Then we can try to get some food into you."

"Hey, sweetie, how are you feeling?" Mrs. Young strokes a loving hand down my cheek.

"A lot better... I don't remember anything from last night. The last thing I remember is getting ready for the party with Hadley in my room. After that, everything's a little blurry... Where's Grayson?"

"He went to handle some things. I told him I'd keep an eye on you for a while."

"You don't have to. I'll be fine," I whisper. I hate being so weak and people feeling like they need to take care of me.

"Piper, you couldn't pay me to leave this room right now. I'm going to make sure you're ok." She brushes my hair out of my face like a loving mother does.

"How's Hadley?"

"She's a mess." Mrs. Young sighs and perches herself on the edge of the bed. "She thinks it's all her fault and she's upset she didn't realize something was wrong until after Grayson and Mac stepped in. I'm pretty sure my son is feeling the same way. Apparently, Mac asked how much you had to drink and that made Grayson realize you were acting too drunk for how much you had."

"I only had one."

"I know. It's fine. I'm not that parent who's going to yell about that. You're a teen, you're going to do stupid things like that... who drove home though? Do you remember? I know it wasn't you or Hadley and I'm really hoping Grayson was smart enough to not let Mac drive."

"Grayson drove, I think," I whisper. "I remember bits and pieces, but not much. For some reason I remember him holding onto the steering wheel so tightly his knuckles were white... I think Mac was worried too. I'm not sure, it's so hazy."

"That's ok. Don't worry about it. I can talk to him later."

"Is he not allowed to drive?"

"It's the first time he's driven since the accident. I'm sure it was difficult for him. When we tried to bring him home from the hospital, he shook the entire way. It took us weeks to get him used to being in a car."

"Hadley said he almost died."

"He's a lucky little shit." Mrs. Young stares up at the ceiling and tries to blink back tears. "I was terrified I was going to lose my son. He had internal bleeding and a liver laceration. A broken arm and a concussion. He slept for days, only waking up when he was in pain. It killed me. Now it feels like it was all just a bad dream."

"How'd the accident happen?"

"Grayson told us he was going out to Connor's house. He was planning on sleeping over. Apparently, Connor thought it would be fun to drag race against a bunch of punks from a nearby school. He convinced Mac and Grayson to race while he watched. It was the middle of December. There was still snow on the ground from a storm a few days prior. They met up with the other guys late at night, it was after midnight when we got the call from the hospital."

Mrs. Young stares off into space like she's watching everything play out like a movie in her head.

"Mac raced first and was fine, but he didn't win. Connor was down his throat, yelling that they needed to win the next one. He got Grayson all hyped up and told him to go as fast as possible. Grayson was an idiot and listened. This time they decided to make the race longer. Add in some turns and winding roads. He was an idiot,

Piper. He agreed to all of it. He had this mindset back then that nothing could touch him. Nothing could hurt him."

She pauses and sucks in a shaky breath. Swiping at the tears gliding down her cheeks. It takes her a few minutes before she's able to continue.

"He gunned the engine and took off too fast. He was barely able to keep his car on the road at the first curve, yet he sped up before he got to the next one. Like I said, he thought he was untouchable. When he got to the third curve, he hit a patch of wet leaves and lost control of the car. He spun in a circle a few times before he finally stopped. He was fine... but then the kid he was racing slammed into him and pinned his car against a tree."

Her hands shake as she reaches for a tissue from the box beside the bed. She blots below her eyes and flashes me a sad smile.

"The other kid died on impact. Grayson was unresponsive. Mac's the one that found him. He climbed in the other kid's car and reversed it just so he could get to Grayson, but he still couldn't get my baby out. He called 911 even though Connor tried to convince him not to. If Mac had listened... Grayson wouldn't be alive today. They had to use the jaws of life to get him out and they rushed him straight to the hospital. Mac went with him and called us right away. He stayed by my son the entire time."

"What did Connor do?" I'm almost afraid to ask, but I have to know.

"Connor got in his car and drove home like nothing ever happened. Later he tried to tell Grayson it was because he couldn't handle the idea of losing his best friend, but I don't believe a damn thing that bastard says."

"I can't believe he'd do that. He's such an awful human."

"Mac didn't step foot in school until Grayson returned. He somehow convinced the principal and teachers to let him gather all the work him and Grayson were missing. As long as they completed all of it and took finals, they didn't have to repeat the year. Mac helped Grayson with physical therapy, he waited on him hand and foot. He did whatever he could to help his best friend. The entire time Connor stayed away. When he went back to school, Connor acted like nothing ever happened."

"Why is Grayson still friends with him?" I frown, that makes no sense. Connor's response and actions are more than enough reasons to drop him as a friend.

She shakes her head and lets out a humorless chuckle.

"I have no idea. Every time Grayson's ever gotten in trouble was because of something Connor had a hand in. We've never been fond of Connor, but the accident was our breaking point. We told Grayson to stay away from him, but he convinced us to give him until graduation. That's the thing about Grayson, he's loyal and has the biggest heart in the world. If he's chosen to let you in, it takes a hell of a lot for him to push you away... Piper, I've never seen him let anyone get as close to him as he lets you."

"I love him," I state simply. There's nothing else to say, no other way to explain how I feel for her son.

"I think he loves you too. I saw him falling for you that time you and Mac stayed over and the four of you slept in the den... I hope the two of you stay together. I think you're good for each other. I've never seen him this happy before."

"I'm not going anywhere, Mrs. Young."

There's a knock on the door and we glance up to find Tim standing in the doorway. I blink several times, swearing I must be seeing things. When he's still standing there, I shake my head and grin.

"What are you doing here?" I laugh in surprise.

"Well, I heard someone had a little too much fun last night and I wanted to check on you." He smirks, moving into the room.

"Mrs. Young, this is Tim. He's my best friend from home."

They say hello and make small talk for a few minutes before she excuses herself to give us some time alone.

"What the hell happened, Pipe?" Tim settles on the bed next to me and waits while I explain everything that's happened since I moved.

As much as I hate that this is what brought him to town, I'm so happy to see him. I didn't realize just how much I missed him until now.

Chapter 35
Grayson

My hands are shaking in my lap as we pull up outside of the Cooper's house. I narrow my eyes on the structure like I'm trying to figure out the best way to destroy it. To a certain extent, I am. I'm going to destroy Will's life and watch with a smile as he loses everything.

"What's the plan?" Mac asks from the driver's seat.

"I need to make a call before we do anything." I lean to the side and tug my phone out of my pocket. Moving through my contact list, I find the number and press call.

"Hello?" His Italian accent rings through the line, calming me the smallest amount.

"Fernando, it's Grayson, Piper's boyfriend."

"Hey, is everything ok? Where's Piper?"

"Piper's safe, but everything is not ok. Someone drugged her last night and I have a feeling your cameras might've caught the guy on tape. Can you check them? It would've been around ten last night."

"Yeah, just give me a minute. I'm pulling them up on my computer now..."

He's quiet for almost ten minutes. I would've wondered if he hung up if it weren't for the muttered curses and him complaining about teenagers being in his kitchen.

"There's a guy with three cups. He put some sort of pill in one of the cups. I can't see who he gives it to, though." He adds in a few muttered words in Italian, but I don't know what he's saying.

"Can you send a picture of him to this number? Bonus points if you can send me the video."

"I've always loved extra credit... so, this is the guy who drugged her?"

"Yes. And I'm going to make him pay for it," I growl into the phone.

"Piper's a sweetheart and doesn't deserve any of this shit. Let me know if you need help. I'm good with a knife and a shovel."

"Thanks. I'll let you know if I need you." I'm about to hang up when he stops me.

"Hey, Grayson?"

"Yeah?"

"You really care about her, right? This isn't just a ruse to ruin her completely, is it?" The uncertainty in his voice makes me smile. I'm glad she has someone looking out for her. With Connor, she's going to need an army of us.

"No. It's all real. Connor doesn't know that though, so let's keep this between us."

"Always. I'm going to keep checking this camera feed. I feel like Connor had a hand in this," he mumbles.

"Let me know if you find anything. I have the same gut feeling, but I don't have any proof."

I end the call and turn my attention to Mac. I show him the video that just came through of Will making three drinks and signing his death sentence with proof of him slipping the pill into Piper's drink.

"How do you have Fernando's number and how'd you know about the cameras?"

"Piper."

Mac nods his head like that answers all of his questions. Everyone loves Piper and wants to help her. Everyone except Connor.

"I think I should go knock on the door and tell him we're going for a little ride if he doesn't want me to burn that shitty house to the ground." Mac's jaw is clenched tight. Him and Piper have been growing closer lately. He hates watching her in pain just as much as I do.

Mac broke down last night and told me how much he regrets helping Connor with his vendetta against Piper. He was more willing to help since day one than I was. I knew there was something different about her, I just kept quiet and watched everything until I didn't have to anymore.

He has severe remorse over his actions and now he's questioning everything. What if all of the women we ran off really loved Mr. Ward and we destroyed his happiness? Did any of them actually deserve the things we did to them?

It's going to take him time, but eventually he'll accept what his role in things was and move on with his life.

"I like that idea. If he sees me, he might run."

"I'll be right back." Mac climbs out of the car and slips an easy smile over his face. You'd never be able to guess he's seconds away from losing his shit. He's skilled at keeping his emotions locked down. He lets you see what he wants and nothing more.

I'd be scared of his ability to hide behind a mask if I didn't have the exact same talent.

Mac knocks on the door and a few seconds later a middle-aged woman opens the door. I can tell he's charming her from here. She smiles and giggles at something he says. Then she waves him into the house and I know there's no way Will can get away from him now.

I try to relax into my seat and let Mac work his magic, but I'm itching to release my anger on someone. Will fucked with the wrong girl and now he's going to pay for it.

The entire time Mac's inside, I have to remind myself to stay calm. If I lose it now, nothing good will come of it. I need to remain in control for Piper.

Chapter 36

Mac

I knock on the front door and take a step back. My easy-going smile is fastened on my face. It's all a mask, all fake. But I'm comfortable behind this mask. It's what I show the world most of the time.

No one knows who I really am. No one gives a shit about what I hide behind this smile.

"Can I help you?" A middle-aged woman opens the door.

"Hey, is this the Cooper residence?"

"Yes, how can I help you?"

"I'm looking for Will. I'm a friend from school. I forgot my math homework at school and Will said I could come over and copy down the problems. You must be his older sister, I'm Mac." I hold out my hand and flash her a smile that makes all the girls melt at my feet. All of them except the one who matters to me.

"Oh, hush. I'm Will's mom." She giggles just like they all do. Moms love me. "C'mon in. You can make yourself comfortable in the living room while I get Will." Mrs. Cooper motions to the living room before disappearing up the stairs.

"Don't mind if I do," I mutter to myself, dropping onto the couch and propping my feet up on the coffee table. I cross my arms over my chest and wait.

Footsteps race down the stairs a few seconds later. They slow right before Will comes into view with a scowl on his face.

"What the fuck are you doing here?"

"Aww, that's no way to talk to your friend." I stick out my lip in a pout.

"We both know you're not my friend," Will hisses.

"And who's fault is that? It sure as hell isn't mine. I'm friends with everyone." I stand to my full height and look down at him.

Will's tall, but he's nowhere close to my six-foot five frame. I tower over everyone in the school. Grayson's the only one that comes close to my height and he's only an inch or so shorter.

"Let's go for a ride, Will." I grab his arm and tug him towards the door.

"I'm not going anywhere with you," he growls, trying to break free from my hold.

"Ok, then I'll just burn this shit hole to the ground with you and your sweet mama in here. I can only imagine how crappy the wiring is in this old house. You know, you really need to get these things checked every once in a while, or someone could get hurt." A slow smile spreads over my face when his eyes widen. "You don't wanna fuck with me, Will."

"Grayson's going to beat the shit out of me!"

"Did you expect anything else when you drugged his girlfriend? I mean, c'mon! You can't be that fucking dense. He'll let you off lighter if you man the fuck up and march out of this door with your head held high."

He hesitates at the door, glancing around for something. I'm sure he's looking for something to use as a weapon. I'm not nearly as stupid as everyone thinks I am.

"Or... burning the house down is still an option." I shrug like I don't give a shit. And honestly, I don't. Fires can be just as fun as punching someone. I just need to find some marshmallows to roast.

"Fine!... Ma! I'll be back in a little bit."

"Ok, sweetie. Stay safe!"

"Oh, Mama Cooper." I shake my head and chuckle. "If only she knew where I was taking you."

I shove Will out the door and into the backseat of my car. I made sure to turn on the child safety locks before we got here. After all, I care deeply about safety. I wouldn't want Will to jump out of my moving vehicle and get hurt.

"Grayson! I can explain," Will cries the second I climb behind the wheel.

The idiot pulls at the door handle, a soft whimper escaping his mouth when he realizes he can't get out.

"Don't talk. You'll have your chance to talk when we get there. I want silence until then." Grayson leans his head back against the headrest and closes his eyes.

He looks so calm and peaceful, but I know there's a nasty storm raging inside of him. As Connor would say, his little monster is seconds away from coming out to play. And mine's right there with his.

Chapter 37
Grayson

Will's smart enough to keep his mouth shut the whole drive. I'm a little worried he might've pissed himself in the back of Mac's car, but that isn't my issue.

I relax into the seat and let my eyes close. I'm exhausted. The little bit of sleep I got last night wasn't enough. I'm practically running on empty.

Every time Piper made a noise or moved, I'd wake up. I was so terrified of something happening to her. I can't wait to go home and see her with my own eyes. I'm hoping she's awake and back to normal by the time I'm done with this prick.

"We're here," Mac whispers, shifting the car into park and turning off the engine.

I climb out of the car wordlessly and open the back door. Will swallows hard and gets out. He refuses to meet my gaze. He knows exactly what he did and I'm sure he can guess what's going to happen now.

Mac leads us down the hill and into a big garage located at the back of his property. He slides open the heavy metal door wide enough for us to enter, then he's pushing it closed and locks it behind us.

We're blanketed in darkness until he flips a switch and I have to squint until I get used to the bright lights.

There's a single chair sitting in the center of the open concrete floor. The rest of the garage is practically empty. There are a few boxes off to the side, but the rest is bare. I don't even know why they have such a big garage if they don't use it.

"Sit. We're going to have a little talk." I point to the chair and wait for Will to follow my instructions.

He hesitates for a moment, but when Mac raises a brow at him and flicks open his lighter, Will practically runs for the chair.

"This is how things are going to work. I'm going to ask you questions and you're going to answer them. Once you've answered all of my questions, I'll give you a chance to plead your case before I beat the shit out of you. I'll be honest, it will take a pretty convincing argument to get you out of here without some part of you being broken." I pace back and forth in front of him.

"Grayson-"

"I said I'd ask the questions first. You're a really shitty listener." I shake my head. "This isn't helping your case... Did you drug Piper?"

"Yes," he whimpers, hanging his head.

"Did you know she was my girlfriend?" I stop in front of him and glare down at the pathetic man in front of me.

"Yes, but I know it's fake. You're not actually dating."

"Huh... how do you know that?" Mac steps next to me, stroking his chin.

"Uh, rumors are going around. The cheerleaders said you'd never actually date someone like her. They all think this is just a ruse. Some way to help Connor get rid of Piper."

"What the fuck does it matter if it's real or not? I have an image to uphold. Do you really think I'm the type of man to stand by and watch my girlfriend get roofied and do nothing about it?"

"No."

"Exactly! Whether or not I want to do this, I have no choice but to take action against you. I won't be seen as weak or vulnerable. I'm strong and a force to be dealt with. Why the hell would you go against me?"

"He must be an idiot, it's the only reason I can think of. What other option could really explain it? Also, he seemed surprised to find me in his living room. Did you think we'd just brush this shit off?" Mac stares at him like he's crazy.

"I didn't have a choice!" Will roars. He's smart enough to stay in his seat. He glares at us, his nostrils flaring with each exhale.

His hands are clenched at his sides, but he knows he can't do anything. If he makes a single move, we'll both attack him and he has no chance against us. We're bigger, stronger, and a hell of a lot more pissed off.

"We always have a fucking choice! You had a choice to drug Piper or not to. Don't sit here and tell me you didn't have a choice." Mac shakes his head and walks away.

He grabs a baseball bat and starts swinging it through the air like he's practicing his swing. Will's attention is focused on him and nothing else. His face drains of color and I'm a little worried he might pass out before we get to the good part of this evening.

"Was Piper the target or Hadley?" I fold my arms over my chest.

"Piper," he whispers so quietly I almost can't hear him.

"Did you give Hadley anything?" Mac growls.

"Just beer. I didn't slip anything in her drink. I would never do that."

I throw my head back, letting my deep chuckle bounce off the walls of the empty room. It's a little creepy how much everything echoes in here. I'd be terrified if I were in Will's position.

Maybe Mr. Barnes is part of the mafia and he comes here to torture people. There are more than enough stains on the concrete floor, and it's not like they're storing cars in here.

"You expect me to believe you wouldn't drug my sister after you just drugged my girlfriend? I wasn't born yesterday, Will. You're a fucking snake in the grass. You always have been," I growl, stepping closer and cracking my knuckles in his face.

"I'm still stuck on how he didn't have a choice. Did someone stick a fucking gun to your head?" Mac lets the bat fall against the floor, the clang reverberating several times.

"No... I made a mistake and got caught... the person told me if I did this, they'd forget everything I did." Will rubs his sweaty hands up and down his thighs.

"What'd you do?" Mac's interest is piqued.

"I'm not telling you," Will spits.

"I don't see how you have a choice." Mac smirks, throwing Will's words back at him. "Pretend this bat is a gun, it's pointed at your brain... or what you'd consider your brain. I'm not exactly sure there's anything between your ears."

"I'm having an affair with one of the teachers," Will whispers.

"Oh, now things are getting interesting. I have so many questions." Mac rubs his hands together and grabs another chair from the corner of the room.

He places it in front of Will and straddles the seat. He rests his arms across the back of the chair and drops his chin onto them. He looks so entertained.

"Who'd you fuck?" Mac flashes him a devious grin.

"Mrs. D," Will's words are barely loud enough to hear.

"Damn, she's hot. How'd you get her attention? Didn't she just get married last year? I guess Mr. D isn't too great if she decided to turn to you." Mac looks Will up and down with disgust.

"I don't know, ok? I have no clue how it happened. I was at the school most of the summer getting things ready for this year. Being class president means you have to actually do things for the class. I was working with Mrs. D on things like the pep rally at the beginning of the season and handling things like prom and formals. It was just the two of us and... she just kissed me. One thing led to another and soon we were fucking in the classroom after the other teachers left for the day."

"Who caught you?" I stare at him, looking for any changes that could indicate he's lying to us.

"He'll kill me if I tell you." Will swallows hard and glances away.

"You think Grayson won't?" Mac snorts with laughter. "Dude, you can't seriously be this stupid. Out of all the people in my life, there are only two I wouldn't fuck with. Grayson and... Connor," Mac whispers our friend's name. His gaze snaps to mine and I nod my head subtly.

My gut's been pointing to Connor since before we even left the party last night. I didn't want to believe it. I figured there had to be another explanation, but there isn't. Connor's behind this, just like he always is. Everything bad in my life is a product of him.

My phone rings before I can say or do anything else. I tug it out of my pocket and find Fernando's name flashing across my screen.

"Yeah?" I answer without a hello. I don't have time for that shit right now.

"Connor gave Will the pills. I have it on video," Fernando whispers into the phone. I'm sure he doesn't want Connor or James catching him during this conversation. I can only imagine the rath he'd incur if Connor caught him feeding us information.

"Can you send it to me?"

"Yes. It should be on your phone any second. What are you going to do?"

"I'm going to watch the King of Prescott High fall from his throne and shatter into millions of pieces."

"I'm happy to help."

"Thanks, I'll get back to you." I end the call and open the video.

Turning the volume up as loud as my phone goes, I press play and hold the phone out for Mac to watch too.

Connor and Will are in the kitchen, one of them on either side of the island. Will looks like he'd rather be anywhere else, but Connor looks oddly calm and in control for how he's been behaving lately.

"You don't have a choice. If you don't do this, I'll tell the school board. Mrs. D will get fired. She'll never hold another teaching job and I'm sure Mr. D won't stick around very long. Hell, Mrs. D will be lucky if she doesn't get thrown in prison. You're technically still a minor. Damn, she'll be a child predator." A slow smirk spreads over his face. "I'm fairly certain the school board will remove you as class president and I know how much you need that to get your scholarship to college. After all, Mommy and Daddy Cooper can't exactly afford college."

"Why do you want to do this? Piper's really nice. Why don't you just let her stay? You'll both be going off to college in a few months anyway."

"Don't worry about my reasoning. All you have to do is slip this into her drink. One should be more than enough." He pushes a bag of pills across the counter to Will. "But if you feel like doing more, I'm not going to complain."

"What's going to happen after she's drugged?" Will hesitantly grabs the bag and slips it into his coat pocket.

"Oh, don't you worry about that. I'll make sure she gets to her room safely." A sinister smile takes over his smug face.

"You won't do anything to her?"

"I won't touch a hair on her head. I promise."

It's taking everything in me to stay in this garage and not steal Mac's SUV and go to Connor's house. I'm not sure I'd leave there without killing him though. And I really don't want to end up in jail. I want to be with Piper, I don't need a thick piece of glass between us for the next twenty years.

"I feel like a broken record tonight, but are you stupid? You didn't realize he promised he wouldn't touch her, not that she'd be safe? Who knows what he had planned! When it comes to Connor, it definitely wouldn't have been anything good for Piper!" Mac stands up so quickly the chair clatters to the ground and he starts pacing back and forth again.

"I didn't have a choice!" Will bellows again.

Mac jumps to his side and grips his face roughly. He tilts Will's face up until he's forced to meet his gaze. Mac's inches from him, a snarl plastered across his face.

Mac always has an easy smile, I know it's fake, but it's always there. I've never seen him this pissed off and honestly, it's a little scary. He looks like Connor and me.

"Hey, Gray, I wonder if I'll have a *choice* in breaking this fucker's nose. Maybe I won't have a *choice* in squeezing his neck until he stops breathing. Or maybe I don't have a *choice* and I have to swing that baseball bat at his skull."

"It's Connor's fault! Why aren't you going after him?" Will cries, tears dripping off of his chin.

"Connor will get what's coming to him," I growl. "But so will you. You aren't faultless here either. You helped him. I don't give a fuck about your reasoning. You pretended to be her friend!"

"And you're pretending to be her boyfriend!"

"I'm not though. Connor just thinks it's fake. Piper knows everything. It was the only way we could be together." I fold my arms over my chest and give him a smug smile. He knows nothing.

All he is, is a pawn that was easily played. The thing about pawns is, they're disposable. No one cries over their pawn getting taken out, but they protect their king and queen because they're the key to everything. Apparently Will needs a lesson in chess. In how you keep your plans close to your chest until it's your turn and you strike without warning.

Well, guess what, fuckers, it's my turn and I'm about to strike.

"But you've helped him with everything he's done to Piper since she moved here!"

"Have I though?" I tilt my head to the side like I'm thinking. "Connor stole her clothes after swim class, but magically you never found out about the new girl running naked through the school. Connor planted drugs in her locker, yet Piper wasn't arrested when the police and drug sniffing dogs came. I could go on and on, but it doesn't matter. I've saved her each and every time I could!"

"You were awful to her! You're awful to everyone!"

"I was, but you didn't see us outside of school. I fucking love that woman and I'll do whatever I have to do to keep Piper safe and happy."

I take slow steps towards him, my decision finally made up.

"What- what are you going to do to me? Are you going to kill me?" Will stares up at me with terror in his eyes. He was scared of Mac being near him, but that was nothing compared to how he's looking at me right now. He knows I'm capable of so much more than Mac is.

"No, but I'm going to make you hurt. I'm going to make sure you never want to glance in my girl's direction again."

I close the distance between us. Before Will can utter a single word, my fist slams into his nose. That horrible crunch of bone echoes in the room. I have to fight to keep bile from rising up my throat.

Turning my back on him, I close my eyes and try to calm myself down. If I don't stay in control, I have no doubt Will won't make it out of here alive.

I spin back around to find blood streaming out of his nose, but he doesn't try to protect himself. Will knows he deserves everything I'm about to give him.

Mac steps up beside me and throws a right hook, catching Will's jaw in the process. His head whips to the side and he loses his balance, falling to the floor. He whimpers in pain but never asks us to stop.

Mac kicks him in the ribs a few times. He's not stopping and I know he's not going to. I tug him back by the hood of his sweatshirt.

"Enough," I growl.

"You should kill him," Mac hisses. "Who knows what Connor had planned for her!"

"And if we end up behind bars, we'll never find out. I say we leave him here and go find Connor." My voice is so calm and emotionless that I don't even recognize it.

"Let's fucking go. I want to pound his face in until no one can recognize the fucker."

Tension is radiating off of Mac. Instead of feeding my own anger, he's calming me down. We can't both be loose cannons. This won't end well if we are. I need to step up and save him from himself... even if that prevents me from getting revenge.

Chapter 38
Grayson

As we approach Mac's car, I hold out my hand for the keys. If I let him get behind the wheel, we'll end up at Connor's and I don't want that yet. I need a plan and a good one.

"You're not driving my car," Mac growls, trying to push past me.

"Mac, give me the fucking keys or I'll let you join Will, whimpering in pain on the cold concrete floor."

"Are you fucking kidding me? I'm helping you!" He screams, spreading his arms wide.

I grab the back of his neck and rest my forehead against his. I need him to calm down or I won't be able to reason with him.

"I'm trying to fucking help you, Gray," he whispers, sounding so broken.

"I know you are. Connor's smart, but we need to be smarter. He's expecting us to come rushing in there. We need to act like we don't give a shit."

"It could've been Hadley, man."

"I know, I know. And we're going to make him pay, just not today."

"Why are we waiting? This is stupid."

"We're going to wait until he doesn't expect it. That's the best time to strike. Haven't you ever heard the saying 'revenge is best served cold'? Let's go back to the girls and check on them for a little bit. Maybe later tonight we can go to Connor's and act like everything is normal."

"Like fuck I can. I want to rip his head off."

"Then you won't be coming," I say matter of factly.

"How can you be this calm? Piper's not even my girlfriend and I want to kill Connor."

"There isn't a cell in my body that doesn't want to see him dead, but if I lose my shit, I'm going to make stupid decisions. I don't have time for that. If I surrender to the monster inside of me, I'm not sure I'll be able to walk away before Connor takes his last breath."

"I expected more blood on you," Dad muses, eyeing me as we walk through the kitchen.

"Connor blackmailed him into doing it." Turning on the sink, I wash away the small amount of blood from my hands. He's right, there should've been more.

"Of course he fucking did." Dad tosses his papers on the table and folds his arms over his chest. "I'm done watching this shit unfold. I think I've stood by long enough."

"I'll handle it. I have a plan."

"Yeah, let's hear this damn plan." Dad rolls his eyes. "I'm so sick of that shithead. You almost died because of him, Grayson! And he considers you his best friend! There's no telling what else he has planned for Piper."

"Don't you think I know that! I'm fucking trying here! I'm doing everything in my power to keep her safe! Just like I have since she stepped foot in Prescott High! I've put my own ass on the line time after time! I've kept her safe and I'm going to keep doing it until she has nothing to worry about!"

Rage clouds my vision. I'm so sick of the stress of dealing with the three ringed circus that is Connor Ward. He's always five steps ahead of me and I'm tired of trying to play catch up.

A soft hand slips into mine, pulling me out of my anger. I glance down and am met with big blue eyes. Piper places her other hand over my racing heart and moves impossibly closer to me.

"It's ok. I'm ok, Grayson."

I snake an arm around her waist and hug her close to me. I was so scared last night that something was going to happen to her. Seeing her standing here, looking just like she always does, it's a huge weight off my shoulders.

Carefully cradling her against my chest, I drop my head to hers. I close my eyes and let myself breathe her in. I can feel my heart rate slowing. My breaths are less harsh, less frantic. My entire body is relaxing now that she's in my arms.

I glance up and find a stranger in the doorway to the den. He's on the shorter side, maybe an inch or so taller than Piper. He stuffs his hands in his pockets and watches us carefully.

"Hey, you must be Tim. I'm Grayson. It's nice to finally meet you." I hold out a hand to him, never letting go of Piper.

"It's nice to meet you too. Thanks for taking care of our girl." Tim nods to Piper. I want to get mad over him calling her our girl, but I get it. She was his before she became mine. I'll allow it as long as he doesn't touch her.

The front door opens and closes, I glance up to find Mac standing in the doorway to the kitchen. His phone is in his hand and he's staring at Piper. There's so much relief in his eyes.

"What's going on, Mac?" I ask softly.

"I just got off the phone with the principal. Piper won't need to return to school for a while. Hadley can get all of her work from her teachers. She just needs to do it and take midterms. She'll still be allowed to graduate no matter how many days she misses."

"I don't know how the hell you do it." Dad shakes his head with a smile. "Thank you, Mac. You're a good kid."

"Thanks, Papa Young."

"I want to go to school. Why wouldn't I?" Piper peers up at me, a slight frown in her brow.

"Piper, seriously? You need to stay away from him." Tim frowns.

"You can't be there until I know what's going on with Connor... how long is James and your mom going to be gone?"

"Two weeks."

"You're moving in here until they get back. I don't trust Connor around you," Dad growls. "You can have your own room or you can stay in either of the kid's rooms. I don't give a shit if I become a grandpa anymore. At least you'd be stuck with us then."

"Did you hear that, baby? He wants us to go fuck." I wiggle my eyebrows, making Piper giggle.

"I don't know why you like him, you could do better, sweetheart," Dad deadpans, rising from his chair and leaving the room.

"Gray?" Hadley's hesitant to enter the kitchen. "Is everything ok?"

"For now. We have some things to deal with. Wanna help?"

I motion for everyone to take a seat around the table and we get to work. We come up with a solid plan to take Connor Ward down. Even Tim's willing to help us come up with ideas.

Piper took my idea and added to it, she made it better. Just like she takes every part of me and makes it better. I don't know what I'd do without her.

Chapter 39

Piper

I take a deep breath and blow it out slowly. I've been staying at the Young's house for three days. Every time Grayson and I get alone time, we get interrupted. I just want to be able to kiss my boyfriend without someone walking in. Is that so bad?

Except tonight I want so much more.

I check my reflection in the mirror one last time before I exit the bathroom and stare at Grayson. He's lying in the center of his bed in nothing except a pair of gray sweatpants. I swear that's all he wears. His closet is full of them. I'm not complaining though. I love seeing him in them.

Mr. and Mrs. Young went out to an event tonight and won't be back until late. Mac came over to hang out with Hadley and to give us some alone time. I practically begged him to keep her downstairs and occupied. Not that Mac wouldn't normally jump at the chance, but I know he's going to do anything I ask of him right now.

I'm not going to take advantage of it, but I'm fairly certain if I needed a lung, he'd rip his out of his chest and present it to me on a silver platter. He feels so guilty when it comes to me and that kills me.

"Where's Hadley? I haven't seen her in a while. Normally she's all up in our business." Grayson doesn't look away from his phone, he hasn't seen me yet.

"Mac's here. I asked him to entertain her for the night."

"Why would yo-" The words die on his tongue as soon as he glances in my direction.

Grayson's on his feet in seconds. He slams his bedroom door shut and twists the lock. He stalks towards me, darkness swirling in his eyes, making his emerald eyes so dark I can barely make out the color.

"What are you doing, baby?" His gaze slides up and down my body. I can feel it, like he's running his hands over me and not his eyes.

"I thought we could have some time to ourselves," I murmur, taking a step closer to him. I place one hand on his chest and one on his stomach.

"Oh yeah? What's going through that pretty head of yours?" Grayson carefully plants his hands on my hips. He's been more gentle than necessary since the party.

The heat of his skin seeps through the thin lace fabric and warms me. I swallow the lump in my throat and lock my eyes on his. Once the words come out of my mouth, there will be no taking them back.

"I want you," I whisper, sliding the hand on his stomach lower, over the bulge in his pants.

Grayson sucks in a sharp breath and lets out a low groan. The noise goes straight between my legs, making me clench my thighs together.

"I love you, Piper," his voice is low and gravely, like he just woke up. I'm addicted to the sound of it.

"I love you too." I stroke him, wanting him to throw me on the bed and make me see how much I mean to him.

"I'm serious." Grayson cradles my face in his hands and stares deep into my eyes. "You're the most important person in the world to me. I don't ever want to lose you."

"I'm right there with you." I place my hands on top of his.

"I know Dad keeps joking around about it, but I plan to get down on one knee sooner or later."

"I hope it's sooner," I whisper.

"Me too."

Grayson slowly lowers his mouth to mine. He's soft and gentle. Taking his time to savor me. He gently parts my lips with his tongue and runs it over mine. Goosebumps spread over my skin. I've never had someone kiss me like this. Like I'm their entire world and nothing else matters.

Grayson's intoxicating, all-consuming, and all mine. I always dreamed of being with someone like him, but I never thought it could happen.

He walks me backwards until my knees hit the edge of his bed. I let out a small gasp. It gives him the opportunity to deepen our kiss even more. He slowly lowers me to the bed and hovers over me.

"You're so damn beautiful. I don't deserve you."

Kisses get placed along my jaw before he moves up and down my neck. He licks and sucks, making me moan the entire time.

"Did you buy this for me?" Grayson murmurs against my skin. He tugs on the lace lingerie, barely covering anything.

"Yes," I gasp again when he positions his mouth over my nipple and sucks on it through the fabric.

"I fucking love it. I want to see all of you though."

Grayson stands to his full height and helps me sit up. I slip the lace over my head and toss it on the floor. I stand in front of him, slide my thumbs under the edges of my thong and push them down my legs.

"You're all mine. Do you understand that? No one else will ever touch you again. I'm going to marry you one day soon and I'm going to make you the happiest woman in the world. In the bedroom and outside of it."

"Yes," I whimper, wanting him to touch me more than anything.

Without a word, Grayson drops his sweatpants to the ground, leaving him naked, and helps me onto the bed. He climbs over me, making sure to keep his weight off of me. He rests a hand on either side of my head and dips down until his mouth meets mine.

This kiss is more passionate, more frantic, more everything than the last one was. He's losing control and I'm loving every second of it.

Grayson's always in control. Always several steps ahead of me, so to see him slipping because of me, it's addicting. I want to see him fall over the edge and find his orgasm. I'm sure it's a beautiful sight.

"You're positive you want this?" Grayson slides a condom over his thick cock and positions himself at my entrance. Instead of answering him, I raise my hips and push him inside of me. "Fuck, baby! You're so tight."

He doesn't slide in further. He gives me a chance to adjust to his size. While he waits, he kisses a path down my neck to my breasts. He licks and sucks my nipple into his mouth before moving on to the other side. He gently bites down on it, making me buck my hips, pushing him deeper inside of me.

"You're killing me," he groans, his eyes falling shut. He drops his head to the crook of my neck and takes a deep breath.

I know he's not going to last long, but that's ok. Neither will I. Grayson feels like he was made for me. He's absolutely perfect and I don't plan on only going one round tonight.

"We can go slow next time," I whisper into his ear.

"Fuck, you're perfect," he growls.

Grayson lifts his head and meets my gaze. He presses a rough and passionate kiss to my lips. Thrusting his tongue into my mouth, he matches the rhythm of his cock going in and out of me.

I already feel my orgasm building inside of me and I know I won't last much longer. I can feel Grayson's heart pounding against my chest and it's making me feel so much closer to him.

"Fuck," Grayson groans. "Come for me, baby."

His words push me over the edge. I squeeze around him and feel him pulsating inside of me. Grayson's brows furrow and his mouth parts. He lets out several small grunts and groans. Watching him come apart is the sexiest thing I've ever seen and I want to watch it happen over and over again.

He drops his head to the crook of my neck and stays there while we both catch our breaths. Grayson presses one last kiss to my lips before he climbs out of bed and goes into the bathroom. He comes out a few minutes later with a washcloth and helps me clean up. He tosses it in the hamper and climbs back into bed with me.

Laying so we're facing each other, Grayson traces a finger from my temple, down my jaw and over my lips. I nip at his skin, making him smile.

"You're it for me. I don't want anyone else for the rest of my life."

"I don't either. I want to be in your arms forever," I whisper.

"Do you think your mom would let you move in here? I'm not sure I'll be able to sleep without you in my bed after they come back."

"I doubt that will work." I chuckle. "I'll make sure to have a few sleepovers with Hadley though."

"I'll pay Hadley to invite you over every night," Grayson growls.

I shriek when he flips us so he's lying on his back and I'm on top of him. He wraps his arms around my waist and holds me close.

"I sleep so much better when you lay on top of me like this," he admits softly.

"You're such a weirdo." I giggle into his neck. I don't tell him, but I sleep better like this, too.

"I say we take a nap before going for another round, because I'm going to need you more than once tonight."

"That sounds perfect."

Chapter 40
Grayson

It's been a week since Piper was drugged. She hasn't been to school since then and neither have I. Connor's kept his mouth shut and if I needed more proof he was behind things, this would be it.

Hadley and Mac went back to school a few days ago and bring home our work every day. Piper and I have been studying together and making sure we don't fall behind.

There's no reason we can't go back to school, but I think she should wait until Lauren and James come back. More than anything, I'm pushing for her to stay out until I can handle Connor. And tonight's the night I plan to do just that.

"Who wants more homework?" Mac smirks at us, dropping a pile of papers in front of each of us.

"It's never ending," Piper groans.

"Well, your school photos are in there too. You look hot so that should make you happy," Mac tells Piper. He flashes me a devilish grin and takes a few steps away from me. He's purposely creating space between us.

I'm not going to react though. I know he doesn't have a thing for Piper, he's obsessed with my sister.

"Let me see this photo." I snatch the school photos out of Piper's pile and grin down at it. She looks gorgeous in it.

I slide the sheet of wallets out of the pack and grab a pair of scissors. I cut out one and slip it into my wallet.

"Who said you could have one of those?" Piper arches a brow at me.

"Nobody. But I need a picture of the woman I love for my wallet."

"That's really cute. Can I have one of you?" A slow smile spreads over Piper's kissable lips.

I cut out one of my pictures and hand it over to her. Then I change my mind and grab a larger photo out of the pack and give it to her.

"What's this for?"

"You need a picture of your hot boyfriend next to your bed. I'm going to need one of you too." I give her a *gimmie* motion and wait for her to hand it over. Piper rolls her eyes, but gives me what I want.

"Are you ready to go to Connor's house?" Mac eyes me.

We both know this interaction with him is going to take a hell of a lot of deep breathing and hiding behind our masks. Connor can't know we're pissed. He has to think the plan is still in place.

"What are you guys doing here?" Connor asks as soon as he sees us. I can sense his anxiety and it makes a smile spread over my face. I love that he's scared of me.

"Well, we need to talk about the party." I keep my tone neutral even though my blood is boiling. Every time I think about how out of it Piper was, I want to kill Connor all over again.

"Before we start this little bromance talk, can we go find something to eat? I'm starving." Mac pushes past us and heads towards the kitchen, just like we planned.

"Fernando's off today. I don't know what you're going to eat." Connor almost sounds annoyed.

"I'm a big boy, I'm sure I can find something," Mac calls over his shoulder.

Connor drops onto a stool at the island counter and glares at Mac as he opens one cabinet after another. He finally moves to the fridge and finds something to eat.

"What do you want to talk about?" Connor stares at me with a bored expression. I can see through it though. He's nervous. He knows he went too far.

"That shit can't happen again. You told me I could do whatever I wanted with Piper and you wouldn't get involved. Yet you seem to keep getting involved." I cross my arms over my chest and glare at him.

"What are you talking about? I didn't do shit at the party."

"I'm not stupid. I went to Will after he drugged Piper. It took a little bit of patience, but I finally got him to admit you were behind all of it. Will's not smart enough to do it."

"That little fucker! I'm going to ruin him!" Connor roars, jumping off his stool.

I place a firm hand on his shoulder and push him back down onto the wood. I need to focus and get what I came here for.

"We'll deal with Will later. We can only take down one person at a time," Mac mumbles around a bite of food.

"You'll help me take down Cooper?" Connor raises a brow.

"Sure, but first we deal with Piper." Mac waves him off.

"What's the plan? You haven't seemed to be making any progress with her, Gray."

"I've made plenty of progress with her. She told me she loves me before the party and just this week she let me fuck her." I flash him a smug smile.

I feel sick to my stomach talking about Piper like this. She's the center of my whole world and talking about her like she's trash is painful. I'm going to do everything I can to make this up to her. I'm going to confess every sin and beg her for forgiveness.

"You're supposed to be destroying her, not fucking her!" Connor hisses.

"I have her right where I want her. Give me a few weeks to get her to think I'm her future, then I'll rip the carpet out from under her. She's practically eating out of the palm of my hand." I smirk in triumph.

"So, what do you need me for?" Connor eyes me. I think he's starting to question my loyalty, but he's too stupid to know what I'm up to.

"Well, I need to plan my move. What have you done so far? I need to make sure I top all of it. I need to hit her where it really hurts. I'll probably do several things at once to make sure I completely destroy her."

"I stuffed her locker with condoms and wrote 'whore' across the front. I took her lunch card and left her with no way to buy food, but Will stepped in and fucked that up." He ticks off the things he's done on his fingers like he's talking about who he wants to invite to a party. "We stole her clothes and left her with nothing. I still don't know how she got out of that locker room with clothes. It makes no sense." Connor glares at the table.

"She probably broke into someone's locker and stole their shit." Mac shrugs a shoulder.

"I told the school counselor she was harming herself. The counselor still checks in with her weekly, but it did nothing to get her angry enough to leave. I paid someone to hack into her school records and change her grades, but I don't think she's realized that yet." He chuckles.

I make a mental note to tell Piper to log onto the system and check her grades. If she asks her teachers about it now, they'll be able to fix them before it causes any problems.

"Cherie was supposed to steal her clothes and take pictures of her naked. I was going to spread them around town, but she didn't shower that day after swimming. I even planted a bunch of cocaine in her locker and then had someone report. I have no idea how she got out of that one unless she found where I hid it and got it out of the school." Connor strokes his chin.

I glance at Mac, hoping he keeps his mouth shut. The day he found out Connor stashed enough drugs in Piper's locker to land her in jail, was the day he decided he was done with Connor.

I decided I was done soon after he set his sights on Piper. The way he's been attacking her is uncalled for. Piper and Lauren haven't started asking for money or acting like they deserve everything they could ever want. They've actually tried to turn down James' help whenever they could.

They're a complete contrast to all of James' former wives. Those women only cared about his money and status.

"The cheerleaders were supposed to pour paint over her head at the first game of the season, but you screwed that up when you asked her out. I've done a bunch of small things to her at home, like spiders in her bed and replacing

her toothpaste with mayo. And then the shit at the party."
He waves it off like the party was no big deal.

"What was up with drugging her? Like what was the plan?" Mac raises a brow.

"Yeah, you were pretty set on me putting her in her room." I narrow my gaze on Connor.

"It was a great plan until you had to act like the loving boyfriend and fuck it all up. I told a couple guys they could do whatever they wanted with her." He shrugs like he just told me what he had for breakfast and not that he was handing over his stepsister to be raped and who knows what else.

I snap. I can't explain it, but in the blink of an eye I have Connor pinned against a cabinet with my forearm pressing into his throat. I don't remember moving. I don't remember responding at all. Everything went red and then I found myself in this position. It seems to be a common occurrence where he's concerned these days.

"You were going to have her fucking raped?" I growl, pushing even harder on his neck.

I don't give a fuck if I kill him at this point. He deserves so much more than being killed.

If I had listened and put Piper in her room... Bile rises in my throat and I swallow hard to keep it down. I can't even think about it. That would've destroyed her. Connor definitely would've won.

But the lasting effects something like that would have on her is horrific. This has gotten so out of hand. More than beyond what would be acceptable to pull on any person no matter how much you hate them.

Piper and Lauren would've left, I have no doubt about it. They would've been out of here faster than I could blink and I wouldn't even blame them.

Lauren's an amazing mom. Sure, she doesn't know any of the things Connor's been doing to her daughter, because Piper's kept her mouth shut. She cares about her daughter's feelings and how her life is. James does too, at least where Piper's concerned.

I think James cares about Connor just as much, but Connor's done everything in his power to keep James at arm's length. He never tells him about anything going on in his life and they definitely don't talk about how he feels.

"I didn't tell them to rape her! I just said they could do whatever they wanted!" Connor's gasping for air, barely able to get his words out.

"Gray... you're gonna kill him." Mac places a hand on my shoulder. He doesn't try to pull me back, he feels the same way I do.

Mac's skilled at hiding his feelings, but I can read him like an open book right now. He wants to cause Connor as much pain as possible and I know exactly how we're going to do it.

"I thought you wanted her gone too? Don't tell me you've fallen in love with that trash." Connor sneers.

"It doesn't matter how I feel, you can't just drug someone and hand them over to a bunch of teenage guys to do as they please! I'm supposed to be her boyfriend. This reflects on me too!" I slip back behind the mask a little too easily for my own liking. "People are going to think I'm a piece of shit if I let something like that happen to my girlfriend and I just stood around, watching it happen! It makes me look weak if people don't respect me enough to stay away from my girl."

I push off of him and pace the length of the kitchen. I'm losing control and I'm not sure how long I can stand to be in the same room as him.

Connor falls to the ground, clutching his neck as he gasps. It's not surprising he's dropped the tough guy act, unlike the last time when I pinned him against the car. Now, no one's here to witness him being weak.

"You two only care about yourselves!" Connor roars.

"Are you fucking kidding me?" Mac growls. He crouches down in front of Connor and glares at him. "Grayson and I have been helping you with these stupid vendettas for years! We've always done your bidding without saying a word against you! I'm so fucking done with it!"

Mac thrusts his hands through his hair so hard I'm worried he's going to take a chunk out.

"Grayson almost got killed last year because you had to beat those guys from Graverson. Don't you understand that! He almost fucking died! You weren't there to help him recover. You didn't see his parents or sister sitting by his bed, crying day and night. We all thought he was going to die!"

Mac's entire body shakes. I never realized how much the accident affected him. I thought he was just trying to be a good friend. Maybe he had a little bit of guilt over what happened, something similar to survivor's guilt. I didn't realize it traumatized him this much.

"You didn't give a damn about him, Connor. It's you who doesn't care about anyone except yourself. Piper's actually a really cool person. If you got your head out of your ass for five seconds maybe you could recognize that and develop a real relationship with her. Instead, you constantly surrender to this monster inside of you. We all have them, Connor, we just don't let them win."

"C'mon, Mac. Let's go. I'm not dealing with his ass anymore," I hiss, holding my hand out to Mac. I tug him to his feet and move towards the door,

Before I think better of it, I move back to Connor's side and stare down at him. I make sure he sees the murderous rage in my eyes and knows I'm serious.

"You're not going to go near Piper again. You're not going to try to make her life worse. You're going to let her live here without a single complaint out of your mouth, do you understand me?"

"And what if I don't?" He scowls at me. He thinks he holds all the cards, but he doesn't.

My phone pings in my pocket. I tug it out and find a notification for an email from Fernando. It's the exact evidence I need to keep Connor quiet. I quickly forward the email to Dad before turning my attention back to Connor.

"Well, if you don't leave her alone, I'll make sure I fucking destroy you. I'll knock you off that damn pedestal you've placed yourself on and watch your life shatter like a piece of glass. I'll make sure you can't pick up the pieces and your future is completely ruined," I growl.

"You can't. You're not smart enough to take me down. Neither of you are." Connor rises to his feet, his confidence coming back quickly. He's always been unstoppable, but he's never gone against me.

"Do you really want to take that bet? Do you really want to risk everything?" I cross my arms over my chest. I'm not afraid of him.

Did I ever want to willingly go against Connor? No, but I'm not going to back down. Not when it comes to the woman I love.

"I have no doubt I can take you down. I just hope it's all worth it to you. Is a pussy really worth losing over a decade old friendship?"

Before I can even react, Mac flies past me and punches Connor in the face. I planned to keep our opinions of Piper quiet tonight, but clearly neither one of us are as skilled at hiding our feelings as we thought we were.

"Don't you fucking dare talk about Piper like that!" Mac punches him again.

"Wow, I didn't know you were harboring a crush on her too. I thought your dick only got hard for Baby Young. Does Hadley know you're cheating on her?" Connor spits blood onto the floor.

"Don't you dare talk about Hadley! She's better than all of us combined!" Mac pulls his fist back one more time and drives it into Connor's face.

I'm sure Connor's going to be sporting some pretty nasty bruises tomorrow. I'm a little upset I didn't hear any bones breaking, but you can't disfigure everyone.

It takes all my strength to pull Mac off of him. When it comes to my sister, I have no doubt he's not going to stop punching Connor until he can't move or talk.

I grab his neck and rest my forehead against his. This is the only way we can calm each other. The only way to get the other to focus on what needs to be done.

When Mac's calm enough for me to let go of him, I grab his arm and tug him towards the door. Connor's not going to stop running his mouth and if we stay here any longer, one of us is going to kill him.

"I won't stay away from her. I'll make her life miserable until she's running back to the shithole she came from. I want her out of my house, out of my school, and out of my fucking life forever!"

Connor continues yelling a bunch of shit until I slam the door behind us and shove Mac down the stairs. He tries to turn around three times, but I won't let him. I promised

Mom I wouldn't let Connor ruin Mac and I'm sticking to it. I need to get him away from here.

I grab my phone and dial Fernando. He's helped us out a ton, but I need more.

"Hello?"

"I need the rest of the video from our conversation. I thought threatening him would be enough, but I was wrong. I have to destroy his life as he knows it."

"I'll have it sent to you in the next ten minutes."

"Thank you. I don't know what I'd do without you."

"I'm just happy someone's helping her."

Chapter 41
Piper

Grayson's been like a caged animal since he returned home. I watch him pace the room again and try to think of what I can do to help. Tension radiates off of him and I swear it's only getting worse as the minutes tick by.

"Grayson... talk to me." I reach out a hand from my spot on the edge of his bed and my heart swells when he takes it in an instant.

"He's not going to stop, baby."

"It's ok, we'll figure it out."

"You don't get it! It's going to get worse. He's fucking crazy, but it's more than that. Mac and I were able to protect you before because we knew what he had planned. Now, we'll be kept in the dark. He's going to come after all of us. It'll be hard and fast. I don't know how to protect you." He drops his forehead to mine and sucks in a deep breath.

"It's not your job to protect me. I can handle myself. I've stayed silent and tried to play nice with him. I was giving him a chance to adjust and act like a decent human, but clearly that's not going to happen. If he's not going to stop coming after us, I'm taking the kiddie gloves off and hitting him where it hurts."

When Monday rolls around, I somehow convince Grayson we should all go back to school. As the minutes tick by throughout the day, everything is eerily calm. Mac, Hadley, Grayson, and I are constantly looking over our shoulders, waiting for Connor to strike.

The only difference in my normal school day is now Grayson and Mac sit with us during lunch, while Will sits with a group from the football team. He's still a bruised mess from whatever the guys did to him. He keeps his distance from me even if the boys aren't around. I'm not sure if he feels guilty or if he's scared of getting punched again.

Connor walks over to the table he used to share with Grayson and Mac. He drops his lunch tray on the table and scowls as he scans the cafeteria. His murderous gaze stops when it lands on me. It's a silent conversation.

Bring it on.

Tuesday isn't as pleasant. During my second period class, the counselor and two officers appear in my classroom.

"Miss Lawson, please come with us," Mrs. Gowen eyes me like she's afraid of me. I stand and move towards her, leaving my things behind. "Bring your things, Piper. You're not coming back."

My gaze snaps to Hadley. She stares back at me for a heartbeat before she whips her phone out and her thumbs start dancing over the screen. I'm sure she's texting Grayson and Mac to let them know that something is up.

I grab all of my things, stuffing them into my backpack. I move to sling the bag over my shoulder, but one of the officers steps forward and takes the strap out of my hand.

"I'll take that, ma'am." He motions for me to go ahead of him.

I glance over my shoulder one last time at Hadley before I exit the room. She mouths *'I'm coming.'* And I have no doubt my best friend is only a few steps behind me.

"What's going on? Why am I being taken from my class and why are there police officers here?"

I'm not going to silently follow them and wait for them to share information with me. Nope, I want to know all of it now.

"Piper, this can wait until we get to my office." Mrs. Gowen huffs.

"No." I stop walking and refuse to move. "I'm not going with you unless you tell me what's going on." I cross my arms over my chest and stare her down. "Last time I came to your office I was accused of doing things I didn't do. I want to know, or I'm calling James."

"If I could go back in time, I'd slap myself silly for thinking being a school counselor would be fun. I thought I could make a difference in the lives of teens. I couldn't have been more wrong," she grumbles under her breath and pinches the bridge of her nose. "We received an anonymous tip from a student, that you had plans to bring weapons to the school in order to hurt students and teachers."

I stare at her for several long seconds like she's absolutely crazy because she has to be. Why in the world would someone tell her that? But then I remember who my stepbrother is and it all clicks into place. He's trying to get me kicked out of school.

"When are you going to learn Connor's full of shit!"

"Piper, we have to take these things seriously. Please come with us so we can speak to you and get to the bottom of this. And I never said who the student was." Mrs. Gowen motions for me to follow her and I do because what else am I supposed to do?

"I want my mom and James called. And I want a lawyer."

"I've already called Mr. Ward and he's on his way here. I believe he already has his lawyer on his way too." She waves me off like it's not important and I wouldn't be surprised if she's lying.

No one's going to listen to a damn thing I have to say. And the police officers walking on either side of me prove they think I'm a loose cannon. I'm sure Connor spun a wonderful story about how crazy I am.

As soon as the counselor's office door shuts behind us, an officer steps up to me and almost looks apologetic as he grips the back of his neck uncomfortably.

"Ma'am, I'm going to have to pat you down to make sure you don't have any sort of weapons on you."

"Of course you do. Do I have to have a fucking strip search too? Do you want me to pee in a cup? Take a little bit of blood? Fuck this school. You're all a bunch of idiots if you believe anything that leaves Connor Ward's mouth is truth!"

"Ma'am, I don't have a choice. I don't want to do this anymore than you do." He looks so sincere I actually believe him. He's only a few years older than me and he's been very kind so far.

The older officer is probably in his mid-thirties. He hasn't said a word, but he's not looking at me like he's judging me. He almost looks bored.

"Fine," I sigh and hold my arms out for him.

He moves up and down each leg before patting all around my abdomen and my arms. He looks almost relieved when he doesn't find anything.

"She doesn't have anything and her backpack was empty. I think she's telling the truth."

"Did you check her locker?" Mrs. Gowen raises a brow.

"Mrs. Gowen, how would I check her locker? I don't know which one is hers, nor do I have the combination." I can see how hard he's working to not roll his eyes.

"Can I trust the two of you to escort Miss Lawson to her locker and check it?" Mrs. Gowen eyes both of the officers.

"Yeah, I'm sure I can handle a teenage girl. If she gets super rough and tells me I'm ugly, I promise not to run and hide in my safe space," the older officer deadpans. He doesn't try to hide his eyeroll and in that second, I decide I really like these guys.

"C'mon, Piper." The younger officer places a gentle hand on my back and leads me out the door.

"That lady's fucking crazy. I'm Jack by the way and that's Jacob," the older officer motions to his partner. "I'm not an idiot, Piper. This is all a bunch of bullshit, but we have to do our jobs anyway."

"You know I'm innocent?" My brows reach for my hairline, I thought I was going to be arguing with everyone until I was blue in the face.

"I'll never know for sure, but I suspect you are. Connor's an asshole. I've known him since I was little. The kid has all the adults fooled and wrapped around his finger. Most of the time he's full of shit though." Jacob rolls his eyes.

"And let's be honest, Mrs. Gowen's an idiot in general. She's useless as a counselor. I went to high school with her and she was never the smartest person in a room. Normally, she would be trying to recover from whatever she snorted in the bathroom or was nursing a hangover. She was the queen bee on the cheerleading squad. She's a Connor through and through," Jack grumbles under his breath.

We stop in front of my locker. I quickly twist the lock and open the door. I scan the contents and breathe a sigh of relief when there's nothing out of the ordinary. I was a little worried Connor had planted something in here. I wouldn't have been surprised in the least to find some sort of weapon in my locker.

"Does this help my case?" I flick my attention from my locker to each of the men with me.

"I'm just going through the motions and doing my job. Right now, my job is to figure out what the fuck is going on." He places a gentle hand on my shoulder. "We'll go back to Mrs. Gowen's office, where I'll tell her we didn't find anything. Then, Connor will get called down and questioned. You were smart by asking for your parents and a lawyer, now I have to follow the law and wait for them to show up." He shrugs a shoulder. "I just hate when the right to counsel gets in the way of my job." He smirks.

I'm led back to Mrs. Gowen's office and she's eager to find out what was in my locker. I think she was almost hoping they'd find something. If I'm gone, Connor won't have a reason to bother her anymore.

Chapter 42

Grayson

Hadley: Piper was just led out of class by Mrs. Gowen and two police officers. Meet me down there.

My entire body goes numb when I read Hadley's text. What the hell is Connor up to?

"Mrs. D, I'm not feeling well. Can I go to the nurse's office?" I don't bother raising my hand, I'm not going to wait for her to call on me. I don't have a second to spare. I need to make a call and help my girl.

I'm already gathering my things when she glances in my direction. I'm walking out of here with or without her permission.

"Mr. Young, can't this wait?"

"Only if you're cool cleaning up puke... maybe diarrhea too." It's gross and I'm sure there will be a whole rumor spreading about me, but I don't care. She can't keep me here if she thinks I'm going to shit myself.

"Go. Get out of my classroom." She grimaces when I walk past her, plastering her body against her desk to keep as far away from me as possible.

As soon as the door shuts behind me, I'm lifting my phone to my ear.

"What's the matter, Gray?" Dad answers on the second ring.

"Hadley texted me. Two officers just escorted Piper out of class. She said the counselor was with them. I don't know what's going on, but I guarantee she was framed for it."

"I watched the videos you emailed me. I have no doubt he's behind all of this."

Dad was away on business when Mac and I confronted Connor. I haven't gotten a chance to talk to him about the videos, but I wanted him to see what I was facing. He begged me to let him in, to let him shoulder some of the burdens I'm dealing with.

For the first time in a long time, I'm letting someone help me. I'm taking Mom's advice and admitting I can't handle this alone.

"What do I do?"

"I'm getting in my car now. I'll be there in ten minutes. Stay on the phone with me."

"Ok." Noises come from down the hall. I move into an empty classroom and listen.

Piper walks by with the two officers and stops in front of her locker. I watch her open the door and they search it, but don't find anything.

"Dad, I'm in an empty classroom and I'm watching Piper open her locker for the officers to inspect, they didn't find anything. Why would they be checking her locker?"

"Because Connor's a son of a bitch! He's so conniving. I'm calling James. I know you wanted to handle this yourself, but this is too much, Gray. It's time real action is taken against Connor. If the police are getting involved, it's too big for you."

"I know," I whisper.

"You can't save everyone, son. Sometimes you have to watch the ones you love dig their own graves. Sometimes you wake up and don't even recognize who they've become. It's the hardest thing to come to terms with, but Connor isn't the boy you were friends with in elementary school. That boy was buried right along with his mother. Let me call James and I'll call you back. I know they're still on their honeymoon, but they're cutting it short."

We hang up and I take a minute to gather my thoughts. How are we going to deal with this?

My phone rings a few seconds later and I answer it without checking to see who it is.

"Where is she? What's going on?" Mac sounds almost as frantic as Piper looked.

"Where's Hadley?"

"She's right next to me. She met me at my class. Where's Piper?"

I tell them where I am and the second they enter the classroom, I spill what I know, which isn't a whole lot.

Dad: I'm here. Meet me in the lobby so we can handle this shit.

"Let's go. Dad's here." I lead Hadley and Mac to the lobby and Dad joins us to head to Gowen's office.

Dad doesn't bother knocking or anything, he strolls right into the office like he owns the place.

"Excuse me! You can't be in here!" Mrs. Gowen's brows furrow.

"Actually, I can. See, Piper's parents are on their honeymoon and they're about..." He glances down at his watch and twists his lips back and forth. "Eight hours away from being back in town. I'm going to stand in as her guardian until then. Piper's actually been living with me while they're gone."

"I'm sorry, who are you?"

The officers start chuckling. I'm fairly sure everyone knows who Grayson Young is. Everyone except Mrs. Gowen, apparently. Principal Bell enters the office and his eyes widen when he sees Dad.

"Gray, I didn't know you were here. Is something wrong with Grayson or Hadley? I thought only Piper was called to the office?"

"Yeah, well, Piper's my concern now. I'll be here until James shows up. Now, what's going on?"

"Excuse me! This is my office. You don't get to order people around. You have no authority here!" Mrs. Gowen stands to her whole five-foot three frame and plants her hands on her hips.

Poor woman has no idea who she's dealing with, but she's about to find out.

Chapter 43
Piper

The second Gray walks through the door, I breathe a sigh of relief. It's nice to have more people on my side. I know he'll do everything in his power to help me and he won't believe a word Connor says.

"You have no authority here!" Mrs. Gowen stomps her foot and glares at Gray.

"How are you doing, Piper?" Gray drops onto the couch next to me. He wraps his arm around my shoulders and pulls me into his side.

"I'd be great if I never moved here. I can't fight him, I can't win," I whisper as the thought really settles over me.

I'll never be able to win against Connor because he has no morals, no conscience, and not a care in the world. There isn't a single person he loves other than himself. You can't go against someone like him and think you'll win.

"It's ok, I'm going to handle everything. I'll do what Grayson can't," Grayson's dad says softly.

"Am I allowed to ask Piper questions now that this man is here?" Gowen motions to Gray with a scowl. "I want Hadley, Grayson, and Mac to go back to class. They have no reason to be here." She's so mad no one's listening to her.

"Hadley and Mac can wait in the hallway, Grayson stays," Gray growls, making Gowen jump in the seat she just took.

"But he-"

"I'm staying!" Grayson pulls me to my feet and spins us around. He takes the spot I just occupied on the couch and tugs me into his arms.

The door opens and closes, but I can't see through the wall of people to know who's left or entered.

"Fine! Let's get this over with!" Gowen throws her hands up in the air.

"Actually, I'd like a chance to talk to my client in private before we begin anything." He steps around everyone and pushes his way in front of me. "Miss Lawson, my name is Barrett and as of this second, I'm your lawyer."

After a brief argument, everyone leaves the office except Gray, Grayson, the lawyer, and I. Barrett tugs a chair in front of me and takes a seat. He looks every bit as important and respected as Gray or James.

"Tell me your side of the story. I don't give a shit what they're saying you did." Barrett has a big yellow legal pad on his lap and a pen poised above it ready to take notes.

I take my time, telling him how there was an anonymous tip about me threatening to harm students and that I had weapons at school, but nothing was found. When I'm done, Barrett lets out a long breath.

"I can get you out of this without a problem. Do we know who this anonymous tip came from?"

"Connor Ward." Grayson keeps his tone even, almost emotionless.

Barrett sits back and stares at us. He's a little shocked to say the least.

"This is going to be a bit of an issue. Does James know his son is involved? I can't represent both parties."

"I want you to watch this, then you can decide who you want to represent." Gray hands over his cell phone and Barrett presses play.

Connor and Grayson's voices fill the small room. They're discussing all of the things Connor's done to me like it's nothing. But then Grayson snaps. Then Mac snaps. And Connor promises to finish what he's started.

"Has James seen this?" Barrett raises a brow.

"No. I was waiting for him to get back from the honeymoon, clearly that was a stupid move on my part," Gray admits.

"I'm going to get everyone back in here. Piper, don't answer a single question without my approval. I'm officially your lawyer and I won't rest until this asshole pays."

Everyone files back into the room. The officers lean against the wall off to the side, while Gowen and Bell take seats across from me.

"Do you have any proof that Piper really planned to hurt anyone or is this just like the claims she was self-harming?" Barrett's expression is blank.

"I have to investigate every claim!" Gowen defends herself. "I have a note! The student who reported his concerns gave this to me. He says he found this on her desk at home. A sort of goodbye-"

"Let's stop beating around the bush. Connor Ward was behind this and we all know it. I want to see this note Piper supposedly left and Connor found." Gray's getting more and more annoyed with this.

Gowen hands over the note to Barrett and he scans whatever it says. When he's done, he gives it to me and Gray to read.

"Piper, did you write this?" Barret asks.

"No! That's not even my handwriting!"

"Do you have any notebooks with you? Anything we can use to prove the handwriting isn't yours?" Jack asks.

"In my backpack. Pick a notebook, they're all full of my writing."

Jack rummages through the bag and my heart is in my chest. I know everyone keeps reassuring me it's going to be ok, but what if it's not. What if Connor's successful this time and he ruins my entire life?

Chapter 44
Grayson

Between Barrett and Dad, they were able to convince everyone they didn't have anything on Piper. He's not wrong. Since there was no evidence and nothing to prove Connor's claims, Piper was free to go. Principal Bell told the four of us to take the rest of the week off and he'd make sure our teachers emailed us anything we missed.

Barrett talked to Dad before we left and discussed what will happen next with him while we grabbed anything we needed out of our lockers.

"What's going to happen now?" Piper looks to Dad for direction.

"We're going to meet James and your mom. They need to see that video and know just what Connor has been up to. It's time James takes responsibility for his son and does something about him."

"Are they going to do anything with Connor for reporting a fake threat?" Hadley frowns, she hates how easily Connor always gets away with everything.

"He's being called into the office. He's going to be taken into custody until James gets home. Let's just go and worry about all of this once your parents show up, Piper."

Dad ushers us into his car and tells us he'll come back and pick up our cars later on. He wants to know where all of us are and that we're safe until after Connor's dealt with.

When we get home, the four of us head into the den and put on a movie. Mac and Hadley sit on one end of the couch while we take the other, just like last time.

"What am I going to do, Grayson? I can't fight him, but I can't ask my mom to give up our new life either. I've never seen her so happy."

"It's not going to come to that, sweetheart. I promise. Dad has a plan, let him work it out."

James and Lauren knock on the door a little before midnight. I don't know how Dad convinced them to come here before going to get Connor from the station, but he did.

"Now that I'm here, will you tell me why I left my honeymoon almost a week early?" James folds his arms over his chest as Lauren hugs Piper. He doesn't look mad, just tired. I'm sure it's exhausting knowing your son is Satan.

"Let's go into the den and get comfortable. I have a little movie for you to watch." Dad starts walking down the hall without another word.

"I don't have time for this, Gray. I need to get my son from the police station. They won't even tell me why they have him in custody."

"Well, this movie will explain everything, plus give you information your son's never going to willingly admit to anyone. I want you to watch the entire thing before you make a single comment though. If you make a move before the end, I'll remove you from my home." Dad pins Mr. Ward with a look, daring him to fuck with us.

He's protecting me. He knows when James sees me pin Connor against the wall or Mac start punching him, he might get mad.

Once everyone is settled into a seat, Dad hooks his phone up the TV and presses play. Instantly the Ward's kitchen fills the screen and I watch as Connor, Mac, and I enter the picture.

This is the second time Piper's heard Connor's words, but the first time she's seen the actual video. I'm sure it's painful to see someone hate you so much that they're willing to do just about anything to get rid of you.

Piper tenses in my arms and I hold her a little closer. When Connor starts listing all of the things he's done to her to try to get her to leave, James and Lauren stare at us in horror.

James knows his son isn't good, but I don't think he knew the extent of Connor's issues. He probably believed Connor was just a teenage boy acting out, not Satan in the flesh.

A tear trickles down Piper's cheek when she watches me get physical with her stepbrother. My brows furrow, I'm not sure why she's upset. It's not like she likes Connor.

"What's wrong, baby?"

"I doubted you. So many times I've wondered if this was all part of Connor's master plan. I questioned your intentions and I never should have. It wasn't until the party that I knew you were serious. I knew you really loved me after you took care of me."

"I think I've loved you since the beginning. I'm sorry for screwing with your head and always being hot and cold with you. I didn't make things easy on you."

"It's ok. I'll always forgive you." She presses a soft kiss to my cheek and snuggles impossibly closer to me.

When the video ends with me practically dragging Mac out of the house and Connor still screaming at us, James and Lauren turn their wide eyes back on us. Lauren swipes at her cheek with a tissue, but it does nothing to help with how quickly the tears are coming. James opens his mouth but nothing comes out for several long seconds.

"Why didn't you tell me? I asked you if he was treating you ok when we went to get the car. You said you could handle him. This isn't handling him, Piper." James motions to the screen. He's still in shock, still hasn't completely processed what his son is really like.

"I didn't realize just how far he was willing to take things," Piper whispers.

"I'm so sorry, Princess. I don't even know if there's a way to show you how sorry I am. I'm horrified and speechless that the man I just watched is the same little boy I was once proud of. I'm not sure what to do." James shakes his head.

"He needs to be stopped and the only way to do that is to take away everything that matters to him," Dad's voice is strong, confident, and commanding.

"But nothing matters to him. He doesn't love anyone or anything." James stares at Dad, looking to him for guidance.

"He loves money and his status. Take both of those away. Reduce him to a poor nobody and you might be able to save him," Mac speaks up for the first time.

"How do I do that? I can't just cut him off. He's a minor." James frowns.

"Don't step in when he faces the judge for reporting false threats. Let him defend his actions. Allow him to stand on his own two feet just like he thinks he is." Dad nods his head slowly. "He's the one who has to be held accountable. It's the only way."

"He'll go to jail. I can't allow that. He'll just get angrier and angrier there. It won't help him." James buries his face in his hands. Lauren hugs his side, trying to comfort her husband.

"I don't want him to go to jail. I'd like a chance to talk to the judge in private before he makes any decisions. Barrett told me I could do that," Piper raises her voice, wanting everyone to support her in this decision. We already discussed it and if this is what she wants, I'll help any way I can.

"Piper? You can't let him get away with it. He's not going to stop," Dad urges.

"I know he won't. I want him to be mandated to go into a mental health facility. I was researching it earlier and there's one about four hours away. They have a program for young adults who struggle with anger issues. They'll give Connor the tools to help him be successful before he ruins his life. He needs to come to terms with his mom dying, that's when all of this started, right?"

"Yes. He changed completely after she died," James says sadly. "I should've stepped in when I noticed it. I failed him. I'm a horrible parent."

No one comments on James' parenting because what are we supposed to say? He's right. He fucked up and now Piper's the one paying for it.

"Then this place should give him the counseling and support he needs. Prison isn't going to help him... Barrett already spoke to the judge. I'm going to talk with him in the morning. And I'd like to do it alone."

Piper peeks over her shoulder at me. I want to argue with her, tell her I'll support her and hold her hand, but I don't think she needs that right now. I can support her by letting her defend herself. I can be available when she's done and help however I can.

I have to let her stand up to him. Since we've met, I've been stepping in to help. Even though she stated several times that it wasn't necessary.

"Are you sure that's what you want?" James asks, watching Piper. "He tortured and drugged you, Piper. It's your decision where he goes. I'll be by your side regardless."

"I know what I want. I'm positive of my choice."

"If we're airing Connor's dirty laundry, I think you should know about the accident last year," Mac speaks up from his spot beside Hadley.

"Mac," I growl. James doesn't need to deal with this right now.

"No! That was fucked up and you know it! He deserves to know just how evil his son is." Mac slaps his hand on his knee, making Lauren jump.

"I want to know, Grayson. Whatever I'm up against, I need to know it all," James whispers in a tortured voice.

I shake my head, I'm not going to tell him. I survived, there's no reason to dredge up the past when it's not related to this.

"He's been doing shit like this for years." Hadley sighs, refusing to meet my gaze. I know she can feel me glaring at her, but she's choosing to ignore me. "Every woman you've brought home to meet him, he's run them off in various ways. I guarantee he's been behind every single thing he's been accused of over the years and you just didn't want to think he could be that bad."

Her voice is strong and full of so much hatred. I know she doesn't like him, but I didn't realize her hatred ran this deep.

"Last year, he made a bet with some assholes from another school. He convinced these two idiots to drag race on ice roads. When Mac lost to his opponent, Connor demanded that Grayson win. My brother's an idiot. He did everything he needed to win... even though it almost cost him his life."

Lauren gasps and her attention snaps to me. Her brows pull together as she looks at Piper and I'm sure she's thinking that if I weren't here, Piper never would've survived all of this.

"The other guy slammed into Grayson's car and pinned him against a tree. The guy died on impact and I'm sure his family is still mourning his death. He had a Connor in his life that put him up to racing. It's rather convenient that neither of them raced, but they demanded that their best friends did. Do you know what your son did?" Hadley's voice grows harder and there's venom practically dripping from her words.

"Hads," I whisper, practically begging her to keep her mouth shut and not to finish the story.

"I can't even imagine. I'm sure I'm not going to like it though." James shakes his head as a fresh wave of tears spills down his cheeks.

"He left him for fucking dead," Mac growls. "He got in his fucking car and drove home. I had to pull the dead kid out from behind the wheel by myself and move his car, just so I could get to Grayson. I called the ambulance because Connor refused to do it because he didn't want to get in trouble."

"Are you kidding me?" James buries his face in his hands. "How could he do that?"

"Grayson had to have the jaws of life used to get him out of his car. Connor didn't visit him the entire time he was in the hospital," Mom continues, dabbing a tissue under her eyes.

I'm fighting my own emotion from bubbling up inside of me as I watch how painful the accident was for all of my loved ones.

"He didn't call or text. Absolutely nothing. When Grayson finally went back to school, that's when Connor started talking to him again. He acted like nothing happened. Like it was just another day in high school. He hasn't brought up the accident since it happened and any time the conversation turned to Grayson's recovery or anything related to it, he'd change the conversation to something else. He's a fucking monster," Mac growls, finishing the story and nailing the final nail in Connor's coffin.

"I'm not sure a mental health facility will be enough," he confesses into the silent room.

"The facility has requirements. He can't leave until he meets them. Barrett assured me that if Connor doesn't put forth any effort to get better, he'll be moved to prison and nothing I say will prevent it."

"I can't lose my boy," James cries.

"Don't you get it? You already have," Dad says sympathetically.

Chapter 45
Piper
Epilogue

"I don't understand this. I thought you'd want to see me behind bars." Connor's eyebrows form a deep V.

The judge listened to my wishes and agreed that he doesn't believe going to a juvenile detention center would benefit him at all. I showed him the mental health facility and he thought it was a great idea.

Connor will spend the next few weeks there. He'll be able to have contact with all of us, but only if he wants to. They'll be working with him to get to the root of his issues.

James spoke to him after the judge made his ruling. If he doesn't complete the program or pulls any of his shit afterwards, he'll be cut off financially. And to Connor, that would be the end of his world. He also won't be allowed to return home unless he completes it. James made it clear that he won't put Mom or I at risk again.

"I never wanted to hurt you. Nor did I want to change your life or make it harder. Hell, I didn't even want to come here! But since I wasn't given a choice, I hoped we'd be friends or at the very least tolerate each other. None of that has changed, Connor. Sure, I could've taken up my own vendetta against you, but it wouldn't have solved any problems... I'm happy, Connor. I want the same for you. I don't think you've been happy in a long time."

Grayson squeezes my hand from his spot next to me. He's been supportive of my decision, standing by my side through it all.

Mom and James don't like how I stayed at the Young's house while they were gone. They definitely weren't thrilled to learn I slept in Grayson's bed every night. However, realizing that Grayson was the reason I was safe made up for it.

"I don't know how to be happy, Piper. I'm not sure it's something I can change either," Connor admits, refusing to meet my gaze.

Without saying a word, I embrace my stepbrother. I think all along he needed someone to show him love and how to love.

Since James picked him up from the police station two days ago, he's been unusually quiet. He knows he went too far and he can't weasel his way out of things this time.

"Get help, go to therapy, and we'll be here when you get out." Grayson clamps a hand down on his shoulder, before tugging him into one of their bro hugs.

Mac's standing off to the side with a scowl and Hadley stands nervously next to him.

"Figure out your shit, Connor. I'm done with this version of you. I won't be here when you get out if you don't change. Don't force me to make that decision, because I will and I'll never look back." Mac wraps Connor in a tight hug.

Hadley stays quiet. She doesn't offer words of support or even a good luck. I can't blame her. She almost lost her brother because of him and now he's done all of this.

"Nothing from you, Hadley? Not a big 'Fuck you, I hope you rot in there'?" His lips turn up slightly at the corners.

"What do you want me to say, Connor? You're an asshole and I wish you never entered my life. Fuck you for all the awful things you've done to my family and friends... I hope you get better, but I never want to see you again." She lifts her shoulder in a shrug.

"I'm glad you're being honest," Connor whispers. "Can I at least have a hug before I leave you alone forever?"

He opens his arms and waits. Hadley stares at him like he's crazy for several long seconds before she steps into his arms and lets him envelope her.

Connor's eyes slide shut and he lets out a slow breath. He visibly relaxes in front of me for the first time ever.

All along I thought he left Hadley alone because of Grayson, but now I'm wondering if he does love someone and no one ever noticed.

Connor whispers something in Hadley's ear before he takes a step back and lets her go. Her brows pinch as she frowns, but she doesn't say anything.

"It's time to go, son." James places a hand on his back and leads him out the door and down the steps.

Right before Connor climbs into the backseat, he glances up and locks eyes with Hadley. I swear something passes between the two of them. He mouths 'I'm sorry' and slips into the car.

"What the hell was that?" Grayson watches his sister for any hint as to what's going on. "What'd he say to you?"

Before she can answer, Mac's phone rings and he tugs it out of his pocket.

"Hello?... What the fuck? What's going on?... Are you serious?... Shit! I'll be right there." Mac runs a rough hand through his hair and ends the call.

"What's happened?"

"I... Fuck! I gotta go. I'll- motherfucker! I'll call you later."

"I'm coming with you!" Hadley grabs his hand and the two of them race down the stairs and hop into his car. Seconds later they're speeding out of the driveway, leaving us wondering what just happened.

What's Next?

Are you dying to know what happens next? If I Cave –
Mac and Hadley's Storyis where this story continues. Who
called Mac and what is going on?

Hadley Young. That woman has been the center of
my attention for as long as I can remember. I didn't have
a choice but to keep my distance from her. Her brother
made sure of that. Now, I'm done playing by his rules and
I'm making her mine. It doesn't matter what stands in our
way, now that I have her, I'm not letting go. I'll burn the
entire world to the ground to keep her safe.

Macalister Barens has been just out of reach my entire life.
I never thought I'd have his attention on me, but now that
I have it, I never want to lose it. He's proving to me over
and over again that he's the guy for me. If we can survive
everything life throws at us, maybe we can finally have our

happily ever after.

You can also download four free books!

Assisting the Bosshole

Believe

Love Noted Prequel

Unknown Caller

Author's Note

I hope you loved If I Surrender! I'd really appreciate it if you could write a review or spread the word about my books! I spent a ton of time writing this book because I felt like it needed to be perfect. I had this whole new world in my head for months before I was able to focus on it. I had so much fun writing new characters that weren't tied to another series, but of course my brain is already working ways to tie this to another book! You're going to love Mac's and Connor's books!

~Kristin

Stay connected with me!

https://linktr.ee/Kristinmacqueenauthor

Also by Kristin MacQueen

The Boys of Mulberry Lane

Believe

Bare

Broken

Bliss

Blessed

Blurred

Breathless

Bold

Never Series

———

Undercover Love

<u>To Protect</u>
<u>To Serve</u>

Ink It Up

<u>Custom Piece</u>
<u>Virgin Ink</u>
<u>Full Sleeve</u>
Cover Up

University Hospital

<u>All-in with Dr. Chipkin</u>
<u>Dr. Devine is Mine</u>
<u>I'm Not Sharing Dr. McLaren</u>
Dr. Miller is Looking Killer

Prescott High

If I Surrender

If I Cave

If I Stumble

Operation Riot

Leading to Love

Rhythm of Love

Managing Love

Touring for Love

Pit Bulls Baseball

Coming Home

Stealing First

Rest of Series Titles Coming soon!

Maple Springs

Don't Forget Me

Rest of Series Titles Coming soon!

Standalones

That's Cockatoo Much

Under the Mistletoe

It's Always Been You

Unknown Caller – FREEBIE

Made in the USA
Thornton, CO
11/04/24 16:14:00